LET'S DP MY WIFE
The Complete 21 Story Collection

HANNAH WILDE

CONTENTS

CABIN FEVER

Sometimes it's hard for me to understand how I ended up with a woman as beautiful as Cindy. Not that I'm all that bad looking myself, and I certainly know what I'm doing between the sheets, but my wife is in a league all her own. It's trained me away for jealousy, that's for sure, because after years of seeing the heads turn while we walk down the street together, I've finally come to terms with the fact that she'll always be a bombshell. I don't get upset anymore, in fact, I'm proud.

Cindy is reasonably tall and slender, but curvy in all the right places and carrying a set of tits that I'd swear were implants if I didn't already know better. She's the kind of girl that puts everyone around her at ease, somehow the life of the party without stepping on toes. Even the less attractive women around her, who should rightfully be green with envy, can't resist Cindy's charm.

She's my wife, and I'm thankful every day that I get to call her mine.

The sex is great, too. She's as loyal as they come but also an animal in the sack, easily capable of flipping a switch that instantly transforms her from good girl to naughty slut in a few seconds flat. Cindy knows what she likes, but will also try anything with a smile and a wink, adventurous to the core.

It's probably our mutual confidence that has brought us to this place in our marriage. Instead of relying on one another for everything, we work as a team, taking any challenge head on and, most importantly, together.

It's that spirit that has kept our social circle fairly large, as well, and on the night of the cabin vacation, it's that spirit that got us into trouble. The kind of trouble that scares you at first, but eventually you start wanting it over and over again. But now I'm getting ahead of myself.

Our friends Andy and Sara have a beautiful cabin up in the woods. A stunning vacation home, it's been in Andy's family for generations and frequently used for friendly get togethers and various outings throughout the year. These days, we get to spend a lot of time up there with the couple because they've been using the place every chance they get; running, hiking, biking, it never stops with Andy and Sara. Cindy and me may be the hottest of our group of friends, but with all of the exercise and time they spend in the great outdoors, Andy and Sara at least give us a run for our money.

It's no secret that my wife has a crush on Andy, too, and the feeling it mutual. I'm secure enough not to mind, but I do sometimes take issue with the fact that Sara truly seems to have no idea what's happening, even when Cindy and Andy are having fun and making it completely obvious.

Cindy and I are driving up the mountains towards the isolated cabin, a six hour drive that's completely worth it but totally exhausting. It would be one thing if there was phone service or a way to check email in the passenger seat, but once we hit the road it's like falling into an instant dead zone of no contact.

Instead, we pass the time by chatting about work and listening to the few songs that I have stored on my smart phone.

"Thom, do you feel like something weird is going on between Andy and Sara?" My wife finally asks, staring out the window as we glide along the edge of a beautiful cliffside. Below us is an incredible canyon view of lush trees and sheer rock face.

"Weird?" I ask, the thought never even crossing my mind. "Like weird, how?"

"Like… They're going to break up soon." Cindy says. "Whenever we have outings like this they are always fighting. Remember last time?"

I remembered. They arrived two hours late and barely talked to each other. Andy tried to hold it together and make things fun, but it seemed like everything he did just made Sara more and more annoyed and irritable.

"Yeah, I guess you're right." I confirm, "I hadn't really thought about it."

We're cruising down a bumpy dirt path now, light dancing across the car in beautiful patterns as it shines through the patchwork of leaves and branches hanging above.

"I guess we're about to find out." I say, pulling up to the cabin where Andy is standing, shirtless and perspiring as he chops wood in the afternoon sun. He almost looks surprised to see us as we climb out of the car.

"What's going on guys?" Andy shouts, a smile crossing his face. "What are you doing here?"

I laugh and give him a high five while Cindy goes in for a hug that last slightly too long. "What do you mean by that?" I ask.

Andy's face suddenly gets a little more serious. "Fuck. You never got the message this morning did you?"

"We haven't had service for five or six hours." I tell him. "When did you call?"

"I must have just missed you, I sent a text, too." He explains. "I mean, it's fucking awesome to see you guys and you're welcome to stay for the weekend, but Sara and I broke up."

"What?" Cindy says in complete shock. "You've gotta be kidding me, what happened?"

"She just wasn't happy, I guess." Andy says, "Honestly, I don't really know, it just happened last night so I'm a little out of it right now, but I figured this would be a good place to clear my head."

"Totally." I confirm. "I'm sorry to hear that, man."

"But, I mean, I don't want to be the third wheel or anything." Andy explains. "I figured we'd just call the couples weekend off but now that you're here you should totally stay."

Cindy nods enthusiastically. "Oh my god Andy, I'm so sorry." She hugs him again.

"Aw, whatever." He sighs. "There's plenty of fish in the sea."

We stand like this in silence for a brief moment; letting the many revelations of the last five minutes fully sink in.

"We're gonna keep you company up here." Cindy finally says. "It's gonna be okay."

I shrug. "I'll get the bags."

"You two take the main bedroom," Andy shouts to me as I head back to the car. "I'll crash on the couch."

Despite the fresh breakup Andy seems to be in decent spirits that night, chatting and laughing over a dinner of steak and salad that we brought up in a cooler from home. The cabin is not nearly as rustic as you might think, with all of the amenities you'd find at a fairly nice hotel. This is roughing it for rich people.

Still, this silence is nice and I'm glad to be away from the big city for a few nights. I can tell that Cindy feels the same way, happy and full of enthusiastic energy. Her and Andy have been especially flirty this evening since Sara's not here to keep an eye on them. I have to admit, it's pretty sexy watching the two of them get under each others skin, escalating the tension and then pulling back just as something is about to get too weird. It's a delicate dance, but they've been doing it so long that it's almost second nature.

"So how does it feel to be a single man?" I ask Andy across the dinner table.

He rolls his eyes and leans back in his chair with his arms above his head, showing of an impressive upper physique. I can see Cindy checking him out from the corner of my eye. "I don't know, Thom, I can't even think like that yet." He says. "It's just too fresh."

"Yeah, I hear you." I admit. "But they say it really helps to have a rebound. The best way to get over someone is to get under someone."

He smirks a little bit as I say that. "True enough, but Sara was a quality girl. The hotness bar has been set a little too high."

We all laugh as he says this. Andy leans forward and takes a long sip from his beer.

"Hey now, there are a lot of hot girls out there." I reassure him. "Just look at Cindy!"

The two of them suddenly get strangely bashful, refusing for a moment to look into each other's eyes.

"See!" I yell, pointing across the table. "She's so cute that you can't even look at her."

Cindy bursts out laughing and Andy finally looks, cracking a wide smile.

"Yeah, you're right, your wife is pretty fucking hot." Andy finally says.

My heart skips a beat as he says this. It's one thing for them to do a bit of flirting, but this is actually the first time that he's just come right out and said it. The strangest part, however, is how fucking arousing it is to hear those words coming out of another man's mouth.

"Now you just have to find someone that looks exactly like me."

Cindy says with a wink. "Shouldn't be too hard to do."

"Oh, it's already hard." Andy says, raising his eyebrows and taking another swig of beer. My jaw nearly hits the table but I keep it together. I can feel my cock getting stiffer in my pants, aching from this strange, jealous desire.

Cindy looks over at me, as if to check and make sure that I'm okay with everything that's happening. I give her a little nod and she smiles happily.

But then, nothing happens. The conversation shifts onto something else and, by the time Cindy brings out the apple pie she'd brought along for desert, the tension has completely dissipated.

Cindy and I are all over each other the instant that we climb into bed that night, tearing each others clothes off and then quietly going to work with our hands. I reach into her panties and start to play with her clit, noticing immediately that she's already soaking wet.

"Damn baby." I whisper, trying my best not to wake Andy as he sleeps out on the couch in the living room. "You're ready to go, aren't you?"

Cindy giggles and wraps her hand tightly around my cock in the dark. "I sure am, you guys have been getting me so hot and horny today."

"Both of us?" I ask.

Cindy stop for a moment, trying to get a read on my expression in the rooms dim light. "Is that okay?" She finally asks.

"Of course it is." I assure her. "Tell me about it."

"Tell you about what?" She asks, curious.

"Tell me about how much Andy turns you on?"

She's silent for a moment, but still grinding herself against my fingers in her tight slit. "Are you sure?" She counters.

"Positive."

My wife starts to stroke a little faster as she tells me, quietly admitting her attraction to Andy softly under her breath. "I just think he's so fucking sexy." She tells me. "His body, everything. I mean, you're handsome too, baby, Andy's just different."

"It's okay." I tell her. "Go on."

"Well," Cindy says, up close against my ear. "Right now it's dark enough that I can pretend you're him. I wish it was his big fucking cock I was stroking off instead of yours."

A pleasant chill runs down my spine as she says this, affecting me in ways that I can't quite yet grasp. Everything about this turns me on to the core, even the anger and jealousy that comes with knowing my beautiful wife would rather be fucking someone else right now.

"Do you want to fuck him instead of me?" I ask.

"Not exactly." Cindy tells me. She kisses me deeply for a moment and then pulls back. "I want to fuck both of you."

"Right now?" I question.

"Right now."

In a moment of inspiration, I push away from Cindy and start to climb out of bed.

"Whoa, where are you going?" She whispers. "It's just dirty talk, I wasn't serious."

I crack a wry smile. "I'll be right back."

Before she has a chance to protest I'm already out the door and creeping into the darkness of the living room. Andy is still up and lying on the couch, silently watching the fireplace while it dances in front of him in a flickering orange glow. He looks up at me as I approach and sit down next to him.

"How are you doing, buddy?" I ask. "Hanging in there?"

He shrugs. "Honestly, pretty good. It's weird because I feel like I should be taking all of this so much harder than I am."

"Well, you probably saw it coming for a while now, right?" I ask.

Andy nods. "Yeah, I guess I did. Was it that obvious that we were having problems?" He asks, turning to me.

I laugh to myself. "Actually, no. I had no idea, but Cindy pointed it out on the drive up here and once I thought about it I realized she was right."

"You've got a good woman." Andy tells me. "You're lucky to call that girl in there your wife."

"I know." I tell him. "That's actually what I came out here to talk to you about."

Andy seems confused, not exactly sure where this could be headed.

"What's up?" He asks.

"I know that you think Cindy is really sexy, and I don't blame you." I say. "I mean, she's a perfect ten and we all know it."

Andy nods.

"She thinks you're really cute, too." I tell him. "She's crazy for you."

"Oh yeah?" He asks, cautiously.

"Yeah man." I confirm. "Anyway, me and her are in a really secure place, and we know that you're having a rough time right now so I wanted to come out here and ask if you'd like to help me fuck my wife."

Andy is stunned, monetarily unable to speak.

"Are you serious?" Andy finally asks, his eyes wide. "I mean… I'm not gay or anything."

I laugh. "No dude, it's not like that. It's you and me fucking her at the same time. Double penetration." I explain.

"And Cindy wants that?" He asks.

"Badly." I tell him, chuckling to myself. "You have no idea."

Andy thinks for a moment. "I'm in."

The door to our bedroom opens up and a figure slinks inside, tall and muscular.

"Baby, come back to bed." Cindy coos into the darkness. "Don't tease me like that."

The figure climbs under the covers next to her and they start kissing passionately, fondling each other's bodies with an animalistic desire.

"Oh fuck." Cindy moans, "That feels so fucking good when you touch me like that."

They continue to make out ferociously until Cindy beings to realize that something's wrong and slowly comes to a complete stop. She puts her hand across the figures face in the darkness. "Thom?" She asks.

Cindy reaches over and turns on the bedside light, revealing that it's actually Andy in the bed next to her. I'm standing in the doorway, watching with rapt attention as the whole thing unfolds.

"Oh my god." Cindy gasps, looking back and forth between Andy and me as her brain spins in circles, trying desperately to catch up. "What the fuck is going on you guys?"

"You said you wanted to fuck Andy." I explain. "This is your chance."

Cindy shakes her head with confused amusement, a smile creeping across her face as her cheeks turn red. "You guys are bad." She says. "Really bad."

I walk over to the bed and climb in next to them, so that the three of us are lying side by side with Cindy in the middle. She rolls over towards Andy and starts to kiss him, pushing her ass back against my ever-growing bulge. I can see her hands moving under the blanket and suddenly realize that my wife is beating off my friend right in front of me. Andy closes his eyes tight and lets out a soft moan.

After a while of this, Cindy rolls over so that she's facing me, with her ass now pushed up against Andy. I can feel him pulling down her cute, flower-print panties and aligning his cock with her wet slit. Cindy kisses me deeply and then shudders as Andy enters her from behind, expanding her tightness with his massive cock.

"Oh fuck." She says, grabbing onto my shoulders tightly as she braces herself against Andy's powerful thrusts. "That feels so fucking good."

I hold her tight as she takes him from behind and then slowly start to pull myself up towards the headboard. Cindy's not quite sure what I'm doing at first, and then suddenly realizes as my cock comes into view of her beautiful, freckled face.

"Someone's excited to watch me get fucked." She says, eyeing my engorged member.

Cindy opens her lips and then takes my shaft inside of her, bobbing up and down on my dick while Andy pounds her at the other end. I find a rhythm with Cindy and soon enough the three of us are all pulsing together effortlessly. Every time that Andy drives her forward, I'll push back, impaling my wife between our two massive members.

She loves it, looking up at me with eyes of admiration and complete satisfaction.

After a while of this, I pull myself out of my wife's mouth and spin her around so that she's now facing Andy in an elegant doggy style position. I give her ass a playful slap and then climb up onto my knees, pushing my dick deep inside of her pussy.

My wife begins to give Andy head as I fuck her, pushing up and down on his dick and then taking him all the way down in a spectacular deep throat. My wife pushes him so deep that her lips are resting against Andy's toned abs, and he forcefully holds her there for as long as she can bear.

When Cindy finally comes up for air she's a sputtering, gasping mess; but hungrier than ever for our cocks.

"Get rough with me!" She yells at the two of us. "Fuck me harder! Use me like the filthy slut that I am!"

I love seeing this side of her and immediately do as I'm told, picking up the pace within Cindy's tightness and giving her ass a few more hard slaps. She's moaning and squealing against Andy's fleshy rod as it pounds the back of her throat, then finally she pulls him out and looks back at me cutely over her shoulder.

"I want you to DP me." She commands. "Lay back."

I find a spot against the headboard and help guide Cindy as she climbs up onto me, straddling my body with her toned, slender legs. She reaches down and firmly grabs my cock, then pushes her body down onto my thickness as it slides into her tight pussy. The two of us immediately fall into perfect sync, my cock slamming up into her as she grinds happily against me.

"Baby, thank you for letting me fuck you and our friend at the same time." She moans. "Thank you for letting me have all this cock."

I smile up at her. "Don't mention it."

Andy soon climbs into position behind her, so we slow down and I reach back to spread her ass open for him. Cindy holds tight onto the bed frame, mentally preparing herself for entry as Andy places his dick against the puckered hole of her backdoor.

"I'm ready." Cindy tells him. "Shove it up my ass."

Andy slowly and powerfully thrusts forward, forcing her asshole to expand around him as he enters my wife's toned body. I can feel him moving through the thin area that separates her two holes, enjoying the extra tightness as Andy becomes fully consumed by Cindy's taut ass.

Once inside, me and Andy go to work, pumping back and forth within my wife's tiny holes. She's moaning with pleasure almost immediately, tightly holding onto whatever she can as our pace quickens until finally we are utterly slamming into her small frame with our cocks. Cindy lets out a howl of ecstasy that echoes out across the forest around us.

"Do you like that cock up your ass?" Andy asks forcefully, slamming her from behind.

"Yes." My wife moans.

"I said, do you like that cock up your ass?" He demands again, grabbing Cindy by the base of her hair and pulling her back. "Tell me you love that cock!"

My wife is enjoying every second of it, her eyes rolling back into her head as she screams. "Yes I love that fucking cock!"

Andy slaps her ass hard and then pulls out, lifting Cindy up off of me and spinning her around so that she's facing him now. My cock hovers just below the rim of Cindy's asshole and she carefully guides me inside, sliding down my shaft as I impale her tightness. She lets out a sharp cry when I reach the hilt, her ass cheeks resting firmly against my stomach.

Moments later, Andy is climbing in front of Cindy, finding the best position for thrusting into her tight little pussy. He grabs my wife by the waist and then pulls himself inside, stretching her limits between our two girthy members.

Andy then starts to slam into Cindy above me, plowing her with all of his force as she squeals with pleasure. She lifts her legs and spreads them open as far as she can, letting them dangle in the air as they shake with every thrust.

"I'm so close!" Cindy moans, reaching down and frantically playing with her clit. I can see her stomach tensing up, her body preparing for the powerful explosion of ecstasy that looms just over the horizon. Moments later. Cindy starts to shake, violently arching backwards as the sensation overwhelms her and she screams out a series of unfiltered profanity. Even from within her ass I can feel the muscles above me contracting and seizing in powerful fits of orgasm.

When she finally finishes it becomes the guy's turn to blow. Me and Andy hammer away at my wife's holes and before I know it we are both cumming hard, spilling pump after pump of our warm jizz up inside of her. I can feel my cock seizing with every forceful ejection, holding her tight against me as I let out a satisfied cry of pleasure.

Andy is pushed deep inside of Cindy, holding tight as he unloads himself completely into my wife. Blinded by the heat of the moment, It's only then that I realize he's not wearing a condom. Nobody else seems to mind, though, the least of all Cindy, who pulls her legs back and lets Andy watch as he removes his cock from its tight hole, pearly white cum spilling everywhere.

"Oh fuck." Is all Cindy can say, her hair tangled and red in the face. "That was so fucking good. Look at all the fucking jizz."

She climbs off of the bed and immediately heads for the shower while Andy and I throw on some clothes and head out to the kitchen. We each grab a beer and take a seat at the table.

"She's amazing." Andy tells me. "You're a lucky man."

"I know," I say, hoisting up the beer bottle in cheers. "I'll drink to that."

"So what now?" Andy asks. "Is this going to get weird?"

I think for a minute, listening to the shower hum pleasantly in the other room as Cindy washes up.

"No," I say, shaking my head. "I don't think so."

"That's good, because you guys mean a lot to me." Andy tells me. "You're true friends."

"Exactly," I tell him, taking a long pull from the bottle. "To be honest with you, she's probably going to want another round in the morning."

GAME DAY

It all started when I caught my buddy Dean, red-handed and no question about it, checking out my wife's ass. As any husband can attest, the first emotion you feel here is jealousy, obviously, and with most guys I'm pretty certain that's where the emotional cocktail ends. But on this particular night, when we were all outside barbequing and she sauntered by in that little yellow bikini, headed for the backyard pool, I suddenly caught myself feeling something more than just jealous pangs.

I was stunned, not exactly sure what to do with myself as all of these complex feelings flooded into my brain. Dean turned his gaze back and suddenly our eyes met, locked in together in an awkward realization that he had been spotted.

Dean held his breath, waiting for me to say something as the hamster wheel spun rapidly within my head. There were so many ways I could handle it, but finally I landed on the one the felt best.

"Nice, huh?" I asked him. "That thing is incredible."

Dean just stared at me for a moment and then took a long sip of his beer. "What do you mean?" He finally said, playing dumb.

"You don't have to pretend, man." I told him. "I saw you checking out Amanda's ass. She's fucking gorgeous, I don't blame you at all."

Dean went silent again. I could tell that he was terrified to break the unwritten bro-code that says you can't check out your buddies' wife, regardless of my coaxing. Finally, a smile crept across Dean's face and he relented. "Yeah, man. She's looking good these days."

As he admitted this I felt another wave of jealous flow through me, but this time it was warmer and more pleasant, like I was growing accustomed to the way that it made my body tingle. I let it simmer for a moment and then continued. "You should see it out of that bikini." I tell him. "She was already a fucking fox, but now Amanda's been hitting the gym like every day. I don't know what I did to deserve this, but I'm thankful."

I was telling Dean the truth. I'm not a bad looking guy by any means, I take care of myself and have never had a problem getting woman, but my wife Amanda was out of this world hot. She's the type of girl who doesn't even realize how gorgeous she is and that makes her even more stunning; an effortless, walking sex bomb that turns every head in her wake. She's got a cute, disarming smile that will instantly charm you with its sweetness, but that face also happens to be connected to the body of a pornstar, massive tits, a slender waist, and legs that go on for days. Don't forget that ass either.

Clearly, Dean hadn't, because once we started talking about Amanda's rump he instantly went back to staring. Amanda was in the pool, laughing and splashing playfully with some of the other barbeque guests.

"She seems pretty innocent, though, right?" I prodded, my cock hardening in my pants.

Dean nodded. "Yeah, I guess so."

I laughed. "That's what I figured when I first met her. Sweet as sugar. But you would not believe the shit that girl is into in the bedroom."

Dean tensed up a bit. I could tell that he was getting just as turned on as I was while we ogled my wife like a couple of horny cavemen, letting our most primal thoughts come to the surface and play around for a while.

"She fucking loves taking it up the ass." I continued as the grill between us sizzled. "The second I put my cock up there she starts to loose it. One second she's the innocent girl next door, the next she's the filthiest slut you could ever imagine."

My heart was racing, thundering in my chest as it rushed to get more blood to my swollen cock. I was on a roll now, and there was no stopping me as I continued to push it farther and farther with Dean.

"You ever DP'd a girl before?" I finally asked Dean.

"DP'd?" He questioned.

"Double penetrated." I explained. I had trouble believing that any red-blooded American male with an internet connection didn't know what a

DP was, but I was willing to play along. "Two guys fucking a chick at the same time. One cock in her pussy and one in her ass."

Dean shook his head. "No, I've never done it."

"Would you be interested?" I asked him.

"You mean in general?" Dean shrugged. I could tell from his body language that he was way more excited about the idea than he was letting on. "Yeah, I mean, why not. The guys don't touch, right?"

I shook my head. "No, it's all about the girl getting filled up."

"I'd been into it then." Dean said, taking another nervous swing of his beer. I noticed that the bottle was completely empty and at this point he was just doing it out of habit.

"How'd you like to DP Amanda with me?" I asked him.

Dean eyed me cautiously. "Yeah man, I'm down." He finally said.

I nod, thinking deeply for a moment. "I'll talk to her and let you know." I told him.

We stood in silence for a brief moment as a smile crept across Dean's face. Suddenly, he burst out laughing.

"That's funny, Pete." He said, completely aborting the conversation. "You really had me going there."

I smiled in return, not buying it but slightly relieved that one of us was willing to pull the plug before things went too far. "Yeah, I'm just messing with you." I lied.

It's after the barbeque and Amanda and I are lying in bed, exhausted but satisfied after a great night of socializing. She's fresh out of the shower and wearing an old, large T-shirt of mine, somehow looking just as sexy as she would in a strappy lingerie set. My mind is still fluttering from my conversation with Dean, and Amanda can clearly tell that something is up. She lies on her pillow for a while, staring at me while I pretend to read my book.

"What's going on, Peter?" She finally asks.

I crack a smile and put the book down on the bedside table, then turn to my wife. "Do I seem like something's wrong?" I ask,

She pouts. "I don't know baby, kinda." She rubs my arms, tracing them up and down with her long, slender fingers. "What's up?"

I've been going over all of the gentle ways that I could start this conversation in my head, and none of them seem to satisfy me. I don't even know where to begin, so finally I just take a deep breath and dive in.

"What do you think of Dean?" I ask her.

Amanda laughs. "What do I think of him? Well he's a good friend to you, I know that, and you guys have known each other since, what, fifth grade?"

I nod. "Yeah, a long time." I pause for a moment, and then try again. "He's pretty handsome right?"

Amanda cracks a smile. "Are you getting jealous because your friend Dean has been working out lately?"

"He has?" I question. I hadn't even realized that, but now that Amanda mentions it I suppose Dean's biceps have been getting pretty big. I'm more stunned by the fact that she was looking closely enough to notice. "I guess I wasn't really paying attention."

"Sure." Says Amanda. "Well, you don't have to worry baby, you're the most handsome man I know." She leans forward and kisses me on the lips, then pauses and goes in again. She holds longer this time as her tongue slips into my mouth.

Suddenly, I pull back. "You didn't answer the question!" I tell her. "Do you think Dean is handsome?"

Amanda laughs and shakes her head. "Why are you asking me this?"

"Because I want to know." I tell her. "Why are you avoiding the question?"

Amanda's hand creeps down my toned stomach and past the waistband of my boxers. "How about you forget about your friend for a while and just fuck me."

Suddenly, she stops, her hand wrapped tightly around my rock hard dick.

"Whoa!" Amanda laughs. "Something sure has you fired up."

I look her straight in the eyes and ask again. "Do you think Dean is handsome?"

There's a flicker in Amanda's gaze now, a flirtatious realization that neither of us quite understand but can't deny. She starts to gently stroke my cock up and down, filling my body with a warm, even pleasure.

"Are you sure you want me to tell you?" Amanda asks.

"I'm sure." I confirm, closing my eyes and leaning back into the pillow. I'm trembling with excitement now, both terrified and aroused at the same time.

"Well," Amanda begins. "I think he's pretty sexy, if you really must know." She checks to see my reaction, and then cracks a playful smile as she realizes that I am far from upset. "Do you want me to go on?"

"Yes." I beg. "Tell me more."

"He's definitively the best looking guy out of your friends." Amanda informs me. "I have to admit I've always had kind of a crush on him. I love wearing something skimpy around the house when you guys are watching the game."

"You do?" I ask, shocked.

"Yeah." Amanda giggles. "He loves checking me out, so I'll throw on some short shorts and pretend I need something from the kitchen just to walk by."

I'd never noticed this before, but she's definitely telling the truth. Now that I think about it, Amanda's behavior had always been a little strange whenever Dean was over to hang out and watch sports.

"Does that turn you on?" I ask her, reaching down and beginning to play with my wife's clit while she touches me. Amanda lets out a quiet sigh and pushes closer, moving her body against my hand.

"Yeah." She gasps. "It does."

"Would you like to fuck both of us?" I question.

Amanda's eyes snap wide open and she stops for a moment, frozen between fantasy and reality. "Seriously?" She asks me.

I take a deep breath, my cock twitching in her hand. "Yes, completely serious."

Amanda almost looks horrified at first but then her expression softens. Finally, she grins. "Let's fucking do it."

The doorbell rings twice and I hop up from my seat, rushing over and throwing it open to greet Dean with a smile and a bro hug. He's generously brought over a case of beer and is ready to go, clothed in the jersey of his favorite player.

"What's the score?" He asks, heading directly for the living room.

"Oh, yeah, the score." I respond, a little taken off guard. I'd been so excited about tonight's festivities that I hadn't even been thinking about the game. Now that he mentions it, I don't even know who's playing,

"We're up." I lie, following Dean back into the living room and collapsing onto the couch next to him. I glance up at the screen and realize that I couldn't have been more wrong. Our team is way behind.

"What happened?" Dean shouts at the screen. "We were up?"

"Yeah man." I shake my head, trying as hard as I can to not be incredibly awkward. "Looks like they had a good run against us. Shit." I relax back into the couch and pass Dean a beer from the case he brought over.

My heart is almost thumping out of my chest, not because of the game but because of what my wife is currently wearing in the back room. It's been a while since the barbeque and I haven't talked to Dean about anything even remotely sexual since, but I know that our conversation still lingers in the back of his mind. I feel like it hangs over our friendship, unmentioned between the words of every conversation that we've had since.

I few minutes pass while Amanda finishes getting ready, and Dean and I make small talk about work and the weather. Eventually, I hear the door down the hallway crack open behind us. I sneak a quick glance back over my shoulder and nearly fall out of my chair; my wife looks incredible.

She's wearing nothing but black panties and a pink, stylized team jersey, which hangs loosely around her in a causal, sexy way. Her makeup is perfect and slutty, just begging for attention which is exactly what she's about to get. Amanda winks at me, and then saunters down the hallway towards us but turns off into the kitchen before Dean has a chance to notice her.

She calls out through the dining room. "Are you boys hungry?"

Dean looks up. "Hey Mrs. Miller, I didn't know you were here!"

"I'm here, just making a snack for you boys." She calls back. "You ready for something to eat?"

Moments later, Amanda emerges from the kitchen carrying a covered tray and walks it over to us. Dean's not paying attention at first but the moment that he sees her his jaw literally drops.

"Whoa." Is all that he can manage to say, looking her up and down. He glances over to me, making sure that everything is cool and I nod in return. "You look great Amanda." Dean says.

"Why thank you." My wife says with a giggle as she steps in front of the TV and sets the tray down on the coffee table before us. "You're not looking so bad yourself."

I can't believe what's happening, my wife and my best friend flirting openly right before my very eyes.

"Would you like a snack?" Amanda repeats.

"Of course." Says Dean, the game now a complete afterthought.

Amanda reaches up and hooks each thumb under the waistband of her panties, and then slowly starts to pull them down as she rocks her hips from side to side. It's as if the whole world has stopped. When they finally reach the floor she kicks them aside and carefully lifts up the covering of her dinner tray to reveal that it's completely empty.

"I thought maybe you could both snack on my pussy for a little bid." She says with a coy smile, then steps over the table and sides down onto it with her legs spread wide open.

"You first, Dean." Amanda commands. "Peter sweetie, I want you to watch."

Dean gives me one final glance, looking for assurance, and then climbs down onto the carpet and buries his face in my wife's pussy. Seconds later, he's lapping away like a hungry dog. I reach down and unzip my fly, pulling out my cock and then going to work on myself as I watch the scene unfold. Seeing my wife pleasured by another man is unlike anything I've ever experienced and it's not long before my cock is so hard that it aches, throbbing as I stoke the length of my shaft.

Amanda's eyes lock with mine as she bites her bottom lip, clearly enjoying the attention. She reaches up and pulls the jersey over the top of her head, revealing a set of beautiful, perky tits.

"Alright," She finally says. "Now you, hubby."

Dean stands up as I take his place on the floor, sucking and nibbling on my wife's swollen clit. I look up into her eyes and watch as the pleasure washes over her body in waves, but our moment is cut short as Dean takes his position next to her and shoves his cock directly into Amanda's mouth. She takes him to the base, pushing down as far as she can go and then coming back up with a gasp.

Dean's dick is absolutely massive, and for a moment I'm wondering if my wife can even take it but, after she collects herself, she tries again and his member slides down to the hilt no problem. Amanda's face is pressed up against Dean's hard abs, his balls slapping against her chin as he slowly pushes in and out of her depths. She moans loudly against the meat of his shaft, the sound vibrating across his cock.

Eventually Amanda pulls him out of her mouth and stands up from the coffee table.

"I want your friends cock inside of me." She tells me, and then turns to Dean. "How does that sound?"

"Fucking fantastic." Dean laughs.

Amanda pushes the coffee table away from the couch and then lays over it doggystyle, her perfect round ass popped out towards us. "Rail me." She says with a wink, looking back over her shoulder.

Dean has no problem following orders and crouches down behind my wife. I watch as he positions himself at the entrance of her tight, wet slit, and the pushes forward forcefully. Amanda lets out a long groan, trembling while Dean pumps in and out of her slowly.

Meanwhile, I walk around to the other end of the coffee table and get down on my knees so that my cock is perfectly level with Amanda's mouth. I push myself between her lips and watch as she's slammed from behind. Every thrust forward from Dean propels her further down my shaft and every slam back from me sends her plummeting onto Dean's massive cock. It's not long before we find a rhythm like this, thrusting into her from either end as my wife trembles and moans between us. We pick up the pace until eventually we are pummeling her with all of our force, slamming her beautiful body like she's nothing more than a filthy slut. Amanda looks up at me, the mascara now running down her cheeks. She winks.

Seconds later, Amanda pulls me out of her mouth. "Flip me over." My wife commands.

Dean and I do as we're told, quickly lifting her up and rolling her onto her back. Amanda kicks her legs up over Dean's shoulders and then arches her back as he slides into her once again.

"Oh my god!" She cries out. "You're so fucking big! I can't believe how well you stretch out this tight little pussy out!"

Dean pounds her hard, rattling the table as her hands grip the edge tightly and brace against the slams. Amanda leans her head back and then swallows me into her mouth, sucking gracefully as my balls dangle directly above her face. She pulls me out and licks my shaft from base to tip, then takes me inside once again and lets me drive down to the hilt. I hold there until she gives me a quick tap for air and I release, letting my wife take in a few grateful gulps.

Looking across the table at Dean, I can't believe this is actually happening. In all the years that Amanda and me have been married, I could have never imagined what it would be like to watch another man with my wife. I especially would have never expected to enjoy it this much, and yet here I am, quaking with excitement as he pounds away at the beautiful pussy that, for years, had only been touched by me. I love seeing her twist and tremble from the pleasure that he causes her, carefully taking in the way that it looks when her gorgeous body is violated by another set of hands that run across her massive tits.

Eventually, I just can't take it anymore. I pull my dick out of Amanda's mouth and lay down on the living room floor, then command, "Get on."

Amanda does as she's told, climbing down onto me and straddling my toned abs. She reaches under and helps my cock along as it slides up into her pussy, then whimpers happily as it reaches the end. She starts to grind against me, eyes closed at first and then opening them to stare me down. I've seen that expression in the bedroom many times before, a blissful place of lustful abandon where she'd be willing to do anything and everything, no matter how dirty.

Dean climbs down into position behind her and for a moment our gaze breaks as she looks back over her shoulder at him. "I want you to fuck me in that tight married asshole." She tells him. "Double fuck me as hard as you can and make me fucking cum."

Dean aligns the head of his shaft at her puckered doorway and then thrusts forward in one slow, powerful swoop.

Amanda grabs onto me tightly as her limits are tested, the rim of her holes expanding just enough to accommodate the massive girth of both Dean and I. I can feel him pulse within her through the thin membrane between her ass and pussy.

Soon the three of us are all rocking together passionately, pumping in and out of her tightness like a set of duel pistons. Every time that Dean pulls out of her ass I push inside, back and forth together as we gain speed until we are pounding away with all of our force. Amanda starts to scream, bucking wildly as she edges closer and closer to orgasm.

Being the gentleman that I am, I reach down between her legs and begin to rapidly play with her clit. Moments later, this sends Amanda over the edge and suddenly my wife is screaming incoherently, crying out in a mess of jumbled profanity and nonsense words.

"Fuck me motherfucking cocksucker ass fucks!" She screams, her eyes rolling back into her head as I try my best not to laugh. She's completely out of it, damn near leaving her body as we exercise the orgasmic demons within her.

"Do you like that you fucking slut?" I yell, not letting up for a second as I slam into her pussy. I look at Dean. "Call my wife a fucking slut!" I command.

Dean grabs Amanda by the hair and pulls back so that she's looking up at him. "He asked you a question, slut. Do you like that fucking dick?"

"Yes!" Amanda cries out, loving the rough treatment.

"Do you like our dicks inside you at the same time?" Dean yells.

"I love them!" My wife cries out.

"Why?"

She looks as though she's about to explode with ecstasy, red in the face and barely able to form the words as they spill out of her mouth. "Because I'm a fucking slut!" She shrieks.

With this final explosion of orgasm, Amanda collapses between us. She's completely spent, fucked into oblivion and reeling from the sensations that still simmer across her body. Dean and I pull out and then stand up as Amanda climbs to her knees between us.

"If your wife is a slut," Amanda says with a grin. "Then you might as well cover her with cum like one."

"Fuck yes." I moan, beating my cock as I stand above her. Dean does the same, looking down at her gorgeous face as he prepares to cover it in his spunk.

"Cum all over my face!" Amanda commands. "Do it! Shoot your fucking loads all over me."

Seconds later, Dean is exploding across her girlish smile, raining down onto her with a massive splatter of milky white jizz. It paints her face and runs down her cheeks on either side. Amanda licks her lips.

"How about you now?" She says, turning to me. "Do I look nice with your buddies cum all over me?"

At this point, I'm almost trembling too hard to beat off, the adrenalin that courses through my blood growing to a level that's getting difficult to maintain. I certainly don't understand it, why it feels so good to watch my perfect bride become such a filthy, depraved whore before my very eyes, but I love the feelings just the same. I can't get enough of the way that she looks with another mans spunk dangling off of her chin, gazing up at me with those gorgeous doe eyes that I'm lucky enough to look into every morning when I wake up.

Suddenly, an orgasm hits me hard and my knees nearly give out beneath me. A gigantic load erupts from the head of my cock, shooting hard against my wife's face and then directly into her open mouth. She giggles and takes it all, swallowing my cum and then sucking the remainder out of my shaft with a few quick pumps.

"Fuck!" I cry, and then pull back and stumble over to the couch where I collapse next to Dean. My wife stays on her knees, staring at us in silence until finally all three of us burst out laughing.

"Thanks boys." Amanda says. "Go team!"

HOT NEIGHBOR

Maybe I'm a little naive about the hard truth of heated female sexuality, because it took me forever to figure out why my wife was so obsessed with tanning in the backyard. She's gorgeous, and certainly takes care of her body with daily trips to the gym and careful consideration of everything that she eats, so I figured the sunbathing was just an extension of this. To be fair, maybe it even started out that way, but eventually a pattern began to emerge.

Our neighbor, Mark, is one of those guys who will probably forever be a bachelor. I've got no idea why someone with his particular interests would move into a big house in the suburbs instead of some fancy penthouse downtown, but now that he's here he's made his presence known. I'm an easy going guy, so the loud music doesn't really bother me all that much, but when I see the beautiful young women that Mark is constantly parading to and from their cars, I can't help but get a little envious. I mean, I love my wife and, with that beautiful girlish face and hourglass figure, she's more than enough to satisfy me for the rest of my life. But, sometimes I can't help but wonder what it's like to be a guy like Mark.

It didn't take long before my wife started noticing Mark, too. There's a trellis covered in vines that separates our mutual back yards, but it's still very easy to see through. Whenever Mark comes out for his daily afternoon swim, my wife always seems to immediately crave a quick tan. As far as I know, they hadn't exchanged more words than a few neighborly pleasantries, but I wouldn't be surprised if that changed any day now.

Was I jealous that this complete stud had caught the eye of my beautiful wife? Sure. But I couldn't help noticing that there was something more to my feelings, something lurking just below the surface that I couldn't quite put a finger on.

"I'm home!" I shout, pushing my way through our large front door and throwing my suitcase into the chair that sits in the entryway. I undo my tie as I walk, trying desperately to relieve myself of the workday constriction that still hangs around my neck like a noose.

Jamie, my wife, comes strutting around the corner to greet me in her yellow bikini, holding a glass of wine. She gives me a long, passionate kiss as I run my hands along the perfect curves of her body.

"It's good to see you baby." Jamie tells me. "How was work?"

"Horrible as usual." I laugh. "What did you do all day?"

"This." She says with a giggle, spinning around in a circle to show off her gorgeous body. "Notice a difference?"

"With?" I ask.

She rolls her eyes. "My tan."

"Oh, sure. Yeah." I stammer, clearly missing my queue to lie about it like the supportive husband that I am. "Your tan looks amazing, baby."

Suddenly a figure comes walking through the back door. "Hey Jamie, I found that root that was blocking the sprinkler." He stops dead in his tracks when he notices me. It's Mark, shirtless and sweaty from working out in the afternoon sun. "Allen!" He shouts, immediately shifting gears and shaking my hand. "It's so good to see you!"

Realizing how it looks, Jamie immediately jumps into explanation mode. "Mark was just here helping me with that sprinkler in the back yard, you know the one that hasn't been working?"

I nod. "Yeah, I haven't had a chance to look at it yet."

"All better." Mark says. "A root was growing up under the pipe and cutting it off, but I got it out of there no problem."

"Oh, thank you." I tell him.

The three of us stand in awkward silence for a moment until Mark finally throws a hand up and announces, "Well, I gotta be heading back over to my place now. Thanks for the lemonade, Jamie."

"Thank you for all the help!" Jamie calls out as the handsome man exits through the backdoor and begins to cross our yard back over to his place.

I can tell that Jamie is nervous about something, but I'm not exactly sure what it is. Of all things, though, I'm definitely not worried about infidelity. If there's one thing I've learned from having a wife as hot as she is, it's how to trust and respect your partner's faithfulness to you. When every man on the planet wants to fuck her and she doesn't do it, that actually says a lot. Of course, it doesn't mean she's not gonna flirt every once in a while.

"You've got yourself a little crush." I finally say.

Jamie's eyes flick downward as the words leave my mouth, an instant giveaway made even more obvious by her slightly drunken state. "On who?"

I laugh. "Baby, don't even try to hide it. I know you've got a thing for Mark."

Jamie sighs with a wide smile. "Okay fine. But I mean, come on, he's ridiculously sexy."

From where I'm standing I can see out the kitchen window and into Mark's backyard, where he's stripped down and jumped in the pool to cool off after all of that difficult yard work. His body is perfectly toned and ripped, moving under the sun like some sort of powerful, sexual machine.

I shrug. "Sure, I get it."

Jamie walks towards me and then presses her half naked body up against mine. Her skin is still hot from lying out. "Don't worry baby, I'm all yours." She says, and then kisses me deeply. "You don't need to worry."

I hold Jamie tight for a moment and then pull back to look down at her. "I know, baby. It's okay to fantasize, anyway."

"I'd never do that." She says. "Come on."

I hold her gaze, clearly not believing a word of it. "You're telling me that you've never even fantasized about fucking mark?"

"No!" She protests walking back across the kitchen and quickly downing the rest of her drink before she sets it beside the sink. She turns around and leans back against the counter to face me.

"Not once?" I probe, skeptically.

Jamie's expression starts to crack, a devilish grin trying desperately not to sneak across her face. "Okay, fine." She says. "Maybe once or twice I've thought about fucking Mark."

I'm suddenly hit with a flash of jealousy that shoots through my veins like a vicious cocktail. I try to push against it but the emotion is just too overwhelming, and eventually I'm forced to give in. Now I'm swimming in it, the envy clouding my thoughts like a heavy green haze. The strangest part is, however, is that I really like it.

It's hard to put my finger on what exactly is so pleasurable about this feeling; is it the helplessness, or maybe just the fact that the emotion itself is so completely enveloping and powerful? Either way, I love it, and I'm helpless as the lustful undercurrent takes hold.

"I don't blame you. He's a good looking guy." I finally say. "So, what exactly do you fantasize about?"

Jamie's jaw literally drops as I ask her this. "Are you kidding me? I'm not telling you that!" She protests.

"Hey, I don't mind if you're fantasizing about the neighbor guy." I explain. "But you've at least got to tell me what you're thinking. I don't think that's too much to ask."

Jamie's look of shock slowly transforms into a smile as she begins to realize something. "Oh my god!" She finally blurts out with an amused chuckle. "You little perv! You're getting off on this!"

"Maybe." I admit. "Just tell me."

My wife lets out a long sigh. "It's not any one thing, he's just so fucking sexy. You know that I love you, and I always will, but you're the only man I've been with in the last five years and…" Jamie trails off, already worried that she's said too much.

"Tell me." I coax. "I want to know." I suddenly realize that my cock is rock hard within my pants, engorged with jealous anxiety.

"It's not like I think about it all the time, but I miss other cocks, you know?" She says.

I nod.

"He's so hot and it makes me wonder what he'd feel like, what he tastes like." Jamie continues. "But, I love you. You know that, right?"

"Of course." I assure her.

"Our marriage is more important than any of that stuff." Jamie tells me. "It's just a fantasy anyway."

I pause for a moment, all kinds of thoughts circling wildly within my head. I take a deep breath, not at all sure if I should say what I'm about to say. The next few words that I utter could change our marriage forever.

"Would you ever want to make that fantasy a reality?" I ask.

Jamie looks confused. "No, baby, of course not."

"I mean, if I was okay with it." I explain. "Maybe if I was there with you?"

"Is this a trick question?" She asks with a laugh, clearly a little uncomfortable.

I shake my head. "I'm totally serious. In fact, I think it would be pretty hot if me and Mark double teamed you."

"What!?" She blurts out. "You've got to be kidding me."

"Not in the slightest." I assure her.

Jamie thinks about this a moment. "Well, even if I say yes, it's not like he would go for it."

I burst out laughing, completely unable to contain myself.

"What's so funny?" Jamie demands to know.

When I finally stop laughing I take a moment to catch my breath. Jamie looks completely confused by my reaction. "Baby, he's a guy. He's just as obsessed with you as you are with him." I tell her. "Besides, you're gorgeous, a perfect ten. There isn't a man on the planet who wouldn't want to fuck you silly."

"Aw stop." She says, blushing. "A perfect ten?"

"You are!" I confirm. "How about this. Invite Mark over for dinner tomorrow, just the three of us, and we'll see where it goes from there."

A smile crosses Jamie's face. "Really, you're okay with that?"

"I can't think of anything hotter." I confess.

I can tell that Jamie is nervous because she jumps when the doorbell rings. We exchange glances and then laugh as I leave her to greet Mark. I stroll into the front entryway and throw open the front door.

"Mark!" I say, offering a firm handshake. "Come on in."

The guy looks good cleaned up, wearing well-tailored suit jacket and carrying a nice bottle of red wine.

Jamie comes out of the kitchen, still drying her hands. "I'm sorry," she says. "I'm just finishing up in there. Dinner is almost ready!"

"It's okay!" Mark assures, giving her a hug.

Jamie grabs the wine. "Oh, let me take that. Thank you."

Mark hands it over.

"This is funny." My wife blurts. "I'm so used to you coming in my backdoor."

The whole conversation stops awkwardly as Jamie and I exchange glances. It feels like the silence lasts an eternity until finally I just can't help it anymore and burst out laughing.

Immediately, a timer rings loudly from the kitchen. Saved by the bell. "Dinners ready!" Says Jamie. "You guys have a seat at the table."

She leaves quickly and I lead Mark into the dining room where some candles have been lit. We sit down and chat for a moment about the upcoming draft of our local football team, until Jamie suddenly emerges from the kitchen with a salad in one hand and a delicious plate of steak in the other.

"Oh my god." Mark fawns. "What can't she do?"

"You have no idea." I tell him with a wry smile.

Jamie sets the food down and then pours everyone a generous helping of Mark's wine. "Alright boys, dig in."

The meal is delicious and the conversation pleasant. Despite my initial reservations, Mark is actually a really nice guy and funny to boot. Eventually, the three of us are all sufficiently relaxed and I decide to change gears.

"So I've noticed you have a lot of young women coming and going from your place." I say.

Mark is too buzzed to even attempt denying his wild bachelor ways. "Yeah, it happens." He says.

"Any of them a girlfriend?" I ask.

He shakes his head and chuckles. "It's been a while since I've had a girlfriend, just enjoying the single life."

"I bet." I say, nodding.

Jamie finally chimes in. "I'm sure it gets pretty crazy over there. Can I ask you a personal question, Mark?"

He smiles. "Of course."

"Have you ever had a threesome?"

Mark hesitates for a moment, trying to decide whether or not the information he's about to divulge goes a little too deep. Finally, he gives in. "Oh yeah." Mark admits. "All the time."

"Really?" She asks, "What's that like? I bet it's great."

Mark considers this for a moment. "It's a lot of fun, really. I can see how some guys would be intimidated by having to take care of two women in the bedroom, but I think that I manage pretty well. Everyone seems to come away satisfied."

"I bet they do." Jamie says with a wink, which make my heart skip a beat. She takes a long sip from her wine glass, eyeing Mark flirtatiously over the rim. "What about two guys on one girl, have you ever done that?"

Mark shakes his head.

"Would you like to?" Jamie asks.

My face is flushed now, all of my anxiety built up into a feverish breaking point. My cock is rock hard, throbbing with anticipation as I await Mark's answer.

"What are you trying to say?" Mark asks, looking back and forth between Jamie and me.

"You know what I'm asking." Jamie says.

My wife slowly stands up from her chair and makes her way around the table until she's standing directly between Mark and I. She puts a hand on each of our shoulders and rubs gently, sending a chill down my spine.

"Turn your chairs around." Jamie commands. We do as we're told, spinning away from the table so that we are now facing outward while we sit. My wife kneels down between us and looks up with her big blue eyes, rubbing up and down our legs seductively.

"Are you sure this is okay?" She asks me. "Is this what you want?"

"Yes." I moan, blinded by arousal and aching to take this all the way, to watch her fuck another man right in front of me.

Jamie reaches up and skillfully undoes the front of both our pants, pulling them down along with our underwear. My dick springs forth in all of its engorged glory, ready to be serviced. I look over and see that Mark is fully erect as well, and that his cock is absolutely massive.

My wife looks back and forth between the two and then decides to pleasure our guest first, leaning over and taking his length between her soft lips. She swallows him down as far as she can, retching a little as his incredible length hits the limit of her gag reflex, and then trying again. This time she manages to relax and take him entirely, engulfing his rod down to the hilt as her face presses up against Mark's toned abs.

He leans back in the chair and lets out a long, satisfied groan, enjoying the sensation of my wife's expert blowjob skills. He puts his hands on the back of her head and starts to bob her up and down on his shaft, taking control as his cock pumps within her.

Without looking up, Jamie reaches over with her free hand and grabs tightly onto my cock, stroking slowly while I watch her and Mark enjoy each other. It feels incredible, the sensation only amplified by the look of pure bliss on my wife's face as she struggles to wrap her lips around Marks gigantic dick.

After a while she comes up for air and then turns her attention to me, scooting across the floor and burying her head in my lap. I'm left speechless as she consumes my entire shaft, swallowing down as far as she can go until my balls press up against her chin. I can feel my wife playfully tickle my sack with her tongue before pulling up and gasping for air.

"Did you like watching me suck off Mark?" She asks me.

I nod. "I loved it."

"Do you want him to fuck me while I blow you?" She continues.

"Oh god, yes." I close my eyes lean back against the hard wooden chair.

My wife hikes up her dress and pulls off her panties as Mark climbs into position behind her on the dining room floor. His massive cock resting firm in his hands, I watch as he pushes into Jamie from behind. She lets out a pleasant sigh as he enters her, bracing against the movement as Mark begins to pump in and out of her tight pussy.

"That feels so fucking good." She cries out. "Oh fuck!"

I take Jamie's head in my hands and force it down on my huge cock, guiding her over the length of my dick while she's pounded from behind. She trembles with pleasure as she services me, clearly being hit in just the right way by Mark's thick rod.

Eventually, I slide down from the chair and position myself with them on the dining room floor. Jaime is impaled between us on her hands and knees while Mark and I take her from each end, pushing her back and forth on our cocks with equally powerful thrusts. We find ourselves in a perfect rhythm, pulsing together in an erotic mess of sighs and moans. Mark is really giving it to her now, and I force myself to keep up in a primal display of competition.

After a while, we flip her over and switch places so that Mark is fucking her face while I thrust forcefully between my wife's open legs. She spreads them out for me, showing off her incredibly toned body and massive tits that bounce with every slam against her pussy. Her neck is long and slender as she leans back to swallow Mark's girth, pulling him out every once in a while so that she can lick his cock from balls to tip.

"I feel so fucking nasty." She moans. "I love being a plaything for two big dicks."

Her slutty confession pushes me over the edge and suddenly I find myself hammering her body with all of my might, rapidly pounding away at her tight little pussy. She starts to groan louder and louder, her face turning bright red as she begins to quake with pleasure. Moments later my wife explodes in a cry of blissed out passion, her eyes rolling back into her head as an orgasm overwhelms her senses. She screams into Mark's cock, which blocks her throat, and then falls back against the floor in exhaustion.

"I want more." Jamie says to me, pulling Mark's dick out of her mouth. "Lay down."

I do as I'm told, lying back against the hard floor while my wife climbs on top of me. She straddles by body with her long legs, positioning herself carefully before sliding down the length of my cock. She bites her lip as I stretch her out, filling her up with my thickness.

Jamie begins to ride me, slowly at first and then gaining speed as she takes my cock within her in a series of powerful swoops. She grabs me tightly by the shoulders and uses the leverage to pump even harder, fucking me like her life depends on it. Finally, once she's grown sufficiently horny and wild, my wife looks back over her shoulder at Mark and commands, "Shove that dick right up my asshole."

The thought of Jamie's perfect little asshole being ravaged by another man is almost too much to handle, but I manage to hold off on cumming just yet. I watch instead as Mark, now completely naked and showing off his muscular body, climbs into position behind Jamie. He aligns his cock with her puckered backdoor and then thrusts forward.

Jamie screams with pain and pleasure as he slips inside of her. Immediately, the sensation around my cock becomes tighter, stretched to the brink as two cocks begin to pump back and forth within her holes. She grabs onto me tightly and grits her teeth while Mark and I speed up, but by the time we reach a full throttle pounding she appears to be whole heartedly enjoying it.

"Fuck me harder!" Jamie demands, practically begging at this point as she loses herself in the heat of the moment. "Pound me like the slut wife that I am!"

We continue to ram her, growing closer and closer to orgasm ourselves until finally I tell Mark. "If you're going to cum, blow it in her fucking pussy."

"What?" Mark asks, a little shocked and confused.

"Cum in my wife's tight little pussy!" I demand.

Jamie clearly likes this idea because she quickly pulls us out of her and spins around, frantically tearing off her dress and throwing it to the side. I remain exactly where I've been and help my wife guide herself down onto me, this time impaling her up the ass while she faces away. Once completely filled, Jamie leans back and spreads her legs in the air. She coaxes Mark to come forward and push his giant dick up into her wet slit.

Mark mounts Jamie expertly and moments later I can feel his cock slipping up into her toned body. My wife trembles with excitement as she takes a leg in each hand and spreads herself open, giving it all to him while the two of us double pound her pussy and ass.

"You feel so good inside of me!" She moans. "Give me your fucking loads!"

Mark and I pick up the pace, railing her as hard as we can until finally neither of us can hold back any longer. We explode at the same time, our cocks ejecting load after milky load into Jamie's tight holes. My wife shrieks as we pump her full of cum, and I suddenly realize that she's right there with us, enjoying her second orgasm of the night. Jamie leans back and lets out a long, powerful string of expletives as her body clenches tightly. I'm still cumming, still erupting with jizz until finally there's just no more room within her tightness and our loads come squirting out from the corners of her pussy and ass. The spunk runs down her legs and mixes together in a mess of pearly white streaks.

Finally, the three of us collapse in a heap on the floor, panting and exhausted. Mark and I pull out of my wife and start to get dressed, woozy and lightheaded after the unexpected but incredibly satisfying workout.

I'm just about ready to leave work when Jamie sends me a text.

'I've been horny all day.' It reads. I smile, happy to hear that I'll be receiving a special treat after this long day at the office.

'I think I can help you with that.' I type back and hit send. I start to collect my things, putting a small selection of important files into my briefcase. My phone vibrates on the desk almost immediately.

'It's a two man job.' Her message reads. 'Hurry home.'

There's a brief pause before a picture message appears on my screen. It's a photo of her beautiful face with Mark's massive cock resting pleasantly between her lips. She stares up at the phone's camera with huge doe eyes, just begging for dick.

I'm not even mad, not in the slightest.

'On my way.' I text back as I head out the door, my dick rock hard and ready for action.

WEDDING NIGHT

Things are going to happen at your bachelor party that, as an unspoken rule, will never be discussed again. It's like your own miniature one night trip to Vegas and what happens there stays there. It's no wonder that so many groups of guys take this concept literally and descend on sin city by the thousands every weekend to live it up before one of their own is locked down in holy matrimony. Tonight, we are no different.

After a fantastic concert and some full on, bottle-service-level clubbing, we somehow drunkenly pile into a taxi and end up at a strip club on the edge of town. The place is jumping though, so I'm not completely disappointed and when we walk through the front doors I'm immediately greeted with a shockingly good selection of beautiful young ladies.

We're seated in a cluster of chairs at the edge of one of the stripper stages, of which there are many. This place is huge, like a department store of naked dancing women.

"See anyone you like?" My buddy Logan asks, glancing around the room at the assortment of pretty young things as they shake their asses to top forty hits.

"I'm good." I tell him, "Thank you, though."

Logan laughs and shakes his head. "No Don, you're not getting out of here without a lap dance. This is your last night as a free man."

"I've been dating Alana for three years." I explain. "I haven't been a free man for a very long time."

"Dude," Logan protests. "Having a girlfriend and having a wife are not even close to the same thing. Trust me." He flashes the wedding ring on his finger. "You are going to be locked down in a whole new kind of way."

"So what if I want to be locked down?" I shout over the music. "Alana is hotter than any of the girls in this place."

Logan shrugs and leans back in his chair, "Yeah, you're got a point there."

For the first time, I can sense the alcohol clouding Logan's judgment. In all the time that I'd known him, he'd never once mentioned Alana's hotness so blatantly.

Not that we didn't all known it was there. Alana is a total bombshell, the complete package with brains, beauty and a great sense of humor. She's got a gorgeous body that looks like it was built in a science lab specifically for sexual arousal, with long legs and a rack that somehow seems to defy gravity, huge and perky. I've never seen anything like it, until now.

Logan notices her too, and for a moment we are both speechless, eyeing up the sexy toned dancer as she struts out from the backroom in a tiny black bikini.

"Holy shit." Logan finally says. "Is it just me or does that look exactly like Alana?"

The other guys aren't paying attention at this point, but I'm right there with him. A part of me wants to be mad at him for comparing my girlfriend to a Vegas stripper on the edge of town, but I really can't deny the similarity. The long brown hair, the cute freckles, and most of all the symmetry of the face is astonishing.

"Dude! That's your girl, Don!" Logan says excitedly, waving her over.

"No man!" I try to stop him but before I can she's already right next to us, offering a cute smile and running her hands along Logan's shoulders.

"Hi boys." She says seductively. "I'm Candy."

"That's not your real name." Logan protests.

"It is!" Candy insists. "I swear."

Logan shakes his head, "There's no way your parents named you that, unless they were convinced that one day you would eventually become a stripper and I doubt that was high on their wish list."

"Dude!" I interject, but Candy just rolls her eyes, unfazed.

"Candy's my real name." She repeats.

"Well, not tonight!" Logan informs her. "Tonight, it's Alana. Sound good?" He hands her a twenty-dollar bill, which she casually takes and stuffs into her bra.

"You caught me!" The stripper says cheerfully. "My names actually Alana, funny how I just forgot like that."

The next thing I know, the stripper is grinding herself all over Logan. Her body is incredible, and in the dim lighting of the strip club she really is almost indistinguishable from my beautiful bride-to-be. I watch as she straddles him and rubs her hands up and down Logan's chest, her perfect ass popped out seductively right in front of me.

"Oh shit!" Logan yelps after a good two or three minutes of this. "I was supposed to pay for you to dance on my friend!" He starts laughing.

"It's all good man." I tell him.

"No, no, no. She's all yours."

I don't want to say it, but watching this fake-stripper-Alana rub all over Logan has stirred something strange inside of me. I'm not quite sure what it is, but I know that I like it and somehow would rather watch her on my friend than have her servicing me. My imagination is already running wild, pretending that it actually is my beautiful fiancé here in the club, half naked and dancing for the both of us.

"I've got a better idea." Fake Alana interjects. "How about you pay me a hundred and I'll dance for both of you in the private room. That way you don't have to fight over me."

"I don't know." I say cautiously, but Logan is already on board, standing up quickly and grabbing Alana by the hand as they head towards the back.

"Don't even think about it." He tells me. "Come on."

I sigh and stand up, following them through the main room until we reach a purple curtain and slide inside. We're now in a tiny, but very comfortable space that's much quieter than the rest of the club, with a big purple couch that the stripper sits us on side by side.

The fake Alana quickly goes to work turning around and bouncing her incredible ass up and down on my lap. She takes my hands in hers and lets me rub up and down the sides of her body, kindly letting me enjoy the perfection of her curves as they slide under my fingertips. Eventually, she pushes herself back onto me and leans hard against my chest, arching her back as she removes her top and throws it to the side. Her tits really are perfect.

Eventually, she makes her way over to Logan, sliding across our laps and then climbing onto him. She rubs her massive tits in his face, giggling a little.

"You guys are cute!" She says. "I'm thinking I could probably do more for you if you were interested."

"What do you mean?" I ask, curious.

She starts to drop further and further down until her knees are on the floor and she's directly between us, looking up with her giant doe eyes.

"I'm thinking I could give you two a little relief." She says with a wink.

Her resemblance to Alana has gone from freaking me out to turning me on, especially as I watch the way that Logan is eyeing her up hungrily. I can't help but wonder if he would be this aggressive with the real Alana, given the right circumstances.

The stripper reaches up with both hands and starts to undo our pants simultaneously. "If you give me an extra fifty I'll suck both of you off." She says.

I'm too turned on at this point to say no and Logan is way ahead of me, immediately pulling out a crisp fifty and handing it over.

The stripper shimmies down the rest of our pants and then promptly pulls out each of our massive cocks. She goes to work on me first, taking my length into her mouth and then bobbing up and down on my shaft with elegant strokes. The fake Alana is beating off Logan as she sucks me, but her skills are still impeccable, running her tongue in rapid circles around my shaft while her lips stay tightly wrapped. I lean back and let out a long moan of pleasure.

Eventually, she switches over to Logan, swallowing his huge cock with equal ferocity. I watch in complete awe as the stripper takes him, and I'm suddenly overwhelmed with a strange, unfamiliar desire. I want so badly for that to be my wife with her lips around Logan's rod, for my gorgeous bride to be stroking me off just like this while she takes another man down her throat. I want to watch her fuck another man right in front of me and I want to join in, plugging every one of her unfilled holes as we rotate through a never-ending series of positions together.

The stripper is beating me off faster and faster as she pumps up and down on Logan. I'm so wrapped up in picturing her as my wife that when I blow my load I'm completely surprised, the orgasm hitting me like a brick truck as a thick rope of jizz launches from he head of my cock. Logan starts to shake and buck as well and seconds later he cries out, emptying his balls into the strippers hungry mouth.

The two of us collapse back in exhaustion as the fake Alana stands up and wipes her lips.

"Thanks guys!" She says cheerfully, all business. "Hope you enjoyed yourself!" She then turns and heads back out onto the main floor.

The ride back home to Los Angeles is actually quite relaxing, thanks especially to the pipe cleaning that Logan and I had just received from Candy the stripper hours earlier. The other two from our group are passed out in the back, enjoying some much needed rest, while Logan and I stay up talking as the sun slowly begins to rise over the endless desert.

"Are you ready now?" Logan asks me slowly, clearly beaten down by the night's festivities.

"For marriage? Of course." I tell him. "I was ready way before this. I love her."

"I know man." Logan says. "She's a catch."

We sit in silence for a moment, both thinking any number of strange things as the car flies briskly across the interstate towards the future scene of a beautiful wedding.

Logan suddenly breaks the silence with a laugh, chuckling to himself. "Dude, it's crazy how much that stripper looked like Alana though."

I crack a smile and shake my head in amazement. "Tell me about it."

Logan is still cracking up. "Don't hate me for cumming in your fiancés mouth!"

I punch him in the shoulder.

"What?" He says. "Come on man, at least it's not the real thing."

I pause for a moment, my heart racing. I'm not exactly sure where I'm heading with this but I'm too turned on not to mention it.

"What if it was?" I ask him.

Logan suddenly gets very serious. "What do you mean?"

"What if it was Alana?" I ask him. "Would you be into it?"

"Are you trying to trick me right now?" Logan asks. "Are you fucking with me?"

I shake my head. "I swear on my life. I want to know."

"Are you asking if I want to double team your fiancé with you?" Logan questions, flat out.

"No." I say with a smile. "My wife."

Logan takes his time before speaking, looking out across the desert as a plethora of thoughts run through his head. "Honestly, that was pretty hot." He finally says. "Do you think she'd go for it?"

Surprisingly, this is a question that I actually know the answer to. Alana and I have always had a pretty adventurous sex life, and much of that has amounted to some incredibly dirty talk in the bedroom. Threesomes have definitely come up, although we've never actually gotten up the courage to have one. When questioned on the topic of men that she'd like to take on, Logan is consistently at the top of the list, and with good reason. He's a great looking guy and a lot of fun. I'm secure with the fact that Alana has a crush on him.

"I think she'd love it." I tell him. " I know exactly what to do."

As Alana and me pull into the driveway of our home I'm literally trembling with excitement. The ceremony was amazing and went off without a hitch, leaving me buzzing and ready to spend the rest of my life with the woman of my dreams. Admittedly, I was also pretty excited about the surprise that waited for us inside the house.

"Is that Logan's car?" Alana asks, noticing his blue two-door in the driveway.

"It looks like it is." I say, feigning ignorance. "Weird. He must have left it here and gotten a ride with someone else to the wedding site."

Alana steps out of the car, looking gorgeous in her tight white wedding dress, which opens up around the legs in stunning fashion. She walks around the car, past the 'just married' proclamation scrawled across the back window, and then greets me with huge kiss.

"I'm so happy!" She says with a grin.

"Just wait." I tell her slyly, leading her up the front porch and into our house.

The second that we get inside I have her pressed up against the wall, kissing her hard and running my hands up and down her incredible, toned body.

"Watch the dress!" She says, laughing, then turns around and lets me unzip her from top to bottom. She steps out, showing off the beautiful white lingerie beneath, and then jumps right back into it. I tear off my clothes as we attack each other with lustful gropes and kisses, making our way upstairs to the bedroom.

The next thing I know she's pushing me through the bedroom door, where I fall backwards into the bed and she collapses on top of me. Alana pulls down my boxer briefs and extracts my thick, swollen cock, stroking it up and down while she moves lower and lower. When she reaches the bottom she takes me entirely into her mouth, relaxing enough that I slide easily past her gag reflex and into the depths of her throat. I moan loudly, pressing back into the pillows and closing my eyes. She pulls me out and flicks the tip of my cock with her tongue and then dives back down again, her lips wrapped tightly around my thick shaft.

"Oh my god, that's so amazing." I confess, placing my hands on the back of her head and helping to pump her across my length.

Alana drives deep and holds, taking everything that she can in a stunning deep throat that makes my toes curl. Her face is pressed firmly up against my toned abs and her tongue sticks slightly out, just enough to tickle the skin of my balls. I watch as she wiggles her ass playfully in the air.

"You're really fucking cute." I tell her.

Alana pulls my cock out of my mouth and a gasp and smiles up at me. "Oh yeah? What do you want to do with your cute new wife?"

I'm anxious now, not entirely sure that I have the courage to go through with this. My heart is nearly pounding out of my chest as I collect myself and carefully choose my next words.

"Well," I tell her. "You look so innocent in that white lace, so I think I'd like to do something extra dirty."

Alana winks. "I like that."

"I think it might be a little too dirty for you, though." I tell her. "I don't know if you can handle it."

"Oh, I can handle it." She tells me, beginning to slowly run her tightly gripped hand across my throbbing dick. "Tell me, baby."

"Are you sure?" I counter.

"I'm sure." She says, and then licks me playfully from base to tip.

I take a deep breath. "I want to see you be a total slut." I tell her. "I want to double team you with another guy."

She stops stroking immediately. "Really?"

"Yeah." I confirm. "I want it so badly and I don't know why."

Alana smiles and starts to stroke again, harder now. "Well, I think that sounds really hot, I'd love to."

As the words leave her lips a tremor of arousal runs down the length of my spine. I can't believe this is actually happening.

"Okay then, I have another wedding gift for you." I tell her. "Is that okay?"

Alana looks completely confused as I reach over to the bedside table and grab my phone, then send off a quick text. "What are you doing?" She asks.

"Getting you that other cock." I tell her.

Suddenly, the door behinds us opens up and Logan steps inside, completely naked with his massive cock at full attention. Alana jumps to her feet and tries to cover up, but there's nothing around so she just ends up sitting on the end of the bed, awkwardly holding a hand over her exposed pussy.

"What the fuck!" She shouts amid a fit of laughter. "Logan?"

"At your service." He says.

Alana looks back over her shoulder at me. "And you're okay with this?"

I'm quaking with desire. "More than okay." I tell her.

Logan steps forward suddenly and meets Alana at the edge of the bed, leaning down and kissing her deeply. She stays rigid at first but then slowly allows herself to relax as she accepts the body pressing up against hers. As their lips release from one another Alana lets out a long sigh.

"Oh my god." She says, reaching down and taking her cock in his hand. She glances back at me one more time for approval and I nod.

A look of sheer joy suddenly crosses my new wife's face as she fully realizes the treat that she's in for. She hops back onto the bed and spins around so that she's in the doggystyle positions, facing towards me with Logan lined up perfectly at her back end.

"What are you waiting for, boys!" She laughs. "Fuck me!"

Immediately, we spring into action. I scoot forward so that my cock is once again directly in front of Alana's face and she takes me graciously into her mouth, pushing me deep. Behind her, Logan aligns his dick at the entrance to her wet slit, and moments later he pushes forward, stretching the limits of her tightness. My wife lets out a long moan that vibrates through my cock in her throat.

Logan and I soon find a rhythm within her, pushing back and forth while Alana takes it from either end. When Logan thrusts forward he propels her onto me powerfully and, in turn, I slam her back onto him. We start slowly like this and then gain speed until eventually we are railing my wife as hard as we can from either end, using her body like our own personal wedding night sex toy.

Alana is groaning loudly between us, reaching down between her legs and helping herself along by playing with her clit. She starts to tremble, quaking with ecstasy as wave after wave of orgasm starts to pulse through her. My wife pulls me out of her mouth just long enough to look up and tell me, "Oh my god, I'm going to cum so fucking good!"

Suddenly, she's clenching her muscles tightly with her back arched and a look of absolute bliss plastered happily across her face. Alana's eyes roll back into her head as she lets out a cry of pleasure and slams back hard against Logan, holding firm and baring her teeth. "Fuck!"

Instead of slowing her down, the orgasm seems to kick my wife into an even higher gear. Immediately after finishing, she climbs forward across the bed and crawls up onto me, straddling my body with her slender legs. I run my hands across her toned frame as she reaches down and helps to guide my cock up into her wet pussy. She presses down against me as I fill her tightness and then begins to rock her hips against me in powerful swoops.

"Do you like watching your new wife fuck another man?" She asks. "Do you like seeing your friend fuck me?"

"I do." I sigh.

"That's the second 'I do' of the night." Alana says.

I feel the weight on the bed shift as Logan climbs up into position behind her. Alana looks back over her shoulder at him and smiles, then reaches back with one hand and spreads her ass as wide as she possibly can, an invitation for him to slip inside.

"Fill me up." She commands. "I need to be double fucked."

Logan doesn't need to be told twice. He places his rock hard cock at the rim of my wife's asshole and then firmly pushes forward, brutally stretching her tightness around the girth of his shaft. Between the two members that fill her, Alana is completely maxed out and pulled taut, aching with a mixture of pain and pleasure as we pump back and forth within her.

As I look up at Alana I see a face of pure bliss, her entire body overwhelmed with the sensation of pure lustful freedom as two men penetrate her. She's completely lost in the moment.

This is not a position I ever thought I would find myself in, sharing my wife with my close friend and enjoying every second of it.

"Slam me harder!" My wife screams as Logan rails his huge cock up into her asshole. "Fuck me like the slut that I am!"

I can feel every moment of his cock through the thin wall between her pussy and ass, a strange sensation that only adds to the bizarre and visceral nature of our encounter. Logan is moaning now, picking up speed as he rams her and suddenly it dawns on me that he's about ready to blow his load. Moments later, my suspicions are confirmed as he pushes deep within her tightness and lets out a powerful yell.

I can feel his cock twitching within Alana as he pumps load after load up into my wife's ass. Apparently, it's more than she can handle because, moments later, his milky white jizz is squirting out from the rim of her plugged hole and running down her legs in thick streaks.

Feeling another man's spunk drip out of my wife's asshole is too much for me to bear and it immediately pushes me over the edge, as well. I let out an equally ferocious yell and thrust forward with all of my might, ejecting a massive payload of hot jizz within Alana's pussy. I clench tight against her as all of it spills from me, filling her completely.

As I pull out, I can feel both of the spunk injections running down Alana's legs and mixing together in a cocktail of semen.

My wife rolls off of me and onto the bed, which is now a complete mess. Logan and me flop down on either side of her, panting hard as we reel from the implications of what just happened.

"Oh my god." Alana mumbles aloud, not to anyone in particular but as a pure expression of shock. "That was incredible."

After starting our marriage on such a strange foot, things eventually became shockingly normal again. We fell into our happy, marital lives and didn't much talk about that wild encounter with Logan. Somehow things were never awkward when he was around and, in fact, it almost made the three of us even closer than before.

It wasn't until our one year wedding anniversary that Alana even mentioned it again.

We were lying in bed and she was sucking me off, looking up with those big beautiful eyes as she swirled her tongue around the head of my cock.

"Do you like that?" She asked.

"I love it." I told her, placing my hands on the back of her head and helping to guide her along the length of my shaft.

"Are you feeling dirty tonight?" She asked with a smile.

"Of course!" I confirmed, a shiver running up my spine. I could tell she was up to something.

Alana leaned over and grabbed her phone off of the bedside table, quickly firing off a text.

"What are you doing?" I asked, curiously.

"You'll see."

Moment's later I looked up to see Logan stepping into the bedroom. Not a bad tradition to hold onto, I thought to myself as Alana popped her cute ass into the air and gave it a playful wiggle.

PERSONAL TRAINING

Let's be totally honest, once they get married, people tend to let themselves go. It's only natural that, after finding a suitable mate, folks start to forget why eating right and hitting the gym was important in the first place. Without a constant reminder of the single life and all of the competition that lies just around the corner, husbands and wives routinely fall into the trap of mutual relaxation. Which, I suppose, is just fine. If that's what you're into.

On the other hand, my wife Kristen and I have spent every day since our wedding night rallying against the threat of lazy cohabitation. We're not going to get old, or fat, or unattractive. It's become a mantra around the Lewis household, stay fit.

I prefer jogging myself, but never on a treadmill. Los Angeles isn't exactly known for it's scenic nature, but by now I've found some truly incredible trails weaving up and down the Hollywood Hills near our house. I like to get up with the sun and take off towards the peaks before it gets too hot, then head back down with plenty of time to relax before work. It's refreshing, and it makes the rest of the day feel absolutely fantastic. The brief time spent in what little nature I have available can completely change my entire outlook for the next twenty-four hours.

Kristen, on the other hand, couldn't care less about centering herself and getting in touch with the natural world. She wants results, plain and simple. Not that I mind, because she certainly gets them in the form of a gorgeous, toned yet feminine body. I know that it's my husbandly duty to call my wife beautiful no matter what, but in Kristen's case it's not that difficult. She could be on the cover of a fitness magazine, not in a freaky muscular way either, but in a jaw-on-the-floor-sexy kind of way that everyone shoots for but very few can actually achieve.

Her dedication keeps me on point, as well, and even though we prefer vastly different forms of working out, we make a great team. When Kristen turns as many heads as she does by simply walking down the street, it forces me to keep up with her.

Because of this, I don't think anything of it when Kristen starts spending more and more time at the gym. Her usual five mornings a week turns into seven, and then a few sessions in the evening. She's looking great, no question about it, but eventually I start wondering if there's a reason that she's overdoing it like this.

Finally, one morning when she gets back home from a workout and I'm in the kitchen making lunch, I bring it up.

"How was it?" I ask, turning around against the counter as Kristen appears in the doorway of the kitchen, her hair pulled back in a messy ponytail.

"The gym?" Kristen says, lively and excited. She's definitely experiencing a post-workout boost. "Fantastic."

"You still working out with that trainer? What's his name again?" I continue.

"Blake." Kristen tells me, grabbing a bottle of water from the fridge and then taking a massive gulp. "Yeah, I'm still working with him. He's great. Really great."

I make my way over to my wife and wrap my arms around her waist, then go in for a big kiss. When I pull away, Kristen is looking at me with a lustful gaze.

"Well, he's doing a damn good job." I tell her. "You're looking fucking incredible."

Kristen flashes a flirty smile. "Why, thank you."

She kisses me again and pushes me back against the kitchen counter, losing herself in the moment as we suddenly find ourselves in a heated exchange of passion. She normally gets like this after an hour of hardcore fitness, but today there's something more. Even though I can't quite put my finger on what it is, I know that it's there.

Kristen is all over me now, pulling my shirt up over the top of my head and frantically unbuttoning my jeans. I do the same for her, tearing off her sports bar and shorts and then suddenly we find ourselves crawling back onto the counter in our underwear. Kristen is sitting on the edge with her legs spread open as I move my hands across her body, her eyes closed tightly as she trembles and shakes with an incredible, burning passion.

I pull back for a moment. "What are you thinking about?" I ask her.

Kristen laughs. "Nothing! What do you mean?"

I shake my head. "You're my wife and I know your poker face, don't lie to me."

"I'm not lying, Jordan!" Kristen protests. "I'm not thinking about anything."

I give up and start to kiss her again, but my instincts are still bothering me so moments later I try a much more direct approach.

"Are you thinking about Blake?" I ask.

Kristen stops suddenly and just stares at me. I can see a million different thoughts fluttering by behind her beautiful blue eyes, a conflicted stare that sits at the fork between so many strange and unexplored paths. She bites her lip coyly, instantly letting me know that I've stumbled upon something very real.

"You know that you can tell me anything." I assure her. "I'm not going to be mad."

"You're not?" She confirms. "I don't believe you."

To be honest, there is something very similar to anger brewing inside of me. Its hot and bubbling, a jealous ache that can't be contained and wants so desperately to be unleashed. It's a feeling that I don't quite recognize, but I know that I like it so I play along and continue to dive in head first.

"I won't be mad." I tell her. "In fact, I think it's kind of hot to imagine you flirting with your trainer all morning."

Kristen lets out a long sigh as I say this, as if a heavy, sexual weight has been lifted off of her shoulders.

"Okay." She tells me. "Yes, I was thinking about Blake, my trainer."

A smile slowly crosses my face as I'm flooded with an intense, lustful urge. I've inadvertently stumbled off the edge of something powerful within my deepest, darkest subconscious, and I'm almost immediately aware that, at this point, there's no turning back.

"What were you thinking?" I ask Kristen, slipping off her panties and starting to gently play with her soaking wet pussy. Her clit is swollen and aching to be touched, sending chills up and down her body as I pet it gently with my finger.

"I was thinking…" She starts, then quakes violently and arches her back, gripping the countertop tightly. "I was thinking about what it would feel like to ride him."

"Yeah?" I goad her on.

"Yeah." Kristen says. "I was thinking about sleeping with him. I was thinking about fucking his huge cock while I suck you off."

"What?" I laugh. "Really?" I had never really considered a threesome with another man before, although back in college I somehow managed to get down with two women at a time on multiple occasions. Something about the idea of double teaming Kristen, especially with a guy that she has a huge crush on, really gets me going.

"Is that okay?" Kristen suddenly changes gears, worried that she may have crossed a line and trying to backpedal a bit.

I stop her. "Of course it's okay. I like it." As I say this, I lower the waistband of my boxer briefs and align my thick cock with the tight entrance of her pussy. I push forward slowly and Kristen gasps, then grabs me by the hips and pulls me completely into her.

"Do you flirt with him?" I ask, grinding hard up against my wife's open legs.

"Every day." Kristen moans.

"Do you want to fuck him?"

"Yes." She gasps, and then lets out a long squeal of pleasure. "This is so fucking dirty."

"I love it." I tell her, pounding her at a reasonable pace now as we slam over and over against the cupboards. "Tell me what you want to do to him."

"I want him to shove that big cock up into my pussy. I want him to ride me like the filthy slut that I am."

"Is that what you want?" I yell, suddenly overwhelmed with arousal.

"I want the two of you to double fuck me right there in the fucking locker room at the gym!" She screams. "I want his cock in my pussy while you slam me up the ass!"

"Fuck!" I scream out.

Suddenly, we are both cumming hard. Kristen wraps her legs tight around me as her eyes roll back into her head and a ferocious scream erupts from her body. She is spasming hard while I hold my cock deep inside, letting lose with pump after pump of hot milky jizz.

Once both of us finish we somehow manage to stumble over to the living room couch and collapse onto each other in a naked, fucked-silly pile.

My mood has completely changed, having just blown one of the biggest loads of my life, yet somehow my deviant desires still remain.

"Do you want to know something weird?" I ask Kristen, who turns her head towards me with a dazed yet curious expression.

"Sure." She says, offering a smile. "What is it, baby?"

"Normally after I cum all that dirty stuff sounds like a really, really bad idea." I tell her. "But, honestly, I still want to do it. I think me and Blake should double penetration you."

Kristen sits up to look at me, her eyes overflowing with skeptical inquiry. "Are you serious?" She ask. "I thought we were just fucking around."

"Totally serious." I tell her, despite the pangs of trepidation that still murmur deep within the pit of my stomach. "I want you to book a late session with him, once everyone else has gone home from the gym. You can flirt as much as you want and see how far you can get."

Kristen looks scared, but very interested.

"I'll come by to pick you up at the end of your workout." I explain. "And if things have gotten hot and heavy then I'll join in."

A smile slowly crosses the face of my beautiful wife. "Okay." She says. "Let's do it!"

As I drive towards the gym my heart is nearly pounding out of my chest. Kristen had been texting with me the whole time leading up to her personal training session, but now that it's started I've been dealing with complete radio silence while my mind races with all of the dirty things that could possibly be going on.

It's late, late enough that I'm one of three lone cars in the parking lot as I pull up and shut of my lights.

I take out my phone and stare down at the last message she sent, 'Wish me luck.'

Slowly, I lean back into the seat and close my eyes, trying to calm down enough to subdue the raging hard on the tugs unapologetically at the fabric of my pants. I try not to imagine Blake coming up behind my wife and helping her with a lift, wrapping his strong arms around her and then slowly kissing along the length of Kristen's slender neck. At the same time, that's somehow exactly what I want to be happening.

My phone buzzes suddenly and I jump, quickly looking down at the illuminated screen.

'He wants me to go back into the guy's locker room.' She writes. 'I told him I always had a fantasy about fucking a dumb jock in there.'

'Holy shit.' I text back. 'Are you going to fuck him?'

The silence is excruciating while I wait for her response.

Finally, my phone buzzes again. 'Yes, but I want both of you. Already talked to him about it.'

'Should I come in?' I message.

My phone vibrates immediately. 'Doors unlocked. Come in, we're just getting started.'

I read the words several times as it slowly begins to sink in that my beautiful wife is currently being violated by another man. I start to tremble with excitement and quickly exit the car, crossing the parking lot with a singular determination.

The gym door is unlocked, just like Kristen said it would be, so I slip inside without any problem. The place is dark and empty, lit by only a sparse arrangement of dim work lights and completely silent, at first, but moments later I begin to hear a faint squealing float it's way though the air. My breath catches in my throat as the sound reaches my ears, stopping me in my tracks. I listen intently, trying to discern if the noise is actually what I think it is.

Moments later there is another loud shout, confirming that the sound drifting from one end of the gym to the other is definitely Kristen in the troughs of passion.

I follow the cries across the main floor and soon find myself in a hallway that leads to the locker rooms. There is a light on in the men's side, casting out from a small glass window at eye level in the door. I can now say with absolute certainty that the squeals and moans are coming from my wife, who's clearly enjoying herself just beyond my line of sight.

"Fuck." I murmur aloud. "What the fuck am I doing?"

I mentally prepare myself as much as I possibly can and then approach the tiny glowing window, stepping up and peering inside.

My heart nearly stops. There, on a bench at the center of locker room, is my beautiful wife with her legs in the air, moaning wildly as she is plowed by her muscular trainer. Her feet bob in with every slam, dancing to the rhythm of Blake's hips as he pushes in and out of Kristen's tight pussy. She's loving every second of it, arching her back and crying out as she reels from the overwhelming sensations that blossom within her body.

In the pit of my stomach I can feel a forceful tug, like I've just been punched and the wind has been knocked completely from my lungs. I struggle not to collapse under my own weight and then, moments later, realize that I'm harder than I've ever been. Without thinking, I reach down and begin to stroke my cock.

Despite being completely lost in the moment, Kristen somehow notices me watching through the tiny window. Our eyes meet in a strange, wordless exchange, and then moments later she breaks into a wide smile.

I slowly push open the door and Blake turns his head to acknowledge me with a friendly nod, not letting up for a second on my wife's gorgeous pussy.

"Hey baby." Kristen says seductively. "Care to join us?"

I'm trembling as I walk over to the opposite end of the bench, where my wife happily takes my cock into her hand and begins to stroke it. I let out a long sigh and begin to rock my hips against the movement of her grip, enjoying the sensation of her slender fingers moving back and forth across the sensitive head of my rod.

"Oh fuck." I groan. "I can't believe this is happening."

Moments later, Kristen opens her mouth and takes me inside, wrapping her lips tightly around the thickness of my hard dick. I push into her, deeper and deeper until I hit the edge of her gag reflex. I can feel Kristen try to relax, then she gives up with a retch and a cough. I remove myself quickly, allowing her a large gasp of air as she sputters frantically, trying in vain to collect herself the best that she can. The cock that pummels my wife's pussy is overwhelming her senses.

"One more time." Kristen laughs, swallowing my dick. I plunge deep but this time she's ready for me, taking my entire length and relaxing expertly as I dive well past my wife's sensitive gag reflex. Soon, my balls are pressed up against her nose, my shaft engulfed entirely to the hilt as I hold firm in her warm throat.

When I finally pull back it's as if Kristen has been completely transformed, there is a fire in her eyes and an insatiable hunger for cock.

She's gone wild.

The next thing I know, Kristen is turning over on the bench so that she's sitting doggie style across its length, her ass popped up into the air as Blake trusts back into her pussy and begins again. Kristen takes my dick into her mouth and begins to pump up and down rapidly. Soon me and her trainer and plowing her hard from each end, using her like a beautiful fuck doll that hangs between us. With every thrust forward, Blake propels her back onto my dick, and visa versa as we gain speed. Soon the three of us are moving together like one strange, sexual creature.

Blake slaps my wife's ass hard and she squeals with delight, pulling my cock out of her mouth just long enough to look back and tell him, "Fuck me like a filthy cheating slut!"

"Oh my god." I groan, loving every second of it. "You're so dirty!"

Kristen turns her attention back to me. "Do you like seeing your beautiful bride used up by another man?"

"I love it." I tell her.

"Want to see just how dirty I can get?" She asks.

I nod in approval. Seconds later Kristen is pushing us away and then repositioning herself on the bench. She takes Blake by the hand and pulls him over, then instructs him to lay down across the wooden length with his cock sticking straight up in the air. He does as he's told.

Kristen stands over Blake and then throws a leg over the top and lowers herself down slowly onto his thickness, groaning as his girth stretches the tightness of her slick wet pussy. I watch in a trance as she begins to grind slowly against him, bucking her hips hard while she runs her hands up and down the perfect abs of this other man. They pick up speed and I watch with my cock in my hand, stroking off in time with my wife's swoops until they are fucking at full speed, hammering into each other with all of their might. Kristen lets out a wild scream and then looks back over her shoulder at me.

"Double fuck me right now!" She commands. "I need your fucking cock in my ass!"

Her ferocity takes me off guard and for a moment I'm stunned, the insanity of this entire situation suddenly catching up with me.

"Jordan." She says, snapping me out of it. We look directly into each other's eyes and she speaks in a slow, deliberate tone. "I want you to fuck me up the ass, while my trainer rams my pussy."

I climb over the bench and quickly align myself with her puckered back door. Kristen reaches back and grabs a hold of her ass cheeks, spreading herself open for me as her pussy continues its brutal slamming from below. I press the head of my cock up against her tight rim, pushing lightly against it. The seal doesn't give, so I push harder and harder until finally her asshole gives and I slip inside, stretching her limits in a ruthless double penetration.

Kristen lets out a howl of pain and pleasure as she falls forward onto Blake, grabbing his shoulders tightly as she braces herself against my slow but powerful pumps. She loosens up a bit more with every thrust, allowing herself to relax amid the chaos of having two thick rods forced powerfully into her toned body. Soon we are slamming her at full speed, impaling my wife's body as hard as we can while she moans and groans with pleasure.

I notice now that Kristen has slipped a hand down in front of her and is playing with her clit, a sure sign that a violent orgasm is not far behind. Her vocalizing gains intensity, louder and louder until it transforms into an earsplitting shriek of lustful pleasure. Kristen's body begins to clench and spasm hard, quaking as she cums.

"Oh my god!" My wife yells. "Oh my god, oh my god!" Her eyes roll back into her head.

Finally, Kristen collapses forward onto Blake and then three of us slow to a stop, panting with exhaustion.

"More." My wife mumbles. "I want more cock."

I smile. Blake has been doing his job well, I see, she's got enough energy to last all night.

Kristen climbs off of us and stands on two wobbly, but toned legs. She looks dazed and confused, but the sexual fire still burns brightly behind her eyes as she takes me and Blake each by the hand and drags us to our feet.

Her trainer steps up behind Kristen and wraps his huge, muscular arms around her as I approach from the front. Seconds later he lifts her up into the air, somehow managing to get an arm under each leg so that he's holding her spread open for me with her ass hanging down at waist height. His swollen cock is just inches below Kristen's reamed asshole, and slowly but sure Blake lowers her down onto his thick member, impaling my wife's small toned body. Kristen lets out a yelp as the shaft slips inside, gliding all the way up until it comes to a stop at the hilt. Then, using his muscular arms, Blake begins to lift her up and down on his hardness, using the power of gravity to slam my wife onto his cock over and over again.

Seizing the opportunity, I saddle up to the front of them and position my dick at the entrance of her pussy. Blake lifts her up and then brutally lowers her onto both of our rods in the second double penetration of the night.

"Fuck!" Kristen screams, wrapping her arms around me. "That feels so fucking good. I love getting double fucked like this!"

I can't help but chuckle at her unbridled enthusiasm, my once timid, blushing bride now sandwiched between two large men as she's plowed from below in the sluttiest way possible. Blake and I don't let up for a second, hammering her body down onto our rods with all of our might until we finally just can't take it anymore.

The next thing I know, Blake is cumming hard. He holds her deep and lets out a guttural roar, shaking as he unloads a massive ejection of sperm up my wife's asshole. I can feel his cock twitching through the thin layer of flesh that separates us and suddenly I'm cumming as well, blowing my spunk into Kristen as I clench my eyes tight and grit my teeth.

"Give me your loads!" My wife commands, feeling the hot milky liquid spill out of us and fill her to the brim. "Shoot that jizz up into my ass and my pussy!"

We run out of room quickly and suddenly the cum is squirting from the edges of her plugged holes, raining down onto the floor of the locker room below us. I suddenly realize that Kristen is cumming with us, an orgasm ripping through her body in a powerful, violent wave. She kicks her legs out straight and grabs me tight, screaming into my shoulder as her muscles spasm and jerk.

Finally, the two of us finish and pull out of her, letting the jizz splatter below.

"That was incredible." Kristen says in a haze.

Blake smiles. "Time to hit the showers."

There are all kinds of ways to burn calories. Most people like to run but that can be bad on the joints, at least that's what Blake tells me. Some people prefer swimming, or even a row machine. Basically, anything that gets your heart pumping can do the trick, which is why I'm feeling more fit than I ever have.

My wife and I have found the best workout routine ever; a fat burning, heart pounding three way with her trainer Blake five days a week. Sure it's unconventional, but we couldn't be happier and, at the end of the day, isn't that was being married is all about.

BEACH BABE

On a day like today, it's hard to imagine living anywhere other than the ocean side. The weather is perfect here in Malibu and the beach is full of happy, attractive people, but not so many that it's a bother finding a place to spread your beach blanket in the sand. Fortunately, that's something that my wife, Rachel, and me never have to worry about because we're lucky enough to own our own place overlooking the cove. Depending on our mood, we can go down to the water and lie out in the sand, or simply kick back up here on our deck getting wasted under the hot sun.

It wasn't always this way, though. We started as college sweethearts back in Iowa, where the weather isn't nearly as nice and the people are well meaning but, honestly, a little strange. Rachel was working on her arts degree without any real plan of what to do with it, and I was a struggling programmer who spent most of his time in the dark working on line after line of computer code. It was a rough time, but deep down in my heart I knew that if I could just finish this software and get it up and running, I would become an overnight millionaire. Fortunately, my grand ambitions were more than just a pipe dream, because that's exactly what happened. The second I sold my program to the highest bidder, me and Rachel packed up and headed straight for the sunny west coast, landing in Malibu where we now spend most of our days doing whatever the fuck we want and living off of my investments.

It's not all fun in the sun, though. The lifestyle between Iowa City and Malibu couldn't be more different, and having little sexual experience outside of our long-term college relationship, the temptation was always there for something new and dangerous. Deep down, a part of me wished that Rachel and I had met later on in life, at least after dating around a bit more and experiencing what the vast sexual world had to offer. It's not like we were virgins beforehand, but we hadn't done much fucking, either.

The craziest thing about all this, however, is that the facts make me and my wife sound like a couple of fat, weird trolls who couldn't get laid even if we wanted to. In reality, this couldn't be further from the truth. I've been naturally fit my entire life, with heaps of charm and a confidence that women seem to find boundlessly attractive. Of course, I'm nowhere near as electrifying as Rachel.

Rachel is a complete bombshell, the total package from head to toe with long blonde hair and a perfectly toned beach body. It was a shame watching it go to waist in the Iowa darkness, but now that we've got the California sun beating down on us my wife gets a chance to show off her curves almost every day.

Today is one of those days.

"I'm going to go down and lay by the water." Rachel tells me, walking by with a beach towel as I sit on the deck and think under the shade of our giant umbrella.

I'm working on some exciting new script, pounding away at the keys of my laptop as I watch the endless cycle of waves crash along the beach shore.

"Want to come with?" Rachel asks.

I glance down at my laptop screen and across the endless lines of code that need to be edited, then let out a long sigh. "No, but thanks, baby. I should probably keep on this."

My wife laughs and shakes her head. "You know that you don't need to work ever again, right? We can just be on permanent vacation for the rest of our lives."

I nod. "I know, it's just a habit I guess. Have fun down there, don't get burned, baby."

She walks over in her sexy yellow and blue bikini, planting a kiss sweetly on my forehead. "Love you, Tim." She tells me.

I watch her leave in complete awe, taking in the shape of her gorgeous body as it struts away. I'm a lucky man.

For the next long while I find myself buried in my computer screen and sipping a beer, lost in the barrage of coded text that floods my vision.

Working hard like this puts me in a trance, my focus so tightly wound around the task at hand that sometimes I don't even hear my own name. In this case, I'm so focused that I don't even notice how low my laptop battery is.

Suddenly, the screen goes black and my entire computer shuts down.

"Fuck!" I shout, immediately recognizing the critical mistake that I've made. I fall back into my chair with disappointment, trying to recall when the last time I saved was and forcing myself to relax with a long pull of my ice cold beer.

Focused on my breathing, I turn my attention elsewhere. From where I sit I can see Rachel lying out on the sand, her beautiful body already tanning slightly in the sun. So I lost a little code, I think to myself, like could be worse.

As I watch, a volleyball suddenly lands next to Rachel and comes rolling to a stop just a few feet away. I young guy runs over, looking to be in his mid twenties and completely ripped. He smiles as Rachel hands him back the ball.

I'm much too far away to hear their words as the two of them begin talking, but clearly my wife thinks that this guy is incredibly funny. She giggles and then looks away, an alarmingly coy move which I instantly recognize as a subtle bit of flirting. They exchange a few more words and then the guy leaves, walking back over to the volleyball courts where his friends are waiting. Rachel watches him go, her gaze lingering much longer than I would have expected.

Almost immediately, I realize that my cock is rock hard within my shorts. It's aching to be touched, my arousal defying any conscious attempt that I make to subdue it. More than anything, though, I'm confused by where these intense lustful urges are coming from. Having just seen my wife brazenly flirting with another man, I would expect my feelings to be ones of anger and jealousy and, to be fair, there is a large does of that coursing through my system as well. However, deep down below the wrath and envy something strange and powerful lurks, a sexual desire that I can't quite put my finger on.

I reach down below my waistband and start to stroke my cock slowly, letting the unfamiliar emotions flood into my body. Did Rachel think this guy was hot? I guess it's only natural and nothing to get too freaked out about, it's not like she was down there blowing him in the sand or something.

The sudden mental image of Rachel's lips wrapped tightly around the guys cock pulls me even further down the rabbit hole, and my tight grip quickens as I pump my hand faster and faster across the length of my rod. I'm more sexually excited than I've been for a long, long time, confused and aroused by the idea of my wife fucking this handsome stranger. I'm trembling.

As I edge closer and closer to orgasm I notice something happening back down on the beach. The volleyball guys have packed up and are loading their beach gear into a nearby car, but the handsome one who first talked to Rachel is approaching her again. They exchange a few words and then, unexpectedly, the guy takes Rachel's phone and types something into it. He smiles, hands it back to her, and then immediately turns to walk away with a confident swagger. I instantly recognize what's going on, he just gave my wife his number.

At that exact moment the orgasm hits me hard and my muscles clench tight. I moan loudly as a thick splattering of jizz erupts from the end of my cock and splatters down onto the deck below me.

I'm all cleaned up a watching TV in the living room when Rachel finally strolls in from the beach. She flashes me a smile and approaches the couch, throwing a leg over me as she sits down in my lap and lets my hands playfully wander across her warm, exposed skin.

"Did you finish your work?" Rachel asks me.

"Yep." I offer, shutting off the TV and then lying back into the cushion as I gaze up at her. "How was the beach?"

Rachel laughs and shakes her head. "It was nice, but you'll never believe what happened."

"Some guy gave you his number?" I toss out nonchalantly.

Rachel gives me a playful punch. "How did you know that?" She yells. "Were you spying on me?"

"Maybe I was!" I tell her.

Rachel lifts her phone off the coffee table and scrolls through the numbers. Then reads aloud, 'Tony Reynolds.'

"Are you going to call him?" I joke.

Rachel shrugs, clearly a little uncomfortable with my teasing.

"What about a text?" I offer.

As I say this I can see a little sparkle of exhilaration flash behind her eye. My wife is more excited by the idea than she's letting on, and despite all the playful joking I can suddenly tell that there's more attraction going on here than I previously thought. Oddly, however, I don't feel threatened, just weirdly horny.

"I'm not gonna text him." Rachel tells me. "I've got the hottest guy that I know right here on the couch with me."

She leans in for a kiss and I meet her lips, embracing for a moment, before I suddenly snatch the phone out of her hands.

"Hey!" Rachel protests, struggling to get the phone back but failing miserably. "Give me that, Tim!"

"No way!" I tell her, opening up a new text and starting to type.

Rachel's face is flushed red now but she quickly gives up trying to take her phone back, I'm much too strong for her to compete and my arms just long enough to keep her at bay. "What are you doing?" Rachel groans. "Oh my god, this is so embarrassing."

"Just texting this guy." I tell her with a grin.

I finish my message and hit send.

"What did you say?" Rachel asks.

"I asked him if he wanted to come over later and double team you with your husband." I explain flatly.

Rachel's eyes go wide. "What!? You didn't. Please tell me you didn't say that."

I hand my wife back her phone and let her read the text herself. Rachel just shakes her head, completely blown away by my devilish audacity.

"Are you telling me you wouldn't be into that?" I ask her. "Be honest."

Rachel hesitates for a moment, clearly checking in with her wifely duties. "Of course I wouldn't be into it." She finally offers in a blatant lie.

"You sure about that?" I continue, not letting up for a second. I can tell when she's hiding something, and this is definitely one of those times.

Rachel finally let's out a frustrated sigh and then throws her hands up. "Fine, you caught me! I'd love to fuck both of you at the same time, so sue me."

Her admission has a lot of charm to it, but it hits me hard in the gut, the first real confession of her sexual thoughts about a man other than myself. It doesn't sting as much as I'd expected, however, in fact it feels pretty great as the thought seeps deeper and deeper into my brain. Even though I came hard just minutes earlier, I can already feel myself swelling up once again.

"Would you really like to fuck him?" I ask in confirmation, a tense seriousness in my tone.

Rachel looks me directly in the eyes and then states, very calmly. "I'd love to fuck both of you at the same time."

Suddenly, her phone vibrates.

Rachel reaches over and looks at it, a strange expression crossing her face. "Oh my god." She murmurs, then laughs and turns the phone's screen towards me so I can read for myself.

'Sounds hot.' His text reads. 'I'd love to. What's your address?'

We exchange glances excitedly, immediately realizing that we are secretly on exactly the same page with this. I nod at Rachel and she quickly begins to type something back to Tony.

Suddenly, Rachel pauses. "Should I really hit send?" She asks me, making one last confirmation.

"Do it." I tell her.

The sun is still high in the sky as Rachel lies out on the back deck. She's completely naked, her toned body looking absolutely breathtaking under the warm sun. I'm sitting nearby, sans clothing as well, just waiting and watching her intently. I can't believe that I'm about to share this beautiful woman with some other guy, I think to myself. The idea causes a long, pleasant chill to run down the length of my spine.

I suddenly hear footsteps coming through the gravel on the other side of the house, and watch as the smile slowly creeps across my wife's face.

He's here, following our implicit instructions to meet around back.

Tony rounds the corner and the two of us immediately make eye contact. I can definitely see what Rachel liked about him, large biceps and a cute, boyish smile. He looks down at my wife, who lies stretched out in the deck recliner before him, and then immediately starts to remove his clothes.

Now naked, with his cock fully engorged, Tony kneels down next to the recliner so that his cock is pushed right up into Rachel's adorable face. She looks up at him hungrily, and then back at me just to make sure everything is fine. I give a nod of approval as I get to work slowly stroking my own dick, completely entranced by the explicit scene that plays out before me.

Rachel opens her mouth and licks Tony's shaft from base to top, savoring every moment as his massive rod towers above her face. She reaches up with one hand and carefully plays with his balls, giggling a little before opening wide and then swallowing Tony's dick. Rachel bobs up and down for a moment and then deftly pushes forward, allowing Tony's rod to slip deep into her depths.

I watch as she gags for a moment, reeling desperately when it becomes apparent that Tony's incredible size might be too much to handle. Seconds later, however, Rachel regains her composure and manages to push her head down even further over his cock. Tony let's out a long, satisfied moan as my wife takes him entirely into her throat, his balls resting perfectly against her chin.

I'm completely in awe of what I'm seeing, my once timid wife devolved into a thirsty, wild cockslut. What's even more shocking, though, is how much I actually like it.

Finally, I can't contain myself any longer, standing up and walking over to the other side of the reclining deck chair. I kneel down across from Tony as Rachel immediately takes my massive, swollen dick in her hands, stroking me off while she services the other cock with her mouth. After a while, she turns her attention to me, opening wide and allowing me to gracefully slip down within her in a stunning deep throat. She continues like this, going back and forth between us, until finally my wife just can't wait any longer.

Rachel pops the cock out of her mouth and pulls back both legs as far as they can go, opening herself up to us completely.

"One of you needs to fuck my pussy right now." My wife demands.

Tony immediately repositions himself, swinging a leg over the recliner as he places his throbbing dick at the entrance of Rachel's pussy. Tony then slowly drives forward, stretching her tightness around the girth of his thick rod and causing my wife to gasp aloud at the incredible sensation. She closes her eyes and leans her head back, relishing the feeling of this new man inside of her before opening them again and going to work on my hard cock. As Tony pump's in and out of her, my wife continues to blow me, servicing my rod with expert skill as she tries desperately to keep it together. The faster that Tony slams her from the front, the harder it is for Rachel to focus, but she makes due, taking my cock deep into her throat and running her tongue playfully along the length of my shaft.

Rachel starts to moan loudly, her rampant squeals vibrating pleasantly against my dick.

"Do you like that big fucking dick?" Tony asks, speaking for the first time since he arrived. "How does it feel in your tight little pussy?"

Rachel pulls me out of her mouth and looks down at him in a cock-drunk daze. "I love your dick!" She yells at Tony. "Show my husband how good you can fuck me!"

Tony's rhythmic thrusts become harder and harder now, a deliberate firmness to every swing of his hips. It appears to be working, because almost immediately Rachel begins to shake and tremble, releasing her legs from her hands and kicking them out as wide as she can. Her whole body seems tense and ready to snap, like she's standing directly on the edge of something ruthlessly powerful.

Seconds later, Rachel tumbles over the cliff of orgasm. She lets out a ferocious scream that's so loud I'm worried it might alarm the neighbors, her body spasming and contorting wildly as it's rocked with wave after wave of pleasure. She arches her back and clenches her teeth, the sensation almost too much for her small frame to handle.

All the while, Tony doesn't let up, hammering my wife's pussy with everything that he's got. His passion is admirable, and suddenly I'm encouraged to do the same, grabbing my wife's head and shoving my cock down her throat as she's mid scream. She glances up at me as I cut her off, a look of pure lust behind her beautiful blue eyes.

Me and Tony slam her like this for a good while, taking her toned body from each end and making her our own. My wife has now completely transformed into something filthy and lustful, a sex crazed beach babe who couldn't take on enough cock if her life depended on it.

Finally, Rachel pulls me out of her mouth and commands in a desperate gasp, "Lie down."

She stands up, almost tumbling over as her body readjusts to the lack of stiff cock, and then directs me onto the recliner. I lie down in her place with my cock sticking straight up, watching as my wife maneuvers herself over me. She's facing away and showing off her incredible toned ass, which sinks lower and lower towards my shaft until finally the head of my rod is pressed up directly against her puckered backdoor.

"Do you want to fuck this tight little asshole?" She asks, looking back over her shoulder and flashing me a gorgeous smile.

"Fuck yes I do." I tell her.

"Good." Rachel says. "That's what I thought." She slowly starts push down, impaling my giant rod up her tiny asshole with a long, soulful moan of pleasure. Rachel sinks deeper and deeper until finally coming to rest against my toned abs, my thickness fully inserted into her rectum. My wife then leans back so that her body is pressed tightly up against my chest.

"Fuck, you feel so fucking tight." I tell her.

"Oh yeah?" Rachel laughs. "Well it's about to get a lot tighter once Tony shoves that big cock of his up my pussy at the same time."

I start to move slowly in and out of my wife's asshole as Tony climbs into position in front of her, placing his cock at the slick entrance of her pussy and then pushing forward. The tightness feels amazing as Rachel's holes are stretched to the absolute limit between our two swollen members. She grabs tightly onto Tony's shoulders and braces herself as the two of us begin to pump in and out of her. She's already trembling from the feelings of sexual depravity that flood her mind and body.

"Oh my god, these two dicks feel so fucking good!" Rachel cries out. She looks back over her shoulder at me with a fire in her eyes. "Do you like watching another man ram my tight little pussy?" She purrs.

"I love it." I confess.

"Do you like the way his big dick stretches out your wife?" She continues, prodding me even farther. "Do you like it when your beautiful bride gets violated like a filthy slut?"

"I love it!" I yell. "I fucking love this!"

By now Tony and me are absolutely pummeling her, hammering into my wife's tight holes with all of our might as her legs bounce wilding over Tony's tan shoulders. The three of us have formed a perfectly synchronized sex machine, thrusting and pulsing to the rhythm of our carnal lust. As the pace quickens, so does Rachel's clenching and quaking until finally she just can't take it anymore and erupts with her second orgasm of the day.

My wife throws her head back and lets out a powerful howl, eliminating any hope of the other beach patrons not hearing us. Her eyes roll back into her head as she convulses wildly, cumming harder than I've ever seen her cum before. Rachel rocks forward suddenly and holds, as if every ounce of her being is attempting to brace against an powerful, oncoming wave.

"Fuck!" She moans, stretching the "f" sound out as long as she possibly can. It sizzles in the air.

Moments later, Rachel falls back onto me in complete exhaustion.

Tony and I pull out of my wife and then stand as she immediately kneels on the deck between us. She sticks out her tongue playfully and plays gently with our balls as we beat off ferociously, just inches over her smiling face.

"Cover me with both your loads!" Rachel says encouragingly.

Tony pops first, groaning loudly as a thick rope of jizz erupts from the head of his cock and splatters across my wife's face in a beautiful diagonal line. Much of it lands in her mouth, and Rachel swallows graciously.

The sight of another man's spunk decorating her perfect smile is too much to bear and almost immediately I'm cumming as well, tossing out several pumps of milky payload onto Rachel's tongue. She takes it all, catching as much as she possibly can and then licking up the rest of the jizz that lands around her lips.

"Can you believe that we actually did that?" Rachel asks as we lay in bed together that night, listening through the open window as the ocean waves crash softly against the sand below.

"Honestly." I begin, looking down at her. "I always knew you had it in you."

"What's that supposed to mean?" Rachel asks in mock anger. "You always thought I was a slut?"

"No, no, no." I explain. "But I always knew you were dirtier than you were letting on."

She rests her head against my chest and lets out a long sigh. We silently linger like this for a moment, letting our private thoughts dance through our heads as the minutes drift by. Finally, Rachel speaks again.

"So what do we do about it?" My wife asks. "What do we do with all these filthy, lusty thoughts?"

I smile as I look down at her, then reach over to the bedside table and grab her phone. "Who else's number do you have?" I ask as I begin to scroll through her contact list.

IN THE CLUB

I'm happily married, and I wouldn't have it any other way, but I still appreciate the people out there who've stuck with the single life for this long. Sometimes I think about what it would be like to just go out on the town like I used to, grab a bunch of the guys and get wasted at the local bar, or even hit a club if we were in the mood to let loose and drop some cash. There are even days that I legitimately miss the taste of a juicy, strip club steak.

That's not a euphemism either. It's a little known fact that strip clubs cook the best steaks, although I couldn't tell you why. I can, however, vouch for this theory using my own first hand accounts. But, I digress.

I suppose us married men could still do all that stuff, but the barrage of texts and voicemails from our significant others would just be too much to bare and, eventually, we'd end up calling it an early night, and then head home to curl up with a movie and our wife in her favorite sweatpants.

Of course, if the tables were turned and my wife was heading out to the club with her wild group of friends, I'd be even more jealous than she would about me. And with good reason, my wife is fucking gorgeous, a brunette beauty with a toned waist but curves in all the right places. The thought of another man even looking at her sideways makes me overwhelmed with jealous rage.

I know that it's unhealthy, I really do, but the first step to overcoming a problem is admitting that you have it.

I wish it could be different. I want to be one of those couples who are open and free, somehow still the life of the party even though they've happily labeled themselves as sexually off limits until death do them part. How do they manage this wild and flirtatious lifestyle without freaking out all the time, without immediately seizing up at the precise moment they see their partner talking to another attractive person? It's a question worth getting to the bottom of, I've decided, and tonight is the night that I begin my quest towards a better way.

I may be old fashioned but, if there's one thing I like, it's an opportunity for self-improvement.

Taylor walks into the bedroom with an exhausted look on her face and then throws herself onto our king sized bed with a long sigh. I look up from the book that I'm reading and then set it on the bedside table, rubbing her hair softly.

"Tired?" I ask.

My wife nods slowly and lets out a wordless groan, trying to somehow push herself even deeper into the blankets.

"I bet." I respond. "You think we're working too much?"

Taylor groans again. Based on our previous conversations, I'm deftly able to translate her bizarre wailing into an expression of fear that we won't make rent if we don't work all the time.

"I know, but what is that worth if we don't enjoy living here?" I counter, opting for spoken English over wild moans.

Taylor finally looks up at me with her big brown eyes. "How did you know what I was saying?"

"We're always on the same page." I tell her with a smile. "Which is why I know that you can feel it, too, this fucking haze of boring middle class life that hangs in the air all around us."

My wife climbs up the bed and lays down next to me, rubbing her head into my shoulder. "What is going on with our life?" She asks. "I mean, it's not bad or anything, but it's not like it used to me."

She gets it. It's terrifying to know that our feelings of discomfort are shared, but in some way's it's a relief and makes my half of the conversation that much easier.

"Well," I start, "We both work way too much, and we need to get out more to shake up the routine. Remember going out?"

"We're too old to go out." Taylor protests.

"We're twenty five!" I laugh. "What the fuck are you talking about?"

Suddenly, something appears to register deeply within Taylor, the look in her eyes immediately shifting to one of grave understanding. "Whoa, you're so right Billy."

"So let's do something about it." I tell her. "Me and you, this Friday. Let's head down to the club on the corner or something."

A grin creeps slowly across Taylor's face. "Dancing?"

I have no idea why women this age are so obsessed with dancing, but at least she's excited so I play along.

"Sure, whatever, let's just get out of the apartment and have some fun for a change." I tell her.

"Deal!" Taylor says with as much enthusiasm as she can muster, then falls back against my shoulder and almost immediately drifts off into sleep. I reach over with my free hand and turn off the bedside lamp, leaving us in complete darkness.

"Billy, how do I look?" My beautiful wife asks, stepping out of the bathroom in her short black shorts and a tiny, cut-off halter top. I don't even know how to react, my jaw hanging open as I take in her incredible young body. My wife is a damn goddess.

"I don't even know what do say." I stammer. "Just as long as you promise to leave with me at the end of the night and not the swarm of guys who are going to be buying you drinks."

Taylor laughs as she slips on her shoes. "Is that an actual request, baby? You know that we're married right?"

"This is hard, though!" I tell her. "They're going to be all over you like a pack of hungry wolves."

"Shut up!" She counters. "I'm the one that should be worried you handsome devil."

"Sure, sure." I mumble, trying to collect myself and keep it cool.

Taylor sits up for a moment, noticing the very real concern in my voice. "You know, we don't have to go out tonight. Want to watch a movie instead?"

I shake my head and wave her concerns away. "No, no way, not this time." I protest. "We are going out like we used to and I'm not gonna be jealous. I just want you to have a good time and dance."

"Are you sure?" Taylor asks with a coy smile, clearly impressed with my determination.

"I'm sure, now let's get out of here before I change my mind." I say, throwing on my jacket as we head towards the door. Taylor does the same, covering up at least until we get to the club which is only a few blocks away.

We head out into the hall of our apartment building and then take the elevator down to the lobby, already growing giddy with excitement. It doesn't seem like much but, with the work schedules that Taylor and me keep, simply leaving the apartment after ten is enough to get our blood pumping. The night is young, I think to myself, who knows what could happen.

The walk to the club is quick and getting in is even quicker thanks to the fact that I'm an old friend with the bouncer. He's shocked to see me and let's us pass by the velvet rope with a smile and a sarcastic joke about how I should probably be in some office somewhere getting shit done.

As we enter the building I'm suddenly hit with the rumble of a pounding bass, which vibrates its way through my entire body in a powerful, consistent rhythm.

"It's so loud!" I shout over to Taylor.

"Oh my god, don't say that." She tells me. "Nobody in here says that. We're young tonight, remember?"

"Twenty five is young already!" I protest, but she's already heading straight towards the bar. I follow quickly and post up behind her, quickly getting the bartenders attention and ordering us each a stiff drink.

We pound them quickly and immediate go back for round two, trying desperately to loosen up with the help of a little liquid courage. I have to admit, though, it's definitely working. The next thing I know I'm beginning to sway to the music, the concerned frown on my face transforming into a jovial smile as Taylor and I laugh and joke with each other. Everything that seemed annoying about this club just minutes earlier is starting to become really funny for some reason.

"I want to go dance!" Taylor finally says, trying her best to pull me away from the comfort of the bar.

I shake my head, not quite to the point of wanting to make a complete fool of myself out on the floor. "It's okay, baby, you go ahead. I'll be right here." I tell her.

"Come on!" She begs. "This is our night out, enjoy it with me!"

I shake my head again but then finally cave, with stipulations. "Okay, but I need one more drink first. You go, I'll be there in a second." I tell her.

Taylor wraps her arms around me and gives me a long, hard kiss, then turns away and dances off into the crowd to the thundering beat of the music. I can't help but watch her gorgeous body as she goes, my eyes transfixed on the sway of her ass and the incredible, slender line of her hips. I love my wife.

I turn to the bartender and order my final drink, but when I look back towards the dance floor Taylor is nowhere to be seen, lost in the sea of wild revelers. I squint my eyes and scan the flickering darkness, trying my best to catch a glimpse of her long brown hair bobbing up and down to the music.

My drink finally comes and I'm just about to head in after her when suddenly I notice Taylor on the far side of the room. I hadn't seen her before simply because I would have never expected my loving wife to end up in such a precarious situation, but there she is, grinding up against a well dressed man before my very eyes on the dance floor.

Suddenly, all of the jealousy and confusion that I'd been grappling with throughout the evening comes tumbling back and hits me like a hammer. I literally grip my chest, trying to calm down as the sensation overwhelms me.

No matter what happens, I simply cannot freak out over a little harmless fun. Tonight is all about having a good time, and I need to let Taylor have it.

"We're just having fun." I tell myself in a repetitive mantra. "We're just having fun."

As the feelings of burning jealousy subside I suddenly realize that something equally powerful is taking their place. The longer I sit here with the green-eyed monster, the hornier I seem to get as my cock swells within my pants. Somehow this new arousal seems even more wrong than what I was feeling before, but unlike the last flood of emotion I can't seem to make this one go away no matter how hard I try.

Taylor is lost in the music at this point, a wide smile plastered across her face as she maneuvers her body skillfully against the man next to her. I have to admit; the two of them seem to have an incredible rhythm together, a synchronicity between their swaying hips and the music that feels undeniable. It also feels furiously sexual.

I take notice as the man puts his hand on Taylor's hip, a sharp pang of equal parts anger and lust striking my heart. Half of me wants her to push him away, while some other powerful force is desperately hoping that she takes things even further. My cock is aching now, swollen to the point of a dull, pleasant pain.

Finally, I just can't take it anymore. I stand and walk towards them with an initially confident stride, but realize once I'm halfway across the room that I have no idea what I'm going to do when I get there. With no time to think, I instinctively fall into the groove of the music and then sway up behind Taylor, who immediately pushes back against me in a loving response to my arrival.

Suddenly, I'm locked in with my wife and the stranger, the three of us pulsing together in a lustful groove. Taylor is absolutely lost in the moment, her eyes closed as she leans herself back against me and I run my hands up and down her body. Not knowing that he's dealing with an already married couple, the other man takes this as an invitation and begins to explore Taylor's body, as well. I'm immediately seized with a terrified excitement, but I don't stop him and neither does my wife, who is obviously enjoying the dual attention from two handsome men. I'm not sure if we're taking things to far, but the train has left the station and so far it feels incredible.

Without warning, the man suddenly leans forward and kisses Taylor hard on the lips, pushing her back against me. I stop moving immediately, the spell instantly broken on our fun fantasy as reality hits. A deer in the headlights, I have no idea what to do until I look down and realize that Taylor is actually kissing him back. She's still having a great time, still living it up like we did when we were just married without a care in the world, while I'm here stuck in a mire of cold and relentless responsibility. I need to let go, and my rock hard cock agrees.

I reach down slowly and grab Taylor's ass, rubbing up against her and then kissing down the back of her neck. She turns her head and looks back at me, her eyes glazed over with cock drunk lust and then whispers, "Are you okay?"

I nod and smile. "I'm amazing."

"What are we doing?" She says, barely audible above the din of the pounding music.

"Whatever you want." I tell her. "Do you want to take it further?"

Taylor looks at me with a face full of genuine concern, her eyes like deep pools in the flickering light of the club. We are reading each other, checking in on a level so deep that it only becomes accessible after several years of marriage.

"Yeah." She finally whispers into my ear. "Let's take it further."

Suddenly, Taylor pulls away and grabs me and the other man by the hand, leading us through the swarm of people towards the back of the club.

Surprisingly, there's no line for the men's restroom and Taylor kicks open the door forcefully then pushes the stranger and me inside. She turns around and locks the door behind the three of us and then, seconds later, has the other man slammed up against the wall, kissing him mercilessly.

I watch in awe as the two of them go at it, the first new man that my wife has explored in the last three years. The two of them are all over each other, tearing at each other's clothes like wild animals until both of them are down to their underwear. I follow suit, removing my shirt and stepping forward as my wife drops to her knees between us.

"Get out those fucking cocks." Taylor commands, looking up at the stranger and me with lustful eyes. We follow her orders, quickly removing our cocks as my wife takes one in each hand and begins to stroke. She pumps up and down on our shafts with her tight grip, and then playfully licks from one to the other.

Watching her tease this stranger is equally scary and intoxicating, but when she opens her mouth and swallows his massive dick I can't help but feel a powerful shudder of desire run the length of my spine. She pushes down as far as she can, trying and failing to take the man's dick past her gag reflex.

Almost immediately, Taylor comes up with a loud wretch and then tries again, this time relaxing just enough to consume him entirely to the hilt, his balls resting softly against my wife's chin. Somehow she manages to look over at me as she holds him there in her incredible deep throat, flashing a wink before pulling back and then getting to work as she pumps her head up and down over his long rod.

All the while Taylor is continuing to pleasure me with her hand, pulsing her fingers back and forth across my shaft with an expert touch. Soon she turns her mouth over to me, placing her lips at the edge of her grip and keeping the pace.

The next thing I know the stranger is climbing down to the floor and kneeling behind my wife, pulling off her panties and aligning his enormous dick with the soaking wet entrance of her pussy. Taylor pulls my cock out of her mouth long enough to look back over her shoulder and flash him a devious smile.

"Fuck that tight little married pussy." She tells him.

The guy pauses for a moment. "You're married?" He asks, stunned, and then adds with unbridled enthusiasm, "That's so hot!"

Suddenly he pushes forward, stretching the limits of my wife's pussy with his huge dick. Taylor shoves my cock back into her mouth and lets out a long, loud moan that vibrates pleasantly across my rod. Soon me and the other man are pumping in and out of her from either end, using her toned body as it hangs between us. We quickly find a rhythm, just like we did before when we were out on the dance floor, starting slow and then gradually gaining speed until the stranger and I are absolutely pounding my wife with our thick dicks.

I look down at Taylor as she bounces between us, her eyes rolled back into her head in a lustful state of utter bliss. Her body is quaking with every thrust, not just from the force of our slams but from a deep, blossoming orgasm just waiting to explode throughout her body.

Faster and faster we pound my wife, the stranger doing an incredible job within her pussy until Taylor finally pulls my dick from her mouth and lets out an ferocious scream. She grabs onto my legs, bracing herself against the powerful surges of pleasure the pump through her body in a series of blinding orgasmic waves.

"Oh my god!" Taylor cries. "I'm cumming so fucking hard."

When she finally finishes, my wife collapses onto the restroom floor between us in a state of fucked silly bliss. Instead of slowing things down, however, she's immediately ready to kick it up a notch.

"Lay down." She tells me.

I follow her orders, pressing my back against the hard tile floor as Taylor climbs aboard and straddles me with her long, slender legs. She runs her hands down along my ripped abs and then grabs my cock in her hands, carefully guiding my dick to the tight entrance of her pussy before lowering down slowly. She lets out a soft whimper as I enter her, stretching her taut hole with my impressive girth.

"Fuck." She moans. "That fucking cock is so big."

Taylor begins to grind hard against me, swooping her hips in a tight circle against my body as she picks up speed.

"Oh my god, oh my god." She starts to repeat, over and over again as if the record in her brain has started to skip in an endless loop. "Oh my god, oh my god." Finally, my wife manages to pull herself out of the trance and looks back over her shoulder at the stranger. "Okay, I'm ready! Shove that cock up my asshole!"

I look at her in complete shock and amazement. "Are you sure you're ready for that?" I ask.

Taylor looks back at me with a fire in her eyes and her teeth bared like a lion, then slaps me across the face harder than even she expected. "I want two fucking cocks!" She screams.

"Holy shit!" I blurt. "Okay, okay!"

Taylor looks back at the other man, who's climbing into position. "I said, double fuck me with that big dick right now!"

As soon as he's ready, the stranger pushes forward against the rim of my wife's puckered asshole, which gives way and expands itself around him. Taylor grabs onto my shoulders tightly and let's out a blood curdling scream, completely tense as she reels from the fullness of both holes being stretched to their limits. I can feel the stranger plunging deeper and deeper until finally he hits the end of his cock and holds, allowing my wife some time to get accustomed to his thickness.

A break is the last thing that Taylor needs, however, and almost immediately she gets to work gyrating between us, pumping our cocks in and out of her pussy and ass with the perfect movements of her gorgeous body. We quickly gain speed, thrusting in and out of her with our double dicks and stretching the limits of my wife's maxed out holes.

Eventually, Taylor starts to shake again, quaking as the building pleasure within her searches for somewhere to release itself. She reaches down between her legs with one hand and begins to rapidly play with her clit, edging closer and closer to a second powerful orgasm.

"Oh fuck, I'm gonna cum again." Taylor tells us. "I'm so close."

We continue to rail her as hard as we can, pounding my wife's body with all the force we can muster as she begins to seize and buck wildly.

"I want you to cum with me!" She tells us. "Shoot those fucking loads up into my tight pussy and ass!"

Now the three of us are all slamming each other in unison, trying desperately to make it over that final hump until suddenly it hits everyone in a cascading wave of pleasure. I push forward and hold in the depths of my wife's pussy, blowing my load hard and filling her to the brim with hot white spunk that quickly spills from the corners of her plugged orifice.

The stranger cums as well, but instead he pulls out and explodes in a frantic shower of jizz across my wife's ass and back. He clenches his teeth and let's out a long moan through their sealed grin, shaking with every ejection of spunk that flies from the head of his swollen cock.

All the while, Taylor is deep in the troughs of her second orgasm, gnashing at the air as if frantically trying to escape the overwhelming feelings that consume her body. Finally, she throws her head back and lets out a long scream of the word, "Fuck." It goes and goes for what seems like forever until finally she collapses forward onto me in a panting heap.

The stranger and I pull out, spilling pearly cum everywhere.

"That was amazing." I tell her.

"Fuck yeah it was." The stranger adds, giving my wife's ass a firm slap. "I'm heading back out there, thanks for the good time you two."

Taylor looks back over her shoulder at him and gives a wink as the guy leaves.

"I can't believe I just double fucked you with a stranger at a club." I tell her, trying to catch my breath. "That was fucking crazy."

"I know." Taylor agrees, pushing her hair out of her face. "Are you still okay?"

I nod, cracking a wry smile. "Never better, that was so much fun."

"Think we'll ever do it again?" Taylor asks.

I shrug. "If we ever get the chance."

Suddenly, the bathroom door, which was left unlocked, bursts open and two handsome men stumble in. They stop immediately as they see us, my wife's cum covered ass poking out towards them as we lay naked on the floor.

"Holy shit." Is all that one of the guys can say.

Taylor and me exchange knowing glances, then she looks back over her shoulder at the men. "Care to join us?" She asks with a grin.

MILE HIGH

My wife, Harley, has the dream job; but it's not one you'd expect. She travels around the world like a rock star, meets all kind of people like a politician, and helps families come together like a therapist. My wife's paid pretty damn well, too.

Harley is a flight attendant, and although that might seem like something to shrug off with a casual, who cares? It's really not.

You should see her flight itinerary this month. London, then Paris, then New York today and home to Los Angeles tomorrow. After that, it's three days off in Sydney, Australia, during which I'll be joining her.

But, unlike my wife, it was a pain in the ass to get this time off of work.

I have a normal job. I wake up early, get myself to the office and then slave away under the watchful eye of an angry, bitter boss who hates me almost as much as he hates himself. This is what most of us do, day in and day out while we dream of sitting by the beach in Fiji sipping on Mojitos. Meanwhile, my wife is doing just that, sending me photos of the beautiful sunset as it blossoms across the ocean before her, toes in the sand.

The only think keeping me from being overwhelmed with jealousy at this point, though, is that I truly love her and know that she deserves every bit of it. I don't want to sound to corny, but my wife is the best woman I've ever met. She's hardworking, kind, and most of all, a total bombshell.

We've been together since college, where we met as part of our biweekly travel society. At least one of us got to follow our dreams.

But who am I kidding, it's not so bad. I'm flying to Sydney with her tomorrow, after all.

"Would you like to know how excited I am to see you?" I ask Harley, my phone pressed against my shoulder as I walk back and forth between the closet and my half packed luggage that lies open on the bed.

"Please. Tell me just how excited you are, baby." She confirms, and then suddenly changes her tone completely. "Whoa, watch out!"

"Uh, what was that?" I question.

"Oh my god, sorry. The drivers here in New York are even worse than they are in LA. We almost got hit!"

"I don't think it's possible to be worse than here." I tell her, laughing. "Who's we?"

Harley sounds distant for a moment as she talks to someone with her mouth away from the phone, then comes back onto the line. "Sorry, that's just Nick. He's one of the guys I fly with."

"Oh yeah?" I ask.

"Yeah, he's great. He's gonna be on our flight to Sydney actually." She confirms.

"Cool! Sounds good, I can't wait to meet him." I tell her.

Harley does some more talking with the phone pulled away from her head, clearly distracted.

"Well, I'll let you go." I start to say.

"Oh no!" Harley blurts, cutting me off. "I'm sorry, Paul. I'm here. What were you saying?"

I start back at the beginning. "Would you like to know how excited I am to see you?" I ask her again.

"How excited, baby?" She humors me.

"I'm so excited that when I see you tomorrow in that sexy stewardess outfit I'm gonna pull you off into the restroom and fuck your brains out." I say with a laugh.

"Oh really?" Harley asks, drawing the words out in a long, seductive way that makes me skin bristle ever so slightly. "You're going to get me fired before we even land. Maybe wait until after we get to Sydney."

"I'm just telling you what I want do to. I understand that there's a time and a place for everything."

Harley laughs. "You know, people actually do that. I've caught couples in the restroom more than once!"

"Really?" I ask. "I thought that was just in the movies."

"I've even had to break up a threesome!" She laughs.

"Damn. I can't believe there's even enough room for that." I tell her, shaking my head.

"Depends." Harley explains. "On really long flights like this one, the new first class bathrooms are huge. It's like having your own private cabin."

I chuckle. "Good to know."

"Oh shit!" Harley says abruptly. "It looks like our table's ready, we're just going out to eat before heading back to LA."

"Okay, no worries. I'll see you soon, baby!" I tell her as quickly as I can.

"Love you!" She shouts, and then makes a loud kissing sound. "Muah!"

Her phone hangs up and I toss mine into the bed, immediately getting back to the task at hand. My thoughts are brimming with excitement, but I can't help but linger on this mysterious man who Harley is currently out to dinner with. I have no reason to doubt her faithfulness to me, but when your wife is as drop dead gorgeous as mine, it's hard not to think twice about even the most innocent of situations. I push it away. Tomorrow we'll be together, and that's all that matters.

"Paul!" Harley shouts as she runs up to me and throws her slender arms around my shoulders in a big, wet kiss. I hold her close, enjoying the warmth against my body and the tightness of her little blue stewardess dress.

After a long while of making out in the middle of the airport I pull her back and get a good look at her gorgeous smiling face. "I love you." I tell her.

Suddenly, another figure approaches behind Harley. "Hey, I'm Nick." The man says, reaching out a hand, which I shake confidently.

If I wasn't already worried about my wife flying all over the world with this guy, I am now. He's as handsome as they get; chiseled jaw and broad frame, perfectly sculpted to look like the quintessential all American bad boy.

"I'm Paul." I tell him, forcing a smile. "It's nice to finally meet you. I've heard so much about you."

"Likewise." Nick tells me. "You're a lucky man, it's a pleasure working with Harley."

My wife visibly blushes, swaying her hips side to side like a nervous schoolgirl. "Oh, come on." She says.

Paul laughs. "Anyway, I'm gonna grab a book from the airport shop while I still have time." He says. "We've got a long flight ahead of us. See you aboard."

"Sounds good." I tell him with a wave, and just like that, he's gone; disappearing into the fray of anxious fliers, hustling and bustling their way through the Los Angeles International Airport.

"He seems nice." I tell my wife, trying as hard as I can to hide my bubbling jealousy.

She nods. "Yeah, he's not bad."

We catch up a bit more before Harley has to go back and prepare the cabin, but all the while I can't help but think about the way that she acted when Nick was talking about her. There was something uneasy in her glances, a subtle hint of something more just below the surface of our exchange.

The strangest part, however, is the fact that these feelings of jealous actually kind of turn me on. I can't really explain it, but I know that it's there, a tiny flicker of lust that slowly blossoms and blooms across the landscape of my thoughts. The more wild and irrational my ideas get; the hotter the scenario becomes. I imagine them hooking up in hotels across the globe, fucking each others brains out while the missed calls continue to build up on Harley's phone and I remain completely oblivious. My cock is rock hard in my pants.

"Paul." Harley says again. Suddenly, I'm pulled back to reality, staring right through my wife as she looks me up and down in utter confusion. "Earth to Paul."

"I'm sorry." I say, shaking my head.

"Were you even listening?" She asks, seeming slightly annoyed.

I crack a smile. "I'm sorry baby, I haven't see you for so long and just looking at that beautiful face makes me so horny I don't even know what to do with myself." I'm not lying, either; I've just left out some of the more explicit and strangely overpowering specifics.

Apparently this is a suitable answer, and Harley slowly grows a smile of her own. "Alright, fair enough." She says. "I'm horny, too. I can't wait until we land."

A woman's voice suddenly cuts through the air from a loudspeaker above us, announcing that the flight will be boarding shortly.

"I better go. I'll see you aboard!" Harley says, then gives me a long kiss before breaking away and heading briskly back towards the gate.

I watch her go, my head still overflowing with these strange fantasies that are just as sexy as they are terrifying. I want to watch my wife fuck another man, I think to myself, what is wrong with me?

The flight is only about half full so I end up with an entire row to myself and plenty of space to get comfortable. Harley also has less to do, so she manages to come by and talk to me every once in a while, even sneaking me a few extra bottles of single serving booze.

I try to pace myself, but despite my best efforts I can tell that I am getting a little too drunk. Even more surprising, Harley seems to be secretly knocking back a few herself, which could clearly get her fired. Apparently, she's exhausted and stressed enough after the work week to have stopped caring long ago.

"And how are we enjoying our flight so far, sir?" She asks me, sauntering over to my little corner of the plane.

I look up from my book and smile, very pleased to see her gorgeous face. "Very well, thank you. I literally just finished reading my book."

"Oh, great!" Harley says. "Well you know, we offer a wide variety of movies to choose from on our international flights."

"What's playing?" I ask, genuinely interested.

Harley freezes for a moment, and then bursts out laughing. "Honestly, I have no idea. I really should know this." She admits. "Do you seriously want to find out? It's right there in your control panel."

I shake my head with a slight smirk. "I was just kidding." In a moment of inspiration I reach out and touch her leg. "Unless, you've got some adult programming on there."

Harley smiles coyly, looking up and down the aisle to see if anyone is watching. Fortunately, this section of the plane is almost entirely empty. Harley leans down towards me and whispers in a deep and seductive tone. "We could always make our own."

I think to ask if she's serious, but the smell of alcohol on her breath instantly confirms that Harley is definitely on a roll now. I've seen it before, when the drinks start flowing there's no stopping my wife, especially when it comes to wild escapades in the bedroom. The timing could be more perfect, though, because after my newly discovered fetish of imagining Harley with other men, I couldn't be any hornier.

"You want to show me how much room is in those first class restrooms?" I ask.

Harley closes her eyes, as if her thoughts are just too heavy to even deal with at the moment, then they spring open wide. "Let's do it." She says. "Get up and walk all the way down this aisle until to get to the front of the plane. There are four blue doors. Go into the last one and wait for me."

Without another word I undo my seatbelt and confidently walk the length of the plane. Nobody pays me any mind as I cross through the cabins and then finally reach the restrooms at the helm, opening the final door and quickly slipping inside. I lock it and then turn around.

"Holy shit." Is all I can say, the worlds tumbling out of my mouth in complete shock. I've never seen an airplane restroom this nice; hell, I rarely see normal restrooms this nice.

Everything is covered in black tile, which is probably fake but it looks fantastic. The toilet is fairly standard but the sink is lined with gold inlay and similar detailing, which runs up along the giant mirror that covers one side of the restroom. It's large in here, big enough to stretch out completely if you really wanted to.

Suddenly, there's a light rapping against the door. I open it slowly and Harley immediately slips inside, then pins me back against the wall with a barrage of kisses. She's clearly just as pent up as I am, because the next thing I know she is tearing off my clothes and frantically unbuttoning my jeans.

Moments later, my cock springs forth and Harley drops to her knees, taking my thick member deep down into her throat. She gags a little, getting a bit too carried away during her first attempt, but then collects herself and tries again. This time my wife is ready, relaxing her gag reflex enough to take me down entirely to the hilt. She pushes further and further until her lips are resting against the edge of my toned stomach and my balls hang softly on her chin. Her eyes watering, she looks up at me in her sexy blue uniform and I almost blow right then and there.

"Oh my god." I groan. "You're so fucking amazing."

Harley starts to pump up and down on the length of my shaft, using her hands to help me along as I begin to moan with ecstasy.

"Fuck, baby." I tell her. "You're so good at sucking that dick."

She pulls me out of her mouth for a moment, but continues to frantically beat me off, using her spit as lube as her hand glides rapidly across the length of my thick shaft.

"You like the way I blow you?" She questions frantically. "You like the way these pretty lips feel sliding across your big fat cock?"

"Yes." I cry. "Fuck, yes."

Suddenly, there's a loud, hard knock against the restroom door. The both of us jump in surprise and then immediately freeze, not sure what to do with ourselves.

"You need to come out right now." A voice says firmly from the other side.

"Oh no." Harley whispers, standing up and wiping off her mouth. I quickly button my jeans back up and try to put on my shirt.

"I'm so sorry." Harley begins, opening up the door, and then stops when she sees Nick staring back at her in complete surprise.

A devilish grin creeps across his face and he starts to say something but, before he can, Harley grabs him by the collar and pulls him inside.

"You two are so lucky that it's me who caught you." He says with a laugh. "What the hell is going on in here?"

"What do you think?" Harley says.

Nick just shakes his head, unable to wipe the smile off of his face. He looks over Harley's shoulder at me. "Like I was saying, you're a lucky guy."

At this very moment something deep and powerful grabs a hold of me, a strange recognition that a golden opportunity for sexual adventure lies ahead if I'm brave, or horny, enough to take it. I hesitate, only for a moment, and then say, "How'd you like to join us?"

Nick and Harley both stop and look at me, the tension between them almost too heavy to breath as it fills our tight quarters. Neither of them says a word.

"I'm asking if you'd like to fuck my wife with me." I continue, as if they needed it clarified.

"Are you sure?" Harley finally asks, her eyes unable to mask the excitement lying deep beneath them.

"It sounds fucking hot to me." I tell her, and then nod at Nick. "Are you game?"

Nick still seems to be completely flustered by the situation, but eventually he nods in affirmation.

"Well." I look my wife dead in the eyes. "Why don't you show him that little trick you were just showing me?"

Harley gives a wink and then drops down, quickly unbuttoning the pants of Nick's uniform and then pulling out his swollen cock. She wastes no time, wrapping her lips tightly around his shaft and then pushing down as Nick reels from the sensation, letting out a long, satisfied moan.

I watch in complete awe as Harley forces his length deeper and deeper down until finally she has him entirely stuffed within her neck. Nick places his hands against the back of my wife's head, savoring the feeling as he slowly bobs her up and down on his dick.

Suddenly, Harley reaches out and grabs at the air next to me. I immediately know what she's looking for and place my dick in her hand, which she begins to frantically stroke while she continues to blow her friend. Soon, my wife pulls him out of her mouth and turns her attention to me, then back to Nick, servicing us both equally as we stand on either side of her cock hungry mouth.

After a while of this, my wife is finally just too horny to take it anymore and stands between us, hiking up her uniform and pulling off her panties beneath. She turns to face me and then leans over, swallowing my cock as she pushes her bare ass up against Nick.

I watch entranced as this other man runs his hands along my wife's beautiful curves, appreciating the shape of her toned, feminine body before taking hold of his swollen cock and lining it up with the tight slit of her pussy.

Harley reaches back with one hand and spreads herself open for him, then pops me out of her mouth just long enough to command, "Shove that big fucking cock of yours up my pussy."

Nick pushes forward slowly as Harley grinds back and lets out a soft whimper. He begins to pump in and out of her with a firm, deliberate rhythm, stretching the limits of her tightness with his thick cock. With every slam against her beautiful ass, Nick pushes Harley forward and forces my cock even deeper down her throat. Harley is loving every second of it, her squeals vibrating against the flesh of my dick as we pound her from either end. My wife's eyes roll back into her head and I watch as she reaches her other hand between her legs, going to work with her slender fingers against her clit.

"You fucking like that?" Nick suddenly demands to know, slapping Harley's ass hard.

"Yes." She mumbles against my dick.

"I asked if you fucking like taking two dicks?!" Nick yells, loud enough that I'm certain people out in the plane's cabin heard it, but enjoying myself way too much to care.

"Yes!" Harley cries out in a strange, gargled squeal that escapes around the edges of my huge shaft.

Hearing this, Nick immediately picks up the speed of his thrusts, absolutely slamming my wife with everything that he's got. I follow suit, and suddenly we are pummeling her from either end, pushing Harley back and forth like a beautiful, high-flying rag doll on our cocks.

Suddenly, my wife is overcome with lust and stands upright, pulling Nick's dick out of her pussy. There's not much room to maneuver, but she knows exactly how she wants it, literally jumping up onto me and wrapping her legs around my waist. I hold her in the air and then carefully lower my wife down onto my cock as she moans with pleasure, using the force of gravity to slowly impale her onto my rod.

Harley looks back over her shoulder at Nick and snarls, "I need that dick up my asshole right now."

I'm stunned, blown away by my wife's insatiable sluttiness. "You sure about that?" I ask. "Two cocks at the same time?"

She looks back at me and then cracks a mischievous smile. "You had no idea what your pretty little slut wife could do, huh?"

Nick saddles up behind her, and I hold Harley up so that he can position his girthy shaft against her back door. My wife squirms a little as it presses dangerously against her tight rim, then relaxes with a long sigh as I lower her down onto both of our members.

"Fuck." Harley yelps as she sinks lower and lower until finally hitting the bottom, where she hangs with our dual cocks planted firmly up her holes. We start to lift her small frame up and down onto our rods and my wife closes her eyes tight, leaning back against Nick and wrapping her slender arms around his neck. She looks up at him with a hazy, cock drunk gaze and kisses him deeply.

Even though I've been watching Nick pound my wife for the last fifteen minutes, the sight of her kissing him like this still gives me chills. I can feel my blood boiling as I watch them, the jealousy and arousal mixing together within my veins to form some strange, confusing elixir that quickens my heartbeat and sets my teeth on edge. I somehow hate it and love it at the same time, but more than anything it just turns me on.

Overwhelmed with newfound desire, I find myself picking up the pace until I am frantically pounding my wife down onto both of our dicks, violating her holes with a completely reckless abandon. Harley starts the scream, reaching down and helping herself along as she tickles her clit and begins to tremble wildly. The shaking grows and grows, blossoming in a series of spasms that crawl out across her body until finally it's just too much and she kicks her legs straight out, cumming hard from our two cock invasion. Her eyes are clenched tight and she throws herself forward, grabbing onto me.

"Oh my god, I love having another man in my ass while you fuck me!" Harley screams. "Oh my god! Oh my god!"

My wife finally finishes and then collapses in our arms as we carefully lower her to the restroom floor. Nick and I are following a similar track, our throbbing cocks ready to erupt at any second.

Harley looks up at us with her big pleading eyes. "Please," She begs. "I need your cum all over me!"

Nick starts to blow first, letting out a guttural moan as a thick rope of milky white semen ejects from the end of his dick. It flies through the air and then splatters across my wife's face. Harley giggles happily, licking as much as she can off of her lips and then turning to me and opening her mouth wide.

The pressure had been slowly building inside of me, but seeing her with the seed of another man so recklessly blown across her beautiful face sends me over the edge almost immediately. I let out a long groan and then shoot my load directly into Harley mouth and across her tongue. It comes out in several hard pumps and then my wife happily sucks down the rest, swallowing hungrily and then giving me a satisfied wink.

Now completely spent, the three of us quickly put our clothes back on and try to make ourselves look as convincingly unfucked as possible. Nick opens the door and the three of us step out into the cabin.

The entire plane is staring at us with looks of bewildered amusement plastered across their faces. At least it's not anger and disgust, I think to myself as I make my way back to my seat.

As I gather my coat and carry-on bag, I try my best not to think about the way that my life will chance once I step off of this flight. This could be the beginning of an entirely new kind of relationship for my wife and I but, strangely, I'm alright with it.

I'm on the very end of a long line of passengers who are shuffling there way to the front where my beautiful wife bids them farewell with a smile and a wave. When I finally reach her she gives me a playful wink instead.

"Thank you for flying with us." Harley says. "Cum again soon."

I think I'm going to like our new arrangement.

THE LIST

My wife, Kali, loves music. It's always playing and, thanks to the wonders of wireless technology, it follows us wherever we go. From the house, to the car, to the walls of my social media; when she gets excited about some new artist there's no missing it. Music is forever ingrained in my wife's live, and therefore it's ingrained in mine.

Kali's borderline obsessive about her hunt for new bands, and once she finds something that she like she devours entire back catalogs in a matter of days. It's actually quite impressive the way that she consumes musical information.

I, on the other hand, am a casual listener. I know what I like and I pretty much stuck to it, not really taking any sort of the pride in the artists that I know or don't know. Thanks to my wife, however, my knowledge of up and coming artists is well above average but it's only due to the constant information run off. She drags me along to shows, of which there are plenty due to the fact that we live in Los Angeles, but I tend to get bored early and end up resting my feet at a stool by the bar while she goes crazy in the mosh pit.

The funny thing is, you wouldn't really know it when looking at her. My wife isn't some kind of spiky haired, pierced up punk rocker, although she's got a few subtle tattoos from her college years. With her long blonde hair and absolutely incredible body, you'd probably expect her to be hanging out on a beach rather than fighting her way to the front of the stage at a rock and roll gig.

Lately, she's been head over heels about a new band, called The

Hornet's Nest. They're a pretty raucous bunch, but I have to admit I like the little bit that I've heard coming from the speakers of Kali's laptop while she works. It's a strange blend of psychedelic prog-rock and modern punk that's weirdly easy to swallow given this brief summary. There's an obvious edge, though, and I think that's what Kali likes.

It almost seems to be about more than just the music with her. Kali reads interviews and knows the band member's history backwards and forewords. The lead singer of The Hornet's Nests is the background image on her phone.

At least she's got good taste. The guy is great looking in a bad-ass, leather jacket wearing kind of way. I'd probably mind Kali's obsession more if she was into fresh-faced teenybopper pop.

We're out to lunch one afternoon when the new Hornet's Nest single comes floating down from the restaurant speakers above. Kali immediately perks up and smiles.

"Oh my god." She announces to me. "I love this song."

"I know." I say with a slight eye roll.

Kali starts to nod her head as she eats, following along to the rhythm. Eventually, she starts to hum with the music and then finally looks up at me and begins passionately crooning the words, loud enough for the people eating around us to hear her and take notice.

"Stop." I moan, embarrassed as I glance around at the other tables.

My shyness does nothing but egg her on. Kali launches into the chorus at full volume and suddenly I'm reaching across the table, laughing and desperately trying to quiet her down.

"I can't bring you anywhere!" I joke as she finally stops and lets out a satisfied giggle.

"Come on," Kali says with a smirk. "How can you not sing along with this song?"

"The song is good." I tell her. "But this sandwich is better."

"Please." Kali rolls her eyes. "Tom Jordans is the best lyricist in the last twenty years. Are you even listening?"

"I don't really pay attention to the lyrics." I admit, which is comically upsetting to Kali. I've got no problem admitting that I like to play up my musical ignorance around her.

She throws her hands up in mock anger. "Gah! You have no idea what you're missing."

"You just think the singer's cute." I tell her. "The lyrics are just a front."

Kali cracks a smile. "So what if I do?"

I shrug, playing along. "Well, you're never going to meet him so I'm not too worried about it." I tell her.

"Oh, and you're going to meet Carli Foxx?" She asks, poking back.

I immediately know what she's referring to; our list.

The list is an idea between couples, where they agree to let the other person sleep with a certain celebrity without any anger or recourse should the opportunity arise. This is mostly done as a joke although, due to the fact that we live in LA, it's not actually that unlikely in our case. Still, I'm willing to take my chances, especially with the beautiful blonde porn starlet Clari Foxx at the top of my list.

"Is Tom Jordans on your list now?" I ask her. "I think you're going to have to bump somebody off."

The length of a couple's list can vary, but ours in particular are only three celebrities long.

"I'm bumping off everyone." She teases. "Just Tom Jordans three times."

"Fine, I'm doing the same thing with Carli Foxx then." I laugh. "You know, strategically that makes absolutely no sense, but I see what you're getting at."

Eventually, the conversation dies down into the usual fair for a married couple that's been together as long as we have. Discussions of work, the house that we're talking out buying and whether or not we can afford it as a young couple; that kind of thing. All the while, however, I can't stop thinking about the way that my beautiful wife is so obsessed with this other, very attractive man.

The idea of Kali fucking this guy is not something that would ever happen within the realm of reality, but I can't help being strangely turned on by the thought of it.

I'm not the jealous type, within reason, but I'm slightly jealous of her adoration in what feels like a good way. It's a deep, dull jealousy that aches away within the flesh of my cock, simmering as a powerful lustful desire.

We finally finish and I pay, then head out the front doors of the restaurant into the beaming California sun.

"That was really good." Kali says, grabbing me by the arm and pulling herself close as we walk. "Thank you, Evan."

"No problem." I tell her.

Suddenly, Kali stops dead in her tracks. She's looking at the marquee of large bustling record store, which, these days, is already a rare enough sight in itself.

"What is it?" I ask, completely obliviously of what she seems to notice so plainly.

"The Hornet's Nest are doing an in store performance here tomorrow night!" She squeals with excitement. "Do you wanna go?"

I don't, actually. I've got heaps and heaps of stuff to get done for work on Monday and a concert tomorrow night seems like nothing but another thing to be stressed out. However, Kali is more than a little excited and it would obviously mean a lot to her if I were to come along to watch her favorite band play. Besides, I can't just leave her alone with the guy who makes up all three spots on her list.

"Sure." I tell her with a smile. "Sounds like fun."

The next day we show up to the record store early and find our place in line. The whole street is a complete fiasco with people lined up around the block and hot dog vendors everywhere, preying on the hunger of those trying desperately to hold their place. My wife is done up to the nines, wearing a short black skirt over a tight, pink one-piece.

A guy with a small mechanical device walks past us down the line, clicking once as he goes for every person he sees.

"Do you think that means we got in?" Kali asks me.

"I don't know." I answer.

Suddenly, there is a booming voice from about twenty feet down the sidewalk from us. "Already everybody!" The man with the counter is shouting. "If you're after this person in line, you're not seeing the show today. We're going to be at capacity here. I'm sorry about that."

His announcement is met with a sea of disappointed groans as the less fortunate fans disperse back to wherever they came from. Kali claps her hands together with girlish excitement and suddenly the remainder of us who haven't been turned away start moving foreword towards the entrance.

"Once we get inside I'm going to push my way to the front." She tells me. "You coming?"

I shake my head. "No thanks baby, but you go ahead."

Kali nods as we cross through the threshold of the record store and immediately disappears through the crowd, cutting across the ocean of people like a shark as she cruises directly to the edge of the small, makeshift stage. She gets a few angry glances from the fans that she pushes by, but it's hard to stay that upset with someone as cute as my beautiful blonde wife.

I casually find a place to stand at the back of the room and take in the proceedings. The crowd is what I would have expected, young and hip, with a slight but not entirely disproportionate lean towards the female gender.

It's not long before the band hits the stage, causing the entire packed room to burst into a wild frenzy of adoration. They kick into their first song, an upbeat jam that I've heard a million times before in Kali's car. It's okay.

My disaffected reaction couldn't be any farther from Kali's. I spot her in the front, singing along with her hands in the air as she sways her gorgeous body to the music. It's hard not to notice her, even for the band who make no mystery about looking my wife up and down throughout the set.

Immediately, I can feel that strange jealous and horny feeling return to my bloodstream, pumping through my heart and seeping deep into my brain. It's even stronger than before, probably because I've started to accept it, letting it overwhelm me pleasantly instead of struggling to push it away. The eyes of every man in this room are transfixed on my wife and I love it. I find myself rock hard and aching for release, the strange lust consuming my thoughts while I fantasize about my wife fucking any and all of these other men. Even more exciting though, is imagining her with Tom, the band's singer. I can see the way that she looks at him, the way that her pussy must crave his touch.

I picture him bringing her back onto the tour bus while I'm locked outside, peering through the windows while he undresses her and runs his hands across her smooth, soft skin. I imagine my wife whimpering as he pushes her up against the wall of the bus and shoves his enormous cock into Kali's pussy, which hasn't been touched by another man for years now.

"Thank you, goodnight everybody!" Announces Tom, the singer, slicing through my decadent thoughts and jolting me back to reality. How much time has passed?

The band leaves the stage with confident swagger and a series of playful waves, followed by the drummer tossing his drumsticks into the fray and disappearing behind a curtain.

I step outside quickly to avoid getting caught in the swarming mass of fans as they boil out into the street, watching carefully for Kali to emerge.

"Hey!" I shout as she exits and turns towards me, a look of feverish excitement plastered across her beautiful face. "Did you have fun?"

"Are you kidding me?" Kali asks. "That was the best show I've ever seen!"

"Ever?" I humor her.

Kali shakes her head in amazement, unable to even find the words. Eventually, she looks up at me. "Can we grab a beer? I want a beer."

"Sure." I tell her, grabbing her around the waist and starting up the street towards one of our favorite low-key Hollywood hangouts.

The sun is setting, appropriately, down Sunset Blvd as we make our way up the block, and as it's final rays of light disappear beyond the horizon we turn to head inside the cozy dive bar. The place isn't as packed as I'd expect after a show nearby, and we have no problem finding a booth to climb into after ordering our drinks. I look across the table at Kali in the dim light.

"I love you, baby." I tell her.

Kali smiles. "I love you, too. Thanks for coming with me."

I laugh. "I've been put through worse, that was actually really good."

We chat for a while, going over our favorite parts of the set, which I skillfully improvise after paying such little attention to the actual show itself. If we were to go over my newfound fantasies of seeing Kali with another man, however, I'd have plenty to talk about. But for now, I keep them to myself.

Suddenly, Kali stops talking, her eyes transfixed over my shoulder in a mixture of fear and amazement.

"Uh, are you okay?" I ask.

"Tom Jordans is walking towards us." She says under her breath.

I turn around just as the singer arrives and brazenly slides into the booth next to my wife.

"Hi there." Tom says in a thick British accent, shaking Kali's hand and then mine in turn.

"Hi." Is all that Kali can say.

"I saw you in the front row." Tom tells her, and then turns to me. "Is this your girlfriend?"

"Wife." I tell him. I should be offended but somehow his confidence is more astounding than off putting. The guy seems like an asshole but somehow so much of one that it circles all the way back around and becomes charming again.

"Do you mind if I buy your girl a drink?" He asks me.

It's just about one of the strangest questions I've ever been asked, but my instinctual response is to simply nod. Tom motions to the bartender and drapes his arm around Kali's shoulder, which sends a sting of rage and arousal up mine spine. I'm frustrated by my own horniness, desperately wanting him to take it further but terrified by the consequences.

Someone brings by a single drink and sets it in front of Kali.

"Nothing for you?" I ask.

Tom shakes his head, "Nah, I don't drink."

I can't help but laugh at this and Tom cracks a smile, giving me a disarming wink. I hate to admit that I like the guy, especially given the circumstances, but I do.

At this point I find myself with several options. I know where this is headed and I know exactly how confused Kali must be feeling at the moment. It's natural for her to fantasize about such a powerful figure, but what happens when the fantasy meets reality?

As I see it, I have two options, bail completely or go along for the ride, and based on how hard my dick is under the table, I immediately know which one I prefer.

"Have you ever heard of a list between married couples?" I ask Tom.

Kali immediately turns white as a sheet when she realizes where this is headed.

Tom shakes his head. "What kind of list?"

"A list of celebrities that they're allowed to have sex with if given the chance." I continue.

Tom cracks a devilish smile. "Am I on your wife's list?" He asks me. "Is that what you're trying to say?"

I nod. Tom glances over at Kali who looks like a deer in headlights, happily overwhelmed by the situation as she gazes back at him, trembling.

"Is this true?" Tom asks.

"Yes." Kali says, her voice quivering.

Tom immediately leans in and kisses my wife. At first she pulls away, flashing me a quick glance of confusion, but I immediately nod to her and she goes back in for more. The two of them are suddenly all over each other in the booth while I watch, unable to tear my eyes away from this unbridled display between Kali and another man.

Eventually, Tom sits up. "I've got a hotel for the night across the street." He tells me. "I'm going to be fucking your wife. Care to join us?"

My blood is boiling but I'm on autopilot now, completely at the whim of my overpowering lust. "Let's go." I tell him.

We've barely gotten through the door to his suite before Kali's clothes are on the floor, torn off completely by Tom as he pushes her backwards with a barrage of kisses.

His place is swanky, the luxury penthouse on the top floor of this classic Hollywood hotel. It's easy to imagine the kind of debauchery that has gone on in this room over the years, and I'm happy to be adding to it. I'm aware of a spectacular view of the city lights below us, but all I can focus on is the image of my wife and Tom collapsing onto the couch in the middle of his room.

I stand in complete awe as Kali drifts lower and lower to the floor until she's on her knees before Tom, with the rocker laid back across the couch, his toned abs and chest exposed. Tom's jeans are pulled down just enough for his massive cock to spring forth, a throbbing tower of flesh that Kali quickly grabs before looking back over her shoulder at me.

"Are you sure this is okay, baby?" She asks, genuine concern in her beautiful voice.

"He's on your list." I tell Kali. "Of course it's okay."

She smiles, giving me a wink and then immediately turning her attention back to Tom's giant cock. Kali opens her mouth and swallows him deep, barely able to wrap her lips around his girth as she pushes down onto the tight rod. Moments later, she starts to bob up and down on his shaft, pleasuring Tom as skillfully as she can. My wife reaches up with one hand and cradles the rocker's balls while keeping the other hand wrapped tightly around his dick like a ring. Her pace quickens as Tom let's out a long, satisfied moan, placing his hands behind her head and helping to move her along.

Eventually, Tom takes complete control of the movements and pushes my wife's head down as deep as he can over his thick cock. I watch as she gags, retching loudly while his massive shaft pushes dangerously against the edge of her gag reflex. Tom lets her up for a moment and my wife takes in a frantic gasp of air, a line of spit hanging from her lips. She collects herself quickly and then swallows Tom's dick once again, this time fully prepared to relax against the pressure of his massive length.

I watch with pride as Kali consumes him entirely, her lips finally coming to a rest at the base of Tom's cock while her face is pressed tightly against his ripped abs. She holds here for a long while, letting him fully enjoy the fruits of her labor, then pulls up when she's just about to run out of air.

"Your wife gives incredible head." Tom tells me with his thick accent. "You really should come over here and have a go."

I step forward, removing my clothes as I make my way towards them. Kali looks back at me with a smile and then crawls over, gazing up with a wild hunger.

I unsheathe my cock and let it bounce in my wife's face, then close my eyes as she takes me into her wet lips. Kali immediately goes to work, pulsing up and down over my length and then pulling me out so that she can happily lick my shaft from base to tip.

"Oh fuck." I groan, moving my hips gently to the rhythm of her incredible blowjob.

Tom let's me enjoy this for a while and then leans forward and slaps Kali hard on the ass. She lets out a squeal against my cock and then turns around, popping it out of her mouth.

"Get up here." Tom commands.

Kali does as she's told, standing up and then moving back so that she's directly over Tom's lap, his dick aligned directly with her soaking wet pussy. He grabs her by the hips and then lowers her down slowly onto him.

It's hard to believe this was only a fantasy just hours before and now here we are, me and this handsome stranger fucking my innocent wife like she's some filthy, but gorgeous, slut. A high-class escort to the stars, I think, trembling with strange desires as Tom's cock gets closer and closer to the tight entrance of my wife's aching hole.

Kali let's out a satisfied cry as Tom's massive dick slides into her, stretching out her tightness to the max around his thick member. He uses her huge arms to lift her up and down onto his cock, impaling my wife's small frame with a slow series of powerful thrusts. Her eyes roll back into her head as she reaches down and start to rapidly tickle her clit, trembling as the powerful sensations of orgasm start to make their first appearance.

I step up in front of the pairing and Kali gladly grabs a hold of my swollen cock, beating me off as the member below her steadily speeds up. She matches the pace, and soon the three of us are rapidly moving together as one frantic sexual unit.

"Do you like watching your pretty wife get pounded by another man?" Kali asks me, a devious and cock hungry look in her eyes. "Do you like the way it looks when someone else fucks me?"

"Oh my god." I confess. "I love it so much."

She takes my cock into her mouth and begins to suck me off with equal ferocity as she bounces up and down on Tom's huge member.

After a good while of this, Kali pulls me out of her mouth and stands abruptly, then turns around to face Tom as she climbs back down onto him, her slender legs wrapped tight around his toned abs. My wife reaches back and grabs her ass with both hands, spreading her cheeks as she guides herself lower until finally Tom's cock slips inside. She immediately gets to work, grinding against him with powerful swoops of her hips.

"Oh fuck!" Kali moans, her whole body starting to tremble. "His big cock is going to make my cum so hard!"

I look on with my cock in my hand, stroking as I enjoy the incredible scene that unfolds before me. My wife is in utter bliss, taken to some other world by this new man and his giant dick that hits her perfectly from the inside with every thrust. Her body is absolutely quaking now, spasming in powerful waves until finally Kali lets out a desperate cry and flings herself forward onto the couch.

"I'm cumming!" She screams through clenched teeth, her hands gripped tightly on the back edge. Tom doesn't let up for a second, pummeling her pussy with everything he's got as my wife continues to orgasm. It lasts for what seems like forever, until finally the squealing stops and she sits up on his cock in a state of bewildered bliss.

At this point, I expect Kali to be finished and completely exhausted, but instead the orgasm seems to have given her a lustful second wind.

"I need more!" She stammers, trying to collect herself. "I need more fucking cock."

"What do you want, baby?" I ask.

My wife looks back over her shoulder at me, the cock still planted firmly within her. "I want you to fuck me up the ass while Tom takes my pussy."

My eyes go wide. Never had I dreamed my wife would be telling me to do something so brutally decedent to her body, but I couldn't be happier about it. I immediately step foreword and align my cock with the tight puckered rim of Kali's asshole.

"Shove it in!" She demands. "Double fuck me like a filthy slut!"

I press foreword but it's just too tight, the entrance maxed out and stretched by the substantial girth of Tom's rod. I try again, pushing even harder with the head of my cock against Kali's hole.

"Oh my god." She suddenly moans as the tension releases and I plunge inside, deeper and deeper until my cock comes to rest at the depths of her tightness. I can feel Tom start to pulse in and out of her and I follow suit, slowly at first and then building speed as we ruthlessly double penetrate my wife.

As we pound away at her holes Kali starts to squeal again, already building towards a second orgasm. I can feel her stomach clenching hard, preparing for the visceral eruption of pleasure as she reaches down and frantically plays with her clit.

Suddenly, I find myself in a similar position, succumbing to the sensations that flow through my body as they build towards an inevitable conclusion.

"Oh fuck." I start to mumble over and over again. "Oh fuck, oh fuck."

"I'm gonna cum again!" Kali suddenly interrupts.

"Me too!" I shout, pushing deep within her asshole and holding tight. My cock unloads inside of her, shooting rope after rope of warm jizz up into my wife's tight rectum until there's simply no room left and it comes spilling out of the sides.

Kali is shaking wildly, her eyes rolling back in her head as the powerful feelings of ecstasy consume her. "Fuck, I can't... I don't even..." She screams frantically, unable to figure out what to do with herself.

Suddenly, Tom lets out a guttural howl and thrusts up into Kali's pussy as hard as he can, blowing a massive load of his own. He holds her hips tightly as he unleashes several pumps of semen, and then finally falls back onto the couch in complete satisfaction.

After a brief rest, my wife stands up and heads to the shower, our jizz running down her ass and legs in thick pearly streaks.

The elevator ride back down to the lobby should be awkward for my wife and I, but it couldn't be any less. We're already joking about the encounter, talking about what an incredible story it will make when we tell our friends about our wild threesome with a rock star. Of course, we'll save this particular tale for only the most the sexually liberal of the bunch.

"That was so much fun." I admit to Kali as the floors continue to count down lower and lower.

She smiles at me warmly and then gives me a hug, her wet hair from the shower seeping lightly through my shirt. "I know." My wife says. "I owe you one."

The elevator suddenly stops on the third floor and the door opens as another passenger joins us. She's blonde and absolutely gorgeous, instantly recognizable as pornstar Carli Foxx. My wife and I exchange glances. Here we go again.

ON THE GREEN

My boss, Jeff Peters, is one of the most intimidating people I've ever met, and yet somehow charming to the point that watching his business interactions is downright comical. Everyone who meets the guy falls instantly in love, and from there his powers of manipulation are free to do whatever they please. It's truly uncanny and, as his faithful employee, it's something that I try to aspire to.

Unfortunately, we just don't see eye to eye on a lot of things around the office, and right now it's coming to a head.

I work at a commercial investment firm, specializing mostly in real estate opportunities. We develop land that our company determines to be valuable, turning it into massive shopping centers where slums existed before and, although it's not exactly glamorous work, our business is incredibly successful.

I've worked my way up the ranks high enough now that I'm routinely being put in charge of entire development operations, even finding my own sites and pulling the trigger on multimillion-dollar deals. It's a rush, to say the least, but I'm still only allowed to move forward when Jeff signs off on it.

"Vance, we can't keep having this conversation." Jeff tells me as I sit across the desk in his massive, sunlit office overlooking downtown Los Angeles. "I know you've got your heart set on this deal, but it's not a home run."

"Who knows?" I tell him. "It's a risk, I get that, but isn't that what this is all about? Taking risks sometimes?"

Jeff leans back into his chair and shakes his head. "At this point, no. We're a publicly traded company now, the days of flying solo like that are over, Vance. At this point we need to be cruising upwards slow and steady, and the last thing we need to be spending money on is a project that isn't a sure thing."

"But if this works it's going to be huge!" I protest. "This land has the potential to have five times the value after we get in there."

"*If* it works." Jeff says. "I'm not interested in 'if' right now."

I take a deep breath, trying not to get flustered even though I've lost track of how many times we've had this conversation over the last week.

"Listen, I consider you a friend." Jeff tells me. "We've been through a lot together and that's the only reason I've allowed you to come in here and pitch me this many times, but honestly, if I hear about it again there's going to be consequences."

His words make the hair on the back on my neck stand on end. The guy is equal parts friendly and ruthless, and I'm not interested in flipping over to the ruthless side any time soon.

"I'm sorry about that, sir. You're right." I lie. I know this is a killer project for our company to focus on, but I also know when to quit; at least for the time being. "Thank you for hearing what I had to say."

I stand up to leave, almost making it out the door of Jeff's office when he suddenly yells after me. "Hey, Vance!"

I stop and spin around.

"You golf?" He asks.

I nod. I'm actually quite an accomplished golfer, having spent most of my childhood following my dad around the course and leaning to play like I mean it.

"Me and the wife are hitting the course this weekend. How'd you like to bring the misses and join us?"

"Of course!" I answer, almost too quickly.

Jeff smiles. "Great. Can't wait, buddy."

My wife Paris and I arrive at the course a little early, mostly out of my nervous preparation towards making today's game go smoothly. The thing is, golf is not just golf in the world of big business. The biggest contracts in the world are locking down on the green, and if there is one place for me to make a final stab at Jeff signing off on my little pet project, it's here.

It also doesn't hurt having Paris on my arm. Similar to Jeff's almost supernatural charm, Paris has a way of getting what she wants, although it's not as difficult to pinpoint in her case. As far as beautiful, jaw-dropping women go, my wife is at the top of the list. She's a total bombshell in every way, a slender body with massive tits and distinctly exotic features. Paris turns heads wherever we go, and today at the clubhouse is no exception.

"Hey!" I hear a familiar voice booming suddenly from just behind us. We turn around to see Jeff approaching with his hand extended. I give him a firm shake and then he turns to my wife.

"And you must be Paris." Jeff says, giving her a friendly hug. "Wow, you are absolutely breathtaking." He tells her, his eyes lingering a little longer than they should on my wife's gorgeous body.

I feel a pang of jealousy shoot through me. Not only is this guy handsome, charming and the highest spot on the totem pole at work, now he's checking out my wife.

I glance over at Paris quickly, and find myself even more surprised by the fact that she seems to be loving the attention. Her usual confident swagger has been shot, melted down into the form of a nervous, bashful schoolgirl.

"That's very sweet of you." Paris says.

I reach out and put my arm around her, which seems to break the spell, at least for now.

"Ready to play?" Jeff asks.

It suddenly dawns on me that he's arrived alone, his wife nowhere to be found.

"Where's Dana?" I ask.

An awkward looks crosses Jeff's face and he hesitates for a moment, clearly struggling to find the words. "She's not coming today." He finally says. "We're probably going to be separating soon."

"What?" I ask, genuinely surprised. It's not like I was super tight with them as a couple, but I'd seen enough interactions at the annual Christmas party and random work events to think they seemed utterly ecstatic with the state of their marriage. "I'm so sorry."

"Oh no." Jeff says, waving away my concern. "It's better this way, really."

"I'm so sorry." Paris repeats, reaching out her hand and putting it softly on Jeff's arm. He stops and looks up at her, suddenly back under the spell. This is getting ridiculous.

"Alright, well let's get going!" I interrupt loudly.

Being the natural alpha male that he is, Jeff takes the lead as we head out towards the first tee. We take two golf carts, one for Paris and me and one for Jeff. I'm thankful because it gives me a chance to talk to my wife alone for a moment.

"You seem to like my boss quite a bit." I joke.

Paris looks back at me with a face full of confusion, but I can see right though her. She knows exactly what I'm talking about.

"Don't be silly, baby." She says, wrapping her arms around me and giving me a kiss on the cheek.

"It's okay, you know." I tell her. "To be attracted to other people. We've talked about this before."

It's true, though. My wife and me have the healthiest marriage out of anyone that we know, and it's partially because of the sexual freedom that we allow each other. It's not like we're full on swingers or anything, far from it, but if I see a hot woman walking down the street, I've got no problem mentioning it, and the same goes for her. Some people couldn't do things this way, but the closeness that's developed between the two of us, due to our open minded take on love, has brought nothing but happiness. Strangely enough, some of her little crushes on other men have actually started to turn me on, although I've never actually mentioned it to Paris.

Paris lets out a long sigh. "Yeah, he's very handsome."

I let her words seep into my consciousness, taking note of the way that they play with my emotions. There's something about her attraction that triggers more than just jealously within me; a strange, confusing lust. The thought of her wanting my boss makes my heart rate quicken and my face flush red, but I actually kind of like it.

"Handsome enough to fuck?" I ask her as our golf cart continues down the path.

She pulls away for a moment, looking deep into my eyes as she tries to read my expression. Paris is being cautious, knowing full well that, even though we're honest and open, honesty isn't always the best policy when it comes to sexual fantasies.

"It's okay." I assure her, not quite sure what's come over me. "You can tell me."

Paris shrugs. "Well, I mean, yeah then. He's handsome enough to fuck."

I feel my cock hardening the second that she says this, but I'm still not exactly sure what's going on within my brain. Where is all of this leading? I think to myself. Do I actually want my wife to fuck my boss?

We arrive at the first tee and hop out onto the perfectly manicured grass, Jeff already there and lining up to take his first shot.

"What took you so long?" He asks, not even looking up as he makes a perfect swing that sends the ball soaring high through the air to, moments later, land perfectly on the green for an easy birdie.

Jeff is good, but it doesn't take long for me to realize that I am significantly better than him when it comes to golf. That being said, my game today couldn't be more off. Plagued by missed putts and a few horribly sliced drives, I find myself neck and neck with an adversary that I should be absolutely pummeling.

Paris is keeping up, too, and doing a fine job of it, but the real battle is between Jeff and I as we enter the back nine.

"So, I wanted to take a moment to talk to you about that project." I start, setting my ball down onto the tee while I attempt to casually broach the subject.

"Are you fucking serious?" Vance demands. Clearly, my plan of getting him relaxed on the course and then making a final attempt has backfired, because my boss is anything but relaxed right now. "I thought we talked about this."

"We have." I confess. "More time's than I'd like to admit, but I know that if you let me run with this thing we can do something really special."

Jeff shakes his head, visibly fed up with me and not afraid to show it anymore. He turns to Paris. "Does this ever get to you?" He asks. "Your husband is so stubborn."

Paris laughs and flashes him a flirtatious grin, which causes my breath to instantly catch in my throat. "He can be." She says. "But, he can also be very open minded."

I stop what I'm doing, suddenly picking up a strange vibe from Paris. I'm not exactly sure where she's heading with this, but something tells me she's been thinking about our talk in the golf cart just as much as I have.

"Oh yeah?" Jeff asks. "How's that? Because around the office he pretty much has his mind set on one thing, this new development project."

"Vance is very open minded." Paris informs Jeff. "At home, even in the bedroom."

Suddenly, my heart is nearly pounding out of my chest, my cock stiffening quickly within my pants as I freeze in place. My wife and Jeff don't even notice me standing right here next to them at this point, they're completely focused on the strange verbal dance happening between them.

Fortunately for me, Jeff is in the mood for a little fun and actually starts to laugh. "In the bedroom? You guys making it to third base yet?" He teases.

Paris smiles. "More like anal, and the occasional threesome."

Now Jeff is frozen too, not sure what to make of my wife's sudden aggressive moves. Paris isn't exactly lying either, she happens to love it up at ass and can take all of me like a pro. We've had a few threesomes, too, but always with another girl and it feels as though this conversation is quickly headed in a different direction.

I immediately recognize that I'm at a crossroads. Right now I could easily shut this whole thing down and continue the game as planned, but there is a lustful devil perched on my shoulder and at the moment he's got an incredibly filthy mouth. It makes me boil with anger to imagine Paris with another man, especially my boss, but at the same time just the thought of it is causing me to tremble with lustful excitement. I swallow hard, and then make my choice.

"You know, we've never had a threesome with another guy before." I suddenly interject. Paris flashes me a quick grin, recognizing that we are on the same page.

"What are you trying to say?" Jeff asks, cutting to the chase.

"I'm saying we make a game out of it. Both of us takes a drive. If I'm closer to the hole than you, then I get to do my project, and if you're closer to the hole then you get to fuck my wife with me. Right here, right now."

"Are you serious?" Jeff asks, looking back and forth between Paris and me.

I nod.

"You've got yourself a deal." Jeff says, gladly.

I immediately line myself up for the shot and take my drive, which soars up into the blue sky and then lands with a soft thud near the green. I'm happy enough with it, stepping back as Jeff walks up and pushes his tee into the tightly chopped grass.

As he lines up his shot, it suddenly dawns on me what I'm actually doing, and I'm terrified. What if Jeff's ball actually goes farther than me? Am I really willing to share my beautiful wife with another man? At that moment, I want nothing more than to stop the bet, but before I can say anything Jeff takes his swing and sends the ball flying gracefully through the air. It lifts up towards the clouds and then arcs and falls, hitting the green and rolling to a stop just inches from the hole.

"Fuck." I say aloud.

Jeff turns around to face me with a smirk plastered across his face. "There's a hole down in the valley that's part of the old course, nobody uses it anymore." He says.

"Sounds like a nice spot." Paris chimes in. I look over at her, simultaneously wanting to cry and fuck her silly while Jeff plows her up the asshole. I'm so conflicted, but it's too late to turn back now as my cock throbs with a dull excited, ache.

"Follow me." Jeff says, hopping into his golf cart and then taking off down the hill.

This particular section of the course is slightly overgrown, having not been maintained over the last few weeks as the rest of the place undergoes maintenance. Eventually, this area will be a second clubhouse, hustling and bustling with excited players, but for now it's just me, my wife and my boss all alone on the green.

Our golf carts parked off to the side, the three of us stand just a few yards from the hole, awkwardly wondering who is going to make the first move. Jeff talks a good game, but apparently when it really gets down to it he's as hesitant as anyone else, at least in this particularly weird situation.

"These golf clothes are getting a little hot out here." Paris finally says, reaching down and pulling her shirt off over her head. She tosses it to the side and stands before us, revealing her cute white bra and gorgeous toned body. Her pants come off next and soon she's wearing nothing but her underwear. Slowly, my wife drops down into a squat between Jeff and me. "I guess it's time to pay up." She says, looking up at us playfully.

No longer hesitant, Jeff immediately steps forward and unzips his fly, pulling out an absolutely massive cock that towers above my wife's face as she watches in awe.

"Damn." Paris says, a little shocked. She looks over at me. "Are you sure you want to watch your pretty little wife take some other guys big fat dick?"

Her words send shivers down my spine, the strange lust within me spilling over in a wave of decedent fantasy. I want to watch her do everything, to share my wife's body and see the look of pleasure on her face as she fucks and sucks another man. I want her to do it all.

"It's a little late for that now." I finally say. "Do it."

Paris gives me a wink and then opens her mouth wide, taking Jeff's giant shaft between her wet lips. She lets out a satisfied hum, as if to say that his fleshy popsicle is particularly tasty, then begins to pump her head up and down over the length of his shaft. Jeff throws his head back with a long, loud sigh, his body already quaking with pleasure as he rocks his hips to the movement of my wife's mouth.

Paris pulls him out and then licks him from balls to tip. "Damn, you've got an incredible cock." She tells my boss. "Let's see what I can do with it."

The next thing I know, my wife is pushing down as far as she can on his shaft, taking his entire length into her mouth and forcing her head as low as she can. Jeff's cock disappears into her throat completely as she relaxes her gag reflex, until finally my wife's lips reach the base of his rock hard shaft and hold there.

"God damn!" Jeff cries out, unable to contain himself as Paris stretches her tongue out and somehow manages to lightly tickle his balls. The move may have been too ambitious, though, because seconds later she's choking, pulling back up with a gasp as trails of spit hang down from her red lips.

Paris glances over at me. "Get the fuck over here with that cock of yours." She commands.

I step up and unsheathe my dick, standing opposite from Jeff as Paris begins to move back and forth between or huge shafts. While she's sucking one of us, she's stroking the other, and visa versa until my wife becomes utterly frantic for dick and ends up shoving both members into her mouth at the same time. It's a tight fit, but Paris is a trooper and somehow manages to give a fantastic double blowjob.

After a good while of this, my wife is fired up enough to take things even further, and we're right there with her.

"Fuck me!" Paris demands, kneeling down onto the green in the doggystyle position with her ass in the air. She kicks off her panties and unclasps her bra, tossing them away as Jeff and I frantically remove our clothes as well, but Jeff takes it a step further by walking over to his bag and pulling out a club.

Paris wiggles her ass in the air as he approaches and then smirks as he turns the club around and aligns the soft handle with her tight pussy. "Oh my god." Paris mumbles, the words falling out oh her mouth in frantic desperation. "Shove it in already!"

Jeff pushes the club forward and Paris lets out a satisfied gasp, her hands gripping tightly into the grassy green beneath her. Meanwhile, I kneel down in front as she braces herself and then, moments later, Paris takes my cock hungrily into her mouth, sucking me feverishly while Jeff fucks her pussy with his golf club.

Watching my wife in such an extreme position was something I never thought I'd see in a million years, but now that it's right in front of me I'm loving every second of it.

Eventually, Jeff pulls out the club and takes its place with his fleshy rod, carefully aligning his dick with my wife's pussy and then thrusting forward and stretching her tightness around his substantial girth. She moans loudly into my dick as he pumps forcefully in and out of her, his strong hands gripping tightly onto Paris's slender hips. The three of us find a good rhythm together and start to gain speed, becoming more and more confident with our slams until eventually we are pounding into my wife with everything we've got.

Paris starts to scream into my cock, clearly enjoying herself as her muffled cries vibrate through the shaft of my swollen member. I can feel her body trembling as the first signs of orgasm begin to course through her body. She reaches down and starts to frantically play with her clit, the shaking becoming more and more violent until finally my wife just can't take it any longer and explodes in a fit of wild shrieks. She's cumming hard, every muscle in her body expanding and contracting between us until finally she collapses onto the grass in exhaustion.

At this point I fully expect my wife to be finished and ready for us to join her, but somehow the orgasm has kicked her into an even higher gear. She immediately pushes me back onto the grass and then climbs on top of me, straddling my muscular body with her toned, slender legs. She kisses me hard and then runs her hands down my abs before reaching even lower and grabbing hold of my rock hard dick. I let out a satisfied groan as she lowers herself down onto me, her tight pussy gripping my cock with its slick lips.

Soon we start to rock together in a series of deep, firm thrusts, her hips swinging down perfectly as she impales herself onto my thick rod. My wife whimpers slightly with every push, then quickly switches to a long, drawn out moan as our movements get faster and faster.

"Okay." She finally gasps, looking back over her shoulder at Jeff, who's been waiting patiently behind us. "Now fuck me up my fucking asshole!"

Jeff doesn't have to be told twice, kneeling down onto the green behind us and quickly lining up his dick with Paris's puckered hole. My wife reaches back with both hands and spreads her cheeks open while I hammer her from below, then screams loudly as Jeff pushes forcefully inside of her.

"I'm taking two dicks!" She cries out, amazed at her own unbridled sluttiness. "I can't believe I'm taking two dicks!"

Her words hit me at my very core, forcing me to accept the beautiful depravity of this moment. My loving wife is sandwiched between me and another man who just happens to be my boss, fucking us silly with a cock up her ass and one in her pussy. I don't know exactly how we got here, but at this very moment I'm completely in heaven, watching the pleasure on Paris's face as she's railed from behind.

At this point we're absolutely hammering her tight holes, throttling my wife brutally with our massive, swollen cocks. The three of us are perfectly in sync with each other, a three-person sex creature that pulses manically in the middle of this hidden valley of the golf course. I'm so close to cumming that I can barely contain myself, but as I look up into my wife's eyes and see her orgasm hard for the second time, I just can't take it anymore.

Suddenly, I'm exploding inside Paris, my hot jizz spilling out into her pussy in a series of forceful ejections that send waves of pleasure through my body. Eventually, my massive load is too much to contain and it comes spilling out of her tightness, running down her legs in thick white streaks.

Jeff blows almost immediately after, letting out a loud roar as he pushes deep into my wife's asshole and holds.

"Oh my fucking god!" Jeff shouts, his eyes clenched tight as he loses his entire payload within Paris. Seconds later, my boss pulls out and falls back onto the grass.

Paris rolls off of me onto the ground, as well, and now we're all laying here naked and panting. I close my eyes and listen to the shouts of "Fore!" off in the distance, and the metallic ping of clubs driving balls high into the air. The cool breeze feels nice as it runs gently across my hot skin.

"I know you lost the bet." Jeff finally speaks up. "But, I think you deserve a chance with that development project, Vance."

My wife and me turn our heads towards one another, exchanging glances.

"Thank you, sir." I tell Jeff. "You won't regret it."

COPPING A FEEL

Being married to a cop creates a strange dynamic for any relationship, but we make it work.

Mostly, this is thanks to my wife's incredible ability to turn it off when she gets home from her shift. Being on duty is a high stress environment where you're always on your toes, alert and ready to take on anything that comes your way, including a bullet. Honestly, I'm amazed that she can do it, but then again she's the strongest woman I know.

For me her job creates a whole new kind of stress, though. On one hand, I don't really worry about things like our home getting broken into, especially when my wife keeps a gun in the closet and damn well knows how to use it.

But, at the same time, I hate the fact that she's always in danger when on duty. We work about the same amount, but I'm not going to get shot through the heart while sitting in my office chair filling out spreadsheets.

Because of this, we try to make our time together really count. We're connected on a level that I never thought was possible between two people, at least, before I met her years ago while walking in the park with my dog. I'm not sure I believe in love a first sight, but the two of us are pretty good contenders. It only took three dates for me to know that I wanted to marry my wife, Jasmine, but that didn't happen until a year later.

We're an adventurous couple and like to do something new and different almost every day, even if it means something as simple as a sweet picnic dinner in the park.

"This is fucking fantastic." I tell her, after swallowing a large bite of the pasta salad she painstakingly crafted for our outdoor meal. I look out across the grassy, downtown Los Angeles square as people come and go. There's a group playing basketball nearby and others setting up for what looks like a movie in the park event; the perfect Summer evening.

"Why thank you, baby." Jasmine says, taking another bite of her own.

"So how's work been?" I ask. "How's the new partner."

She quickly tries to finish her bite with a smile and then covers her mouth as she swallows. "He's great. Really easy to work with."

"What's his name?" I continue.

"Parker." My wife informs me. "You'll meet him at the fundraising dinner this Thursday."

"Oh, awesome." I tell her. We try to keep up with everything that's going on in each other's lives, but when you're as busy as we are it's hard to keep track. She's had her new partner for two months now and I still can't remember the guy's name, which I'd rather wasn't the case. I make a mental note this time and try to remember it.

"What about you, Morgan?" Jasmine asks with a coy smile. "How's the new girl at the office?"

I suddenly stop chewing. I know exactly who she's talking about, and the tone in my wife's voice makes me realize that she knows something's up.

"Who?" I ask, doing a terrible job of playing dumb.

"Sarah." She says. "You already forgot about the new girl?"

"Oh yeah!" I say, snapping my fingers in the air. "Yeah, she's good. Really hard worker."

Jasmine cracks a smile. "Really? You seem more interested in what she does on vacation than at work."

Suddenly, I know exactly what my wife's referring to and it hits me like a ton of bricks, nearly knocking me backwards onto the green grass behind me. How could I have been so dumb and not covered my tracks.

"Fuck." I say aloud. I know that I've been caught.

"I found quite a few pictures of her saved on the computer last night when I got home." Jasmine tells me. "Bikini photos, from a vacation to Hawaii that she posted online."

"Yep." I say, swallowing hard.

"So, you were just looking at her bikini photos?" My wife asks.

I have no idea what to say, not even so much as a stammer falling out of my mouth. I'm frozen in complete silence.

Finally, though, Jasmine cracks a smile. "I'm just fucking with you." She says.

I breathe out a sigh of relief. "You mean you're not mad at me?"

Suddenly, an open hand hits me in the face, hard. I reel from the slap, and then try to collect myself.

"No, I'm still fucking mad at you." Jasmine says. "But, it's not the end of the world. I mean, what can I say, the girl's cute."

"I'm so sorry." I tell her.

"I know you are, and I know how you're going to make it up to me." She says with a grin.

I don't know where she managed to find a spare men's police uniform, but she did. I look at myself in the bathroom mirror, turning from side to side as I admire the way the sharp edges of the button up and the well tailored shoulders compliment my already muscular physique. Maybe I should have been a cop, I think to myself, then remember that that would entail getting shot at and revise my opinion.

I step out into the bedroom where Jasmine is waiting for me in a very sexy lingerie set, her hair tousled and wild.

"You look nice." I say, stepping forward, but my wife puts her finger out into the air and stops me.

"What's your name?" She asks.

I sigh. "Officer Parker Reeves."

Jasmine shakes her head. "Not good enough. Are you going to play along or what?"

"I'm sorry." I tell her. "I'll play along."

"If you get to fantasize about fucking your coworker, then so do it." She tells me, then pulls out a set of handcuffs. "Now arrest me, Officer Reeves. I've been a very, very bad girl."

There should be something humiliating about my wife wanting to fuck another man, her partner no less, and in a logical sense I understand the emotions I should be feeling. Somehow, though, another sensation starts to bubble up inside of me, one that I don't completely understand. Instead of some kind of fucked up punishment for my marital indiscretions, I find myself enjoying the roll play. The fact that my wife is turned on by another man is actually kind of hot.

I step forward and take the handcuffs, then latch one of her wrists onto the bed frame.

"Tell me how much you want my cock." I command

"I want that big dick so fucking bad." My wife confesses, running her hands up and down my uniform as I crawl foreword onto the bed, pushing her back into the sea of pillows.

"Do you want to fuck this new dick that you've never tasted?" I ask. "While your husband watches?"

"Yes." Jasmine moans in ecstasy, her eyes closed tight.

I stop suddenly, breaking the mood as my tone changes completely. "Really?" I ask.

Jasmine opens her big blue eyes and looks at me. "Do you honestly want to know?"

"Tell me." I beg. "You know we can always be honest with each other."

Jasmine rolls her eyes. "Oh really, always honest with each other? Even when you're jacking off to that little slut's bikini photos?"

"I'm sorry." I sigh. "I really am, but I think I've got a much better way to make it up to you than this. Just tell me the truth, would you want to fuck me and this Parker guy at the same time?"

Suddenly, Jasmine actually looks kind of shy, a sight so rare that I'm not sure I've ever truly seen it in our three years of happy marriage. "I'd really like it." She finally admits.

I shake my head in amazement, and then tell her. "I have no idea why, but that turns me on so fucking much."

"Really?" Jasmine's eyes go wide.

"Yeah." I confirm. "And I think we should make it happen."

I go into the Thursday night fundraiser fully expecting to be surrounded by a bunch of uptight cops, but instead I'm pleasantly surprised by a warm reception from Jasmine's blue blood coworkers. It's probably the fact that they're consistently under pressure on the job, because these social functions now seem like nothing more than an opportunity to let loose.   Not too loose, though, since they're all still in uniform this evening.

My wife make's it look good, equal parts unapologetically feminine and terrifyingly commanding in her work attire. Her gorgeous face is perfect in the frame of tonight's venue, a massive ballroom that was once used for parties of the old Hollywood elite.

I grab a beer and Jasmine takes a mineral water, thanks to a strict policy of no drinking while in uniform, then we hang back for a moment until she can spot Parker across the room.

"There he is." Jasmine tells me.

The fantasy of my wife with other men is brand new to me, so I'm not quite sure if I was hoping Parker would be attractive or incredibly ugly. Regardless, there's no denying which side of the coin this guy lands on. He's absolutely stunned, a rugged, muscular figure that seems to effortlessly captivate the people around him.

"Are you ready?" I ask Jasmine, who nods in return.

The two of us cross the crowded ballroom floor towards Parker, and he smiles as he sees my wife coming.

"Jasmine!" He says, abruptly interrupting his conversation and throwing his arms around her in a hug, followed by a slightly less than professional kiss on the cheek. This is going to be easy.

"It's good to see you, Parker." My wife says, "This is my husband, Morgan."

I reach out my hand and he shakes it firmly, trying to show off with the strength of his grip.

"I've heard a lot about you." Parker tells me. "It's nice to put a face to a name."

"Likewise." I tell him. "Jasmine tells me you're a basketball fan." I continue, trying to find some common ground.

Parker's eyes light up as I say this, clearly excited to take a break from the constant stream of work talk. "Hell yeah I am!" He confirms.

Our conversation falls into a rhythm at this point, jabbing back and forth about our favorite teams and who's looking good for the finals this year. The rapport between us is fantastic and I can immediately tell that I actually, genuinely like the guy.

Eventually, the circle of listeners dissipates until it's just Parker, my wife and I standing together chatting.

At this point, I decide to switch gears.

"So, me and Jasmine were having an argument about something the other day, I want to get your opinion on it."

"Oh yeah, what's that?" Parker asks.

Suddenly, the words stick I my throat as I realize what I'm about to do. Am I really ready to watch my beautiful wife take another man? The reality of the situation, outside of any wild bedroom fantasy, comes rushing over me as I freeze mid thought.

"Morgan?" Parker questions.

I shake my head, pushing my reservations aside and rallying my thoughts. "I'm sorry." I tell him nervously. "I thought I might have left the car unlocked. It's all good, I locked it."

Parker nods in understanding. "Yeah, I hate that."

My heart is nearly beating out of my chest now, my cock already swelling in my pants as I realize that I'm setting in motion a series of events which could very well lead to my wife's explicit double penetration at the hand's of me and her professional partner. I swallow hard.

"We were talking about threesomes." I say. "Whether or not it's hotter to do them with someone you know and trust, or to just find a stranger."

"Oh yeah?" Parker asks, curiously.

"What do you think? Is it better to do it with someone that you know? A coworker even?" I continue.

As I say this, Jasmine steps closer to Parker and puts her hand on his back, rubbing gently. He looks back and forth between us, cautiously.

"That depends." Parker says. "Because, depending on the job, it could get people in a lot of trouble."

"Not if nobody finds out." Jasmine coos in his ear.

Suddenly, Parker straightens up, breaking the spell. "I don't think it would be a good idea." He says. "I'm gonna go grab another drink."

Immediately, Parker takes off back into the crowd, shutting us down as clearly as he can without making the whole thing even more uncomfortable than it needs to be.

Disappointment and, admittedly, relief wash over me. Maybe some fantasies are better of left this way, I think to myself. Even so, I can't deny the throbbing ache in my cock; the way that it makes me feel to think about my wife wrapping her wet lips around Parker's swollen dick and sucking him off to completion.

The rest of the party is as enjoyable as it can be, given the circumstances, but we don't talk to Parker again for the remainder of the evening.

Eventually, we are all tuckered out and ready to head home, climbing into the car and taking off towards our condo through one of the many canyons of Los Angeles. The roads are surprisingly empty tonight, especially due to this particularly scenic route that I felt like taking.

"I'm sorry it didn't work out." I say from the driver's seat, looking over at Jasmine who smiles back lovingly.

"It's okay, baby." She says with only the slightest hint of disappointment in her voice.

Suddenly, a set of blue and red lights spring to life behind us, followed by the familiar upward sweep of a shortened police siren.

"Fuck!" I say aloud. "Really? I wasn't even going that fast."

At least Jasmine is in the car with me, and in full uniform no less. Whatever it is, we'll definitely get off with just a warning. I pull my car over to the side of the road and roll to a stop.

The police cruiser pulls up behind us and there is a long pause, neither vehicle doing much of anything while Jasmine assures me that it's probably just something like a busted taillight. I wasn't speeding. The lights of the cruiser shine brightly across us as we wait, obscuring our vision.

Eventually, the door to the police car opens and a tall figure steps out into the evening air. It's hard to make out any details of their form, but as the officer steps forward I can see that they are a man and very well built. The figure walks up to the passenger window, which is unusual, then knocks and motions for my wife to roll the glass down.

"How can I help you, officer?" My wife asks, following his instructions.

My heart is pounding at this point, consumed by a strange sensation that something isn't quite right until finally the cop's face lowers down into view and I realize that it's Parker. A wave of relief washes over me.

"Step out of the car, ma'am." Parker says firmly.

"Are you serious?" Jasmine asks, confused.

"Step out of the car, ma'am" Parker repeats.

Suddenly, everything about my wife's demeanor changes as she unbuckles her seatbelt and climbs out. It takes me a moment to realize what's going on, but as Parker leads Jasmine around to the hood it suddenly hits me.

They exchange a few words as Jasmine glances back at me nervously, and then moments later Parker begins to unbuckle his leather belt and lay back against the hood of the car. From where I'm at, I get a perfect view as my beautiful wife reaches down past his waistband and removes the man's enormous, swollen cock.

My first reaction is to jump out of the car and put a stop to this immediately, to throw open the door and run screaming towards Parker while heaving a wild punch. Of course, I don't do any of those things, somehow managing to let the anger and jealously boil off inside of me and reveal a powerful arousal underneath. My dick is rock hard and aching to be touched, so much so that I finally just can't take it anymore and remove my throbbing member from my pants. I begin to stroke myself slowly, watching as Jasmine takes Parker's massive dick into her mouth.

Parker let's out a long moan as my wife swallows him as deep as she can, pushing her face down until she reaches the edge of her gag reflex and then pulls back with a loud retch. Parker's not letting her off that easy though, taking control with his huge, manly hands and pushing Jasmine down onto his cock once again. This time she's ready, relaxing enough to allow his shaft to slip all the way down her throat until her lips are pressed hard against his stomach, his member disappearing completely under the glow of the yellow headlights.

Parker pumps her up and down a bit, controlling every movement as if my gorgeous wife is nothing more than a kinky, personal sex doll. I love seeing my loyal companion fucked like this, right in front of me and by such an imposing figure of authority. It's hard for me to keep myself from cumming right then and there, but I refrain. Jasmine looks up at me with watering eyes, her lips wrapped tightly around this other man's fat cock.

Moments later, Parker stands up again and roughly grabs my wife by the waist, tearing her belt from its belt loops. He says something aggressive to Jasmine and she smiles, then quickly strips off her shirt, pants and underwear until she is standing on the side of the road completely naked. We're lucky nobody ever comes down this way at night.

The next thing I know, Jasmine is being pushed up onto the hood so that her face is looking directly at me in the driver's seat, while her ass is perfectly positioned towards Parker. He saddles up behind her, aligning the girth of his thick cock against my wife's tight wet slit.

"Shove it in there!" Jasmine screams. "Fuck me from behind while my husband watches and beats off his cock!"

My wife tenses up suddenly and then relaxes, reeling from the overwhelming sensation as Parker pushes his cock inside. He thrusts against her in deep, slow pumps that gradually gain speed as Jasmine's naked body rocks hard against the hood, our eyes locked while I pleasure myself to her expressions of pleasure brought courtesy of this other man's massive dick. The tight grip of my hand keeps pace with every thrust against my wife's ass until I am feverously jerking off, my body trembling while I'm flooded with this strange cocktail of jealousy and arousal.

They fuck like this for a quite a while, my wife and I gazing into each others eyes through the windshield as she's hammered by Parker's beast until finally he grabs her roughly and pulls her back towards him.

"You." Parker says, pointing directly at me. "Out of the car."

I climb out of the driver's seat and approach them, my cock tense and swollen as it craves my wife's touch.

"Blow him." Parker commands, bending Jasmine down towards me.

She looks up at me with a wide smile on her face before taking my cock into her mouth and immediately getting to work, sucking me off while she's taken from the rear. I easily find a familiar rhythm between her lips and soon the three of us are pulsing together at a ferocious pace. With every pump from behind, Parker slams her towards my dick, and with every push back from me I impale Jasmine onto Parker's massive cock; the group forming a well-oiled sex machine.

"Oh fuck!" My beautiful wife moans, her words vibrating though the flesh of my dick as it fills her mouth entirely. "I feel like such a filthy slut."

As Jasmine groans, the words start to change and evolve into a squeal that gets louder and louder with every thrust until finally she's howling between us, her eyes rolling back in her head with ecstasy as her body tries desperately to contain the feeling of being taken from either end so ruthlessly. Her trembling becomes a spastic quake of pleasure, resting just on the edge of an orgasm and nearly toppling over when, suddenly, Parker pulls out of her and lies back onto the hood of our car.

"Get on." Parker tells my wife, taking her by the hips and guiding her. Parker turns Jasmine around and then pulls her back onto him, hoisting up her small frame so that her back is pressed tightly against his rock hard chest. Meanwhile, he positions his thickness at the puckered entrance of my wife's asshole, aligning the head of his shaft with her rim and then groaning in satisfaction as Jasmine lowers herself down onto him. I watch as his cock disappears up into her rectum, stretching the limits of my wife's tight little asshole.

"God damn, that's a good dick." Jasmine confesses, then begins to pump herself up and down over the top of his member. Despite the slightly acrobatic position, my wife's incredibly good at it, managing to get herself up to a reasonable speed in no time as she brutally impales Parker's thick dick up her ass over and over again.

She reaches down and starts to play with her clit, trembling once more as she leans back and opens her legs into the air. Her feet bounce with every slam from below, shaking wildly as she beacons me towards her.

"I need two cocks in me." Jasmine says with a seductive smile. "One in my ass, and one in my pussy."

She takes me into her hand and gives my dick a few firm strokes, then lines up the head of my shaft with her slick entrance. Jasmine was already tight before, but the massive shaft that continues to rail her ass from below has tensed up her pussy even more than usual. As I slip inside, I can feel Parker moving in and out of my wife next to me though a thin layer of pulsing flesh, then start in with a rhythmic pound of my own.

"Oh my fucking god." I moan. "That feels so good."

"Do I look nice with another man's dick up my ass?" My wife begs to know.

"Yes." I tell her as the words strike me deep, sending a series of uncontrollable chills down my spine.

"Then fuck me like you mean it!" Jasmine demands.

I immediately start to pound my beautiful wife with everything that I've got. Slamming into her in a rapid series of thrusts that never let up as they escalated the quakes and spasms coursing through her body. Jasmine throws her head back and lets out a scream of pleasure, unable to contain herself any longer.

"I'm gonna cum!" My wife cries out as she grabs tightly onto my shoulders. She bucks hard against me and then suddenly stops, holding tightly in place, her legs kicking out straight to either side. "Oh fuck!"

I watch as Jasmine's eyes roll back into her head and the muscles of her stomach clench tight while she braces against the powerful waves of pleasure that pulse through her.

Eventually, Jasmine finishes, collecting herself and climbing down off of the car's hood. She pulls our dicks from her reamed holes.

"Now it's your turn, boys." My wife says with a grin, dropping down into a squat between us. Parker and I take a position on either side of her and immediately begin to beat ourselves off, our aching cocks swollen and ready to burst.

"Open up!" Commands Parker.

My wife does as she's told, playfully sticking out her tongue as Parker lurches forward and blasts his seed across her gorgeous lips. It lands haphazardly on either side of her face and gets swallowed in the middle, running down her cheeks in pearly white streaks as Jasmine licks the rest off of her lips.

Seeing her covered in another man's jizz is more than enough to push me over the edge, and suddenly I'm cumming as well, covering her with my thick white load of spunk as it ejects from my dick in several hot pumps. My wife catches most of it on her tongue, then gladly sucks the remainder from my shaft until my cock has gone limp.

"That was nice." My wife says with a smile, looking up at us with a dazed, post-orgasmic expression plastered across her cum-covered face.

Parker nods in approval. "Alright, you two are free to go, now. Move along."

BASES LOADED

My wife, Ella, is the type of woman who's always got something going on; book clubs, social gatherings, cooking class... and she's even a member of more than a few recreational sports leagues. In fact, being a part of the team seems to be her favorite pastime activity, especially when it comes to baseball.

How she manages to fit in the time for all of these hobbies, I'll probably never know, but I do enjoy watching the baseball games just as much as she likes playing them. There's just something about rooting for a team when you personally know the players that, strangely, can make the mostly empty park bleachers feel like a roaring Dodger Stadium.

It also doesn't hurt that Ella looks incredibly sexy in her uniform, a tight fitting red and white baseball outfit that could easily come out of a costume catalog for couples looking to spice up their sex life.

Currently, she's up to bat while a look on with pride.

I'm one of only a small handful of supportive significant others here at the park tonight. The turnout for these things considerably drops after a team enters adulthood, and I'm pretty sure there's a guy on Ella's squad who is in his sixties. Turnout is generally pretty low.

"Come on now, Ella! Knock this one out of the park!" I cheer.

She looks back at me and flashes a broad, but slightly embarrassed smile, as if she knows how silly we all are for being here in the first place but not at all caring. She gives me a wink and then turns her attention back to the task at hand, pulverizing this baseball.

The opposing team's pitcher winds up and let's one fly, which sails right down the middle towards home plate as Ella throws all of her force into a powerful swing. She misses completely, misjudging the incredible speed of the ball as it shoots past her. This pitcher's arm is nothing to scoff at.

"That's alright, that's alright!" I shout, clapping my hands together enthusiastically.

Ella manages to catch a bit of the pitcher's second throw, clipping the ball just enough to send it shooting off towards right field. Too far towards right field actually, because it immediately disappears across the foul line but is, luckily, not caught before flying over and bouncing across the green grass.

That's two strikes. Only one chance left.

By now I'm too wrapped up in the game to even cheer, my anxiety getting the best of me as I sit in silence and wait for the next pitch. I'm literally holding my breath, frozen in anticipation while the pitcher kicks the dirt of the mound.

Finally, the ball comes barreling down the middle. Ella goes for it and smashes the small white orb with a resounding crack, which sends it soaring up into the air, high above the heads of the players. From the second it leaves the bat, it's obvious where this ball is going; completely out of the park.

Our smattering of onlookers jump to their feet in as much cheer as we can muster, looking on with excitement while Ella rounds the bases. It might seem like nothing too extraordinary, but I find myself incredibly proud of my wife. Her ability to excel in pretty much anything that she sets her mind to will never stop blowing me away, and is oddly sexy in a big way.

When Ella arrives back at home plate I wave, but she doesn't notice me, instead meeting one of the other players at the dugout for a big hug that extends for much longer than I would have expected. I don't recognize the guy that she's so admit about celebrating with, but then again I don't really know anyone else on the team in general. I do, however, notice how abnormally attractive the man is, tall and fit with huge muscular arms and a perfectly chiseled jaw line. Before they release, he kisses my wife on the cheek and she blushes.

Seconds later, Ella's eyes wander up to me and the second that they meet mine she becomes rigid and pulls away from the man, trying to look natural but failing miserably. I've never once doubted my wife's faithfulness to me, never had a reason to, but at this point there is no denying that something strange is up.

As the game continues my enthusiasm dies down, giving way to a whole new series of emotions that wash over me like a tide. My eyes follow this mysterious man as he walks out onto the field, and I wonder what Ella could possibly be doing with him right under my nose. The jealousy is almost overwhelming, yet, at the same time, weirdly pleasant. I'm not quite sure why, but the thought of them sneaking around has me confusingly aroused, my cock quickly stiffening in my pants as I play through the various scenarios in my head. The more depraved my visions of them become, the more I start to tremble with lustful arousal, barely able to contain myself as while imagination runs wild. Soon, all of the initial jealous is gone, or at least subdued, and a strange lustful craving has taken its place.

The crowd around me suddenly erupts into a cheer and I immediately refocus on the game, completely unaware of how much time has passed while I was lost in thought. I glance up at the scoreboard and it abruptly hits me that the game has just ended.

"Hey baby!" Ella cries as I step down off of the bleachers. She wraps her arms tightly around me a plants a long, firm kiss on my lips.

"Good game." I tell her. "That was a hell of a home run you had there."

"Thank you, Dave." She laughs and gives a cute little bow. "I'm fucking starving. Can we stop somewhere on the way home?" Ella asks.

"Of course!" I confirm, putting my arm around her and heading off towards the parking lot. "You've earned it."

I've almost entirely forgotten about my strange suspicions as we take a booth at the nearby local pizza place.

Ella slides in across from me, still wearing her uniform which is certainly not a problem at all. I love the way it pushes out her tits in a ballgirl fantasy kind of way. We've already ordered two slices, which should be arriving at our table any minute, and have a whole pitcher of beer to share between us. We won't be going anywhere for a while.

"You liked the game?" Ella asks me.

"What's not to like?" I respond, laughing. "Of course, you know that I love coming out and supporting the team. I'd be a fucking cheerleader for you if I could."

Ella laughs to herself and I take a long sip of beer, reveling in my ability to still make her laugh after all of these years.

There is a clanging bell as someone new enters the pizza place, and as I look up my face immediately changes. It's Ella's handsome guy friend from the team, an appearance that floods me with a whole cascade of emotions I had happily pushed away for the time being. I'm unable to hide the reaction on my face, causing Ella to spin around and take a glance.

By the time she looks back at me, the damage is done.

"What?" Ella asks.

"Nothing." I tell her, shaking my head.

"Do you know Mike?" She asks me, curious but cautious.

"Nope." I admit. "Just from the games."

Ella eyes me for a moment, trying to make sense of my expression while also trying to discern how much I might already know. There are so many confusing reactions flying back and forth at this point that I'd be glad to forget about the whole thing, letting it dissipate within the strange web of secrets now hanging between us. Ella, however, would rather cut the bullshit.

"Does he make you nervous?" My wife asks me, bluntly.

"Should he?" I respond, my words coming out more loaded than I intend them to be. We're well out of earshot from the guy as he waits in line, but I still speak in something of a hushed tone.

Ella thinks for a moment and then finally says. "You know that I love you, baby. Why are you getting so jealous?"

That feeling from the baseball field is suddenly starting to tingle again within me, simmering just below the surface of my thoughts as I try to find the best way to broach my feelings. Finally, I just come out with it.

"I saw the way both of you act around each other." I tell her. "I know that you, at least, have a crush on him."

Ella cracks a smile and takes a long sip of her beer, eyeing me over the top of her glass. Suddenly, she doesn't seem to be worried about hiding anything from me, which is something of a relief. Then again, we've always been very open with each other about our sexual fantasies, so honesty is to be expected, even if this time it happens to involve another person.

"Come on." Ella finally says. Her reaction reads like a strange sort of Don't Ask, Don't Tell policy, two words loaded with any number of things that all beg me to back away and not worry about it.

"You can tell me." I say, trying my best to pull my arousal to the forefront and leave my jealousy behind. "I actually think it's kind of hot."

"What is?" Ella asks, her curiosity immediately piqued.

"You having a crush on another man." I admit. "Maybe even wanting to fuck him."

The second that the words leave my mouth Ella turns red with embarrassment, looking back and forth over her shoulders to see if anybody else heard me. She leans forward and drops her voice down even lower. "Seriously?" My wife questions.

I nod. "Seriously. I'll admit, I don't quite understand it myself, but it's the truth."

"You want to see me fuck another man?" Ella clarifies, trying to wrap her head around my strange request.

My heart is pounding out of my chest at this point, already diving into this new fantasy way farther than I ever expected to. Somehow, though, it all feels right, the consistent arousal growing stronger within me as we talk more about my depraved desires. "I do." I confirm. "What's his name again?"

"Mike." Ella says, finally relaxing as she cracks a smile. "And yes, there's chemistry there, but you know I'd never do anything behind your back."

"I know." I tell her. "But what if I wanted you to?"

Ella shakes her head in disbelief. "I can't believe we're having this conversation." She says. "You really want me to fuck Mike? I couldn't ever do that without you."

"Who says I won't be there too?" I ask with a devilish grin.

Suddenly, possessed by the sum of my overwhelming urges, I turn towards the counter where Mike stands waiting for his pizza. We make eye contact immediately and I wave him over. Ella's expression is one of absolute terror, with a hint of girlish embarrassment, but the second that Mike arrives and sits down next to my wife she covers it up nicely.

I reach my hand out across the table and shake his. "Hey Mike, I'm Dave." I introduce myself.

"Nice to meet you." Mike tells me. "You're wife's a hell of a team mate."

I release his grip and then lean back into my chair, trying my best to appear casual and, somehow, just barely pulling it off.

"She's amazing." I agree. "Brains, beauty… and baseball, apparently."

Mike laughs. "For sure."

Eventually, any tension or discomfort that could have existed between the three of us slips away and dissolves over the next few rounds of beer and pizza. It's not long before we are all significantly buzzed and I manage to get up enough courage to start really pushing some buttons.

"Do you have a girlfriend?" I ask Mike.

He shakes his head. "No, man. Not right now."

"That's okay, though. Being single has a lot of perks." I tell him. "A guy as handsome as you probably has a different lady every night."

Mike shrugs. "Honestly, it seems like all of the good ones are already taken."

"Sometimes that's not an issue." I tell Mike, giving Ella a quick wink. "You think my wife's hot, right?"

Mike looks directly at me, searching my face for any clue as to how he should answer this. Helped along by the alcohol flowing through his bloodstream, Mike finally decides on sincerity. "She's beautiful."

"What if I told you that you could hook up with her?" I ask.

"Dave!" Ella shouts. "Stop it!" She's practically drowning in embarrassment right now, but from the way that she bits her lip I can tell she's just as turned on as I am.

"Are you telling me you wouldn't fuck Mike?" I question, literally trembling with excitement.

Ella sighs. "Okay, fine. Yes." She admits.

Mike and my wife lock eyes and all of the embarrassment immediately fades away. It's suddenly like the two of them are the only people here in this restaurant, completely taken by one another as I look on with my cock aching. Somehow, I immediately know that the three of us are all on exactly the same page, an unspoken thread of lust quickly pulling us together.

"Are we going to do this, or what?" I ask them bluntly.

Mike and my wife nod. Immediately, we all stand and head for the door.

There's not a single one of us capable of driving at this point, but our arousal is out of control now and cannot be contained. Within seconds of leaving the pizza shop Ella and Mike are making out in front of me. Soon,

Mike and I are passing her back and forth as we stumble towards the park.

Without any other options, we head for the baseball diamond, which is now completely empty. It's only fitting for us to end up here, seeing as Mike and Ella are still in their uniforms, and the thought of our encounter having some sort of slutty, porno-like baseball theme only adds to the throbbing lust within my dick.

The three of us immediately head down into the dugout, where there's at least a little cover, then quickly get to work kissing my gorgeous wife from either side. I watch as Mike runs his hands up and down her body, caressing her massive tits, which can barely be contained within her tight baseball uniform.

"Oh my god." Ella moans. "I can't believe this is actually happening. Are you sure this is okay?" She asks me.

"Of course." I tell her, our eyes meeting momentarily.

Accepting my sincerity, Ella immediately drops down to her knees between us and begins to frantically undo our belts. My cock feels like it's ready to burst as it pops out of my pants and into Ella's waiting hand, Mike's dick immediately following as my wife takes him in the other. She starts to beat us off slowly, her tight grip running up and down the shafts of our cocks as we brace ourselves for the oncoming sensation that begins to flow through us. It's not long before we are pushing back against Ella's hands, rocking our hips to the rhythm of my wife's pumps while she looks up at me and Mike with those big beautiful eyes.

It feels incredible, and watching my beautiful lover service another cock is a vision beyond explanation. I don't know why, but I love the way that his huge dick looks next to her face, the sheer size impressively dwarfing Ella's beautiful smile.

Suddenly, Ella opens up wide and takes Mike into her lips, which causes me to gasp aloud out of sheer surprise. Ella pushes herself down onto his cock, sliding as far as she can across the girthy pole as Mike let's out a long and satisfied moan.

"God damn, your wife is so fucking good at giving head." Mike tells me.

Ella quickly gets to work pumping herself up and down his mammoth shaft, her lips wrapped tight while her now empty hand gently cradles his hanging balls. Meanwhile, Ella is still servicing me with the other, and soon she begins to trade back and forth between us, taking both of our dicks into her mouth in rapid succession until finally pulling us together and swallowing our shafts at the same time. Hungry for cock, my wife struggles to contain us both, her lips stretched to the limit while our swollen rods vie for position within.

When Ella finally pulls us out, there is an insatiable lust brewing behind my wife's eyes. She is ravenous, any caution or unease completely removed and a frantic sexual energy taking its place.

"Fuck me right now!" Ella commands, standing up and quickly slipping out of her uniform bottoms and panties. She leaves on the top, however, which seems to show off the curves of her delicious rear even more.

Ella struts over to the bench and leans down, her legs locked as she braces herself against it. She looks back over her shoulder and then winks at Mike, who immediately springs into action and steps up behind her.

"You want to see your pretty little wife pounded from behind?" Ella asks me with a sly grin.

"Yes." I tell her, slowly stroking my cock as I stand back and watch the scene unfold.

Mike aligns his dick with the entrance of my wife's tight pussy and then pushes forward in a slow but powerful thrust, stretching Ella's limits as she moans loudly. Her grip tightens on the wooden bench while she takes him, filled completely by his massive member. Mike quickly gets to work pulsing in and out of Ella's depths.

It's now that the reality of this situation truly hits me, sending a chill of uncontrollable arousal down my spine. Another man is inside my beautiful wife, pleasuring her in a way that has been reserved for only me and only me over the last three years. I feel confused and humiliated, yet somehow proud of Ella's supreme beauty, as if sharing her with this other guy is a display of my own power. More than anything, I'm just glad to make her happy, and as she bites her lip and looks back at me, I know that I've made the right choice.

Mike has been slowly gaining speed with every slam, and by now he's absolutely pounding my wife with everything he's got, slamming against her ass in a series of rhythmic slaps that echo within the dugout. Their mutual groans of pleasure carry out across the darkened field.

"Get over here and shove that cock down my throat." Ella suddenly commands me, standing up from the bench and turning so that, when she leans back down, her face is directly positioned at my rock hard dick.

Ella swallows me expertly, taking my dick down her throat as far as she can and then retching when I hit her gag reflex. I pull back, but she's not giving up that easily, trying again and this time relaxing enough to consume my entire length. Ella holds me deep as Mike hammers her from behind, her face pressing hard against my toned abs and my balls slapping against her chin. She looks up at me, eyes watering, and winks.

The three of us soon find a rhythm together, Mike and I using the force of each others pounding to push my wife back and forth across the length of our rods.

"Oh my god!" Ella screams into the flesh of my dick, the words barely audible and they struggle to find their way around the shaft that plugs her throat. "I feel like such a fucking slut."

"What was that?" I ask.

My wife pulls my cock out of her mouth and looks up at me, Mike continuing to slam away at her from behind. "I said, I feel like such a fucking slut!"

"How's this for slutty?" I ask.

Lost in the moment, I pull her to her feet and then lay myself down on the dugout bench, my cock standing up at full attention. I motion for Ella to come straddle me and she does so without hesitation, throwing her legs over the bench and then lowering herself down until she's impaled onto my thick dick. My wife let's out a long, satisfied sigh as she begins to grind against me, her hips moving in slow, firm pumps against my body.

"How'd you like to take two cocks at once?" I ask her.

"Fuck yeah." Ella says, then quickly adds, "Wait, are you serious?" Suddenly realizing the extreme sexual acrobatics that would entail, my wife looks more than a little nervous.

Mike climbs onto the bench behind Ella and begins to align his massive cock with her puckered backdoor, causing my wife to look back at him with worried exasperation.

"I don't know if I can take it!" Ella cries out. "But I want it so fucking bad!"

Mike is ready now, his shaft primed for entry. "Do you need this cock up your ass?" He demands to know.

Ella gulps hard, her hands tightening against my shoulders. "Yes." She sighs, bracing herself for impact.

Immediately, Mike pushes forward, his enormous dick expanding the rim of my wife's asshole around its substantial girth. Ella let's out a yelp of pain and pleasure, which eventually transforms into a long, drawn out moan and then a full on scream as the two cocks within her start to pump in tandem.

Mike and I pulse slowly at first, working together as we fill her tight holes in a steady rhythm, and then growing faster and faster. Soon we are absolutely hammering my wife's tightness in a ruthless double penetration, Ella's eyes rolling back into her head as she reaches down between her legs and starts to help herself along, trembling more violently with every slam against her backside.

"I'm gonna cum." My wife starts to mumble, losing herself in the moment. "Oh my god, I'm gonna…" She trails off as the quakes of ecstasy overtake her. The next thing I know, she's arching back against Mike, her toned abs contracting spastically before my very eyes. Ella clenches her teeth tight, hissing through them until finally she just can't take it anymore and she explodes in a frantic howl of pleasure.

All the while, Mike and I never let up, hammering into her with everything that we've got until the waves of orgasm finally cease and a satisfied Ella falls forward onto me.

"Now fill me up with your fucking loads." My wife demands. "I need some jizz in these tight little holes."

Her words alone are enough to put me over the edge, but I hold off a little bit longer as we pound her, reveling in this incredible encounter. Never in my wildest dreams could I have ever imagined actually double-teaming my wife, let alone letting another man take her so brutally up the ass. I never want this moment to end, but as soon as the thought crosses my mind I just can't take it anymore. I thrust deep into her pussy and hold, crying out as a massive load of cum erupts from the head of my shaft and fills Ella's pussy completely. It quickly becomes too much for my wife to hold, and seconds later my spunk is squirting out of the sides of her plugged hole and running down her legs in pearly white streaks.

Moments later, Mike blows his load as well, opting to pull out right before his climax and blast his warm semen all over the humps of my wife's perfectly rounded ass. It rains down onto her in a torrent of white, milky jizz, gliding down her crack and mixing with mine like a cocktail of spunk.

Ella collapses down onto me, trying desperately to catch her breath.

"What a fucking workout." She says dryly.

I pull out and my wife hobbles to her feet, standing in a fucked silly daze as our cum runs in streaks down her naked lower half.

"Good game." Mike says with a smile.

"Good game." I tell him.

TEACHER'S PET

As she makes her way across the campus parking lot, her long brown hair blowing behind her, I can already tell that my wife is upset about something. This is concerning on many levels, the most obvious being that my wife, Rosie, has thick skin and doesn't usually let anything get her down. She's one of the most levelheaded women that I know, and right now she's absolutely fuming.

Rosie throws open the car door and drops into the passenger seat, slamming the door shut behind her and then staring forward through the windshield.

"Let's go." She says.

"What's up, baby?" I ask as gently as I can.

"Don't even get me started." Rosie answers, continuing to stare straight out the window. "Can we just go home?"

"Yeah, sure." I tell her, starting the car and pulling slowly out of the lot. I start heading back downtown, away from the college and towards our brand new apartment, which is definitely one of those just-married kind of places. A starter home, I guess you would call it, although our particular home happens to be small and surrounded by many others just like it.

I recently graduated college and Rosie is just a little ways behind me, coming in hot on the end of her final year buried under a mountain of textbooks. We're going to celebrate by heading off to Hawaii, and not a moment too soon. She works hard, and she deserves a vacation.

"So, how long are you going to wait before you tell me what happened?" I ask. "Because we're married now, I've got 'till death."

Rosie cracks a smile at this, which is a great sign.

"I saw that." I tell her. "Come on, out with it."

Rosie rolls her eyes and then finally breaks. "I'm just so fucking pissed off right now."

"I can see that." I observe.

"Professor Taylor is going to fail me." She says.

I almost lose control of the car. "What?"

"Well, not almost." Rosie admits. "He kind of already did."

I quickly pull off onto the side of the road and put it in park, then turn to face my beautiful, but incredibly distressed wife. This is the last credit that she needs to graduate and I'm already well aware that a failure in this class means she'll have to attended school over the summer, which means no Hawaii for either of us.

"What the fuck happened?" I ask.

"We took our final last week." Rosie begins. "It was an essay question and it was really easy, honestly."

I nod, listening intently.

"Anyway, this is my human sexuality course, you knew that right?" Rosie continues.

I didn't know that, but I nod anyway.

"In the essay we were supposed analyze an alternative form of sexuality; you know, the bondage community, the gay community, whatever. I did mine about swingers." She lets out a long sigh. "I was just supposed to give a simple overview, it was so easy."

"Well, what did you say about them?" I ask.

Rosie is silent for a moment, not wanting to divulge anything else out of some deep, primal embarrassment.

"Baby, what did you say in your essay?" I repeat.

"I was trying to do a pros and cons thing about the lifestyle." She explains. "And I got done with all of the cons, then suddenly the bell was ringing and everyone was handing in their papers. Time was up."

"Oh god." I say, finally understanding. "So you just handed in a blistering critique of swingers? That's not so bad, I mean it's just an opinion."

"But it's not my opinion!" She shouts. "I'm open! I'm fun!"

I can't help but crack a smile and start to laugh just a little bit, and then catch myself. "So what, it's not like he could fail you for it."

Rosie pulls out her bag and unzips it, then shows me her paper, which features a huge red 'F' scrawled across the top in thick, felt pen lines. "Hal." She says. "Mr. Taylor is a swinger."

"Shit." Is all I can say, suddenly realizing that our vacation had just flown right out the window.

We sit in silence for a moment before I start the car up again and pull back onto the road. We cruise for a while without speaking, looking out our respective windows at the trees crisscrossing above as they pass us by.

In this moment I fell helpless, life I'm failing in my duties as a new husband because we've finally encountered a problem that I just don't know how to fix. Sure, the grade was clearly unfair and not at all based on my wife's abilities as I student, it was just a stupid miscommunication, but there's nothing I can do about it.

After all, Rosie was one of the most sexually liberal girls I've ever known, and definitely knew how to have fun in the bedroom. We'd never actually invited anyone else into the sack with us, but knowing what a freak she was, I'd never considered it completely out of the question. If only there was a way for Professor Taylor to realize that Rosie didn't mean what she said in that essay.

Suddenly, and idea hits me that's so crazy I don't even want to think it. I try desperately to push it away but the harder I try, the more it starts to creep back in. My heart starts to beat a little faster as visions of swaying palm trees start to move back and forth in my head, blown by the warm Hawaiian wind. It's a plan so nuts that I don't think I could actually get my mouth to say it, even if I wanted to. I need more time.

"You wanna stop by the ice cream place on the corner?" I ask.

Rosie looks over at me like I've just asked her to marry me all over again. "How the fuck do you know me this well?"

The two of us sit at a small table in the ice cream shop, devouring our frozen treats happily as we take a short break from the enviable drama that is looming before us. It's a nice moment, and one that completely sums up exactly why I love Rosie so much. When we're together, it's like nothing can stop us.

Eventually, though, my thoughts finally drift back to that crazy idea, the one where Rosie doesn't fail and we get to go on our vacation and everybody wins. I take in a deep breath, then finally start in with it.

"So do you honestly think your grade is based on the fact that you offended him?" I ask. "It was a good essay, right?"

Rosie looks much more put off by my question that I had expected her to be. "Are you kidding me? Do you really think I'm that bad of a writer?" She asks.

"Hey! No!" I quickly defend myself. "I don't mean it like that, I just wanted to make sure."

"I'm sure." Rosie says. "It's because I'm not..." She trails off, poking her ice cream in the bowl with her spoon, and then finally adding sarcastically. "A swinger."

I size her up, trying to make sure I'm not completely out of bounds with what I'm about to say.

"What if you were?" I ask.

Rosie laughs. "Well then I'd probably get an 'A plus'."

"Seriously?" I ask.

Rosie nods. "Oh, for sure. The guy is a total perv, he's always checking out the girls and everything, pretty obvious about it, too."

"So why hasn't he ever gotten in trouble for it?" I question, genuinely curious.

My wife shrugs, thinking about this a moment as she takes down another scoop of ice cream. "Honestly." She begins. "It's probably because everyone thinks he's actually kinda hot."

The second that the words escape my wife's mouth I find myself hit with a hot wave of jealousy, washing over me and causing my heart to skip into double time. I'm not angry, however, in fact the jealousy is mixed with something even more powerful, and certainly stranger.

"Well, what do you think?" I ask.

Rosie looks up at me, noticing the subtle tightness in my voice. "Are you jealous?" She inquires with a slight laugh.

The truth is, I am jealous. Achingly jealous, actually, the emotion overwhelming with me a vicious cocktail of envy that tightens every part of my body. At the same time, however, I find myself oddly soothed. There's something about my wife finding this other man attractive that, as weird as it sounds, actually kind of turns me on.

Rosie rolls her eyes. "Okay, if he wasn't such a fucking dick, he'd be really sexy in an older guy kind of way."

Her words sear me to the core, but the burn is pleasant and I force myself to push farther into it, to let the strange arousal flood into me and see where it leads.

"I think you should show him that you can swing just as good as the rest of them." I tell her.

Rosie chuckles at this and then immediately stops when she realizes I'm not joking. "Wait, are you serious?" She asks. "Hal, what exactly are you saying?"

My heart is nearly pounding our of my chest now, my breathing quickened as I stand at the edge of this cliff that I know there's no turning back from.

"I'm saying we both want you to graduate." I tell her. "And we both want to go on this vacation, and I love you enough to let you get this grade back if you want it."

"Get this grade back?" She repeats, completely understanding my meaning but not quite wanting to say the words herself.

"I think you should fuck him." I tell her.

Rosie just stares at me in complete shock, frozen place as a whole myriad of ideas catapult back and forth within her head. I'm on the edge of my seat, waiting for her response as my cock gets harder and harder within my pants. I've accepted it now, and the thought of her fucking another man turns me on so much that I'm literally trembling.

"I couldn't do that without you." Rosie finally says.

There's too much subtext in her words to even begin wading though, but I know exactly how to answer.

"But I *will* be there, we're swingers now, remember?"

Her face remains totally still, and then suddenly shifts as she bites her bottom lip playfully. Rosie looks down for a moment, collecting herself.

"Are you sure?" She asks.

I reach across the table and take her hand in mine. "Positive, baby."

The campus is fairly quiet this evening, most of the classes long finished and only a few particularly late session still going on. Professor Taylor has a routine, however, and according to Rosie he'll still be there grading papers at his desk in the lecture hall.

I'm looking casually presentable as we enter the social sciences building, but my wife is wrapped in a long trench coat that sweeps just inches from the floor as she walks. It's not the most inconspicuous thing we could find, but it certainly draws less attention than what she's wearing underneath.

We make our way down a series of empty hallways until we find the lecture hall and peer inside, through a tiny glass window in the doorframe. Professor Taylor is here, sitting alone at his desk exactly like Rosie said he would be.

I can see why the girls would be swooning over him. The guy may be a little older, but he's devilishly handsome and clearly has the distinguished look of a man who knows what he's doing with himself.

Rosie looks over at me. "Are you sure you're okay with this?" She asks one last time.

"I'm sure, baby." I smile. "Honestly, I'm really fucking turned on right now."

Rosie give me a long, deep kiss that sends chills up and down my spine, then pulls away. "Here we go." She says, pushing open the door.

Professor Taylor looks up from his table scattered with papers. "Rosie! Can I help you?" He asks.

"I hope so." She says playfully as we make our way down the long row of steps to the front of the room. Soon we're right up at the professor's desk, standing directly across from him. "This is my husband." Rosie says, nodding towards me.

I extend my hand. "Nice to meet you."

Professor Taylor gives me a firm shake and smiles back.

"I wanted to talk to you about the grade you gave me on my final." Rosie begins.

Professor Taylor immediately takes on a new quality, leaning back in his chair and looking at us with a deep annoyance. "I'm sorry." He says bluntly. "The paper just wasn't good, you showed very little understanding of the lifestyle."

"The swinger lifestyle?" Rosie asks.

"Yes." Professor Taylor says. "The research just wasn't there and your conclusions were totally wrong. I understand how, as an outsider, you might have trouble understanding some of these sexually liberal practices, but it still results in a low grade. I'm sorry."

With that, the professor leans forward again and gets back to work, looking down at his desk and effectively dismissing the two of us.

"Outsider?" Rosie asks, letting the trench coat drop to the floor around her.

She looks absolutely incredible, a perfect specimen of feminine beauty done up to the most sexualized extreme. Her hair is pulled back into two long, girlish pigtails that flow down past her shoulders, and her makeup is just the right amount of slutty. My wife is wearing a shot, cropped white shirt that hugs her massive tits and shows off her cleavage, as well as her toned flat stomach. Her schoolgirl skirt barely covers the curve of her ass, and as we stand before Professor Taylor, who's mouth literally hangs open in shock, she lifts up the edge and gives him a playful wink.

"What are you? What is…" Professor Taylor trails off.

"What makes you think I'm not a swinger?" Rosie asks the professor. "I mean, I might be married but I still like to have a little fun once in a while." She starts to walk around the desk now, keeping her eyes locked onto Professor Taylor. "Maybe my husband likes to share me."

She reaches the professor and then drops down onto her knees and slowly unzips his pants, looking up at him with her huge brown eyes.

"Let me show you want I'm talking about." Rosie says, pulling out his huge cock and them swallowing it entirely, pushing her head down as far as it can go across his substantial length. She takes him expertly, relaxing as his giant member hits the back of her gag reflex and then taking him well past it, all the way down so that her face is pressed firmly against the professor's impressively toned abs. Rosie holds there for a moment, letting Professor Taylor savor the feeling of having his adorable student service him so skillfully, and then pulls back with a gasp.

It takes a moment for me to full grasp the gravity of what's happening, but when it hits me it hits me hard. My wife is sucking off another man right in front of me, the first new cock to enter her mouth in several years thanks to our happy engagement, followed by an even happier marriage. There are two forces battling within me, one of them tempting me to leap over the desk and punch the professor right in the jaw, but the other begging for my wife to take things even farther.

Finally, I just can't take it anymore. I unzip my pants and pull out my hard, throbbing dick, then begin to beat myself off in a series of firm, powerful strokes.

"You like watching your filthy wife take another man's cock in her mouth?" Rosie demands to know.

I nod, speeding up the pumps of my hand as I watch her.

Moments later she's back at it with even more lustful ferocity than before, bobbing her head up and down over the professors shaft while his girthy cock stretches the limits of her pink lips. Professor Taylor places his hands on the back of my wife's head and starts guiding her along, controlling her movements as he fucks her face like she's nothing more than some nasty sex doll.

He's more than a little rough with her, but Rosie seems to like it, moaning loudly and then eventually climbing to her feet and throwing herself over the desk in front of the professor.

"I need that fat teacher cock inside of me." She demands. "Now."

Professor Taylor quickly pulls off my wife's panties and then pulls up her skirt, revealing a perfectly sculpted ass, which he playfully slaps before aligning his cock with the slick hole of her pussy.

"Tell me you want this cock." Professor Taylor commands.

"I want your cock." Rosie moans.

"Say it to your fucking husband." The professor continues, grabbing my wife by the shoulders and then pulling her back so that she's looking at me with her crazed, cock hungry eyes. "Tell him that you need another man's dick to satisfy you."

Our eyes are locked and I'm already feeling as thought I could blow my load at any second, but I hold off. I'm quaking with arousal, my body barely able to contain itself as I watch the depraved situation that is unfolding before me.

"I need another man's dick to satisfy me." Rosie repeats. The words nearly push me over the edge, piecing deep into my heart and even deeper into my throbbing cock.

Suddenly, Rosie gasps as Professor Taylor pushes foreword, stretching the limits of her tightness with his enormous member. Her hands grip onto the edge of the desk tightly, bracing herself against the powerful slams as the professor begins to rail Rosie from behind. She's clearly enjoying herself, her teeth clenched tight as a long groan escapes through the cracks. Eventually, her noises morph into words.

"Oh. My. Fucking. God." Rosie starts repeating, a single syllable falling out of her mouth between every brutal hammer against her backside.

Seized with an unbridled passion, I suddenly just can't keep myself from joining in any longer. I step up to the desk with my cock standing proud and at full attention, jutting out towards my wife's face like a spear of flesh. She smiles up at me, then takes me gladly between her lips, pushing her head up and down across my shaft to the motion of the professors fucking from behind her. Professor Taylor and I begin to pulse back and forth, using the inertia from one another's ramming to propel my wife's small frame across both of our cocks, impaling her between us. Rosie quickly starts to moan, the sounds vibrating against my cock as it fills her throat, then coming out like a strange, lustful gargle.

"You've gotta try this." Professor Taylor finally says. I crack a smile, unable to ignore the weirdness of the situation, then follow his lead by walking around to the other side of the table and trading places with the man.

Now my cock is aimed directly at the tightness of my wife's pussy, soaking wet and just waiting to be reamed. I thrust my cock foreword and sigh loudly as I drive deep into her, Rosie's body trembling in reaction to my familiar touch.

Soon we are pumping together at our usual pace, enjoying the slamming as the professor pleasures himself with Rosie's beautiful face.

"Your blowjob skills are above and beyond." Says the professor. "A solid 'A'. But this is an advanced placement course in fucking, so you'll need to work even harder."

Immediately, he pulls out and Rosie stands up. Professor Taylor climbs onto his long wooden desk and lays down across it, his giant cock protruding from his ripped naked body like a manly tower of pleasure.

"Get up here." The professor tells my wife, who happily follows his orders and climbs up onto the desk, straddling his body with her long, toned legs. She reaches down and runs her hands across Professor Taylor's rock hard abs, clearly impressed with the care that he puts into his body. In return, the professor sits up and kisses her deeply, then lies back down onto the hard wood and carefully guides my wife lower and lower until the head of his shaft finally pushes into her tight wet pussy.

"Oh, fuck me!" Rosie cries out as she slides down his pole even further, her eyes closed while she gently massages her clit. When my wife finally reaches the bottom she lets out a satisfied gasp and her eyes fly open, taking in the professor's surprisingly muscular body while she begins to slowly ride him. She moves her hips in a strong, steady pump that circles across his shaft over and over again, milking Professor Taylor with her tight slit.

Rosie bites her lip and looks back at me, smiling as she takes one hand and spreads open her ass cheeks for a better view. It looks just as fantastic as I'd imagine it would, my wife confidently taking the massive dick that punishes her from below, while simultaneously welcoming me into her cute puckered asshole.

"I need two fucking cocks in me!" She calls back. "Get that dick over here and shove it up my ass."

Immediately, I burst into action, climbing up onto the desk and placing my shaft at the rim of my wife's tight backdoor. It's a squeeze to get it in, especially with Rosie already maxed out so brutally from below, and my first attempt is thwarted by the resistance of her tight anus.

Rosie looks back at me wildly, lost in a trance as she's pounded. "I said, shove that fucking cock up my ass!" She screams. "I don't give a fuck how tight it is, your wife needs two dicks, so give her two fucking dicks!"

I try again, this time pushing even harder against her tight rim until finally the tension gives way and I slide in forcefully, spreading her open and completely destroying the previous limits of her rectum. Rosie let's out a yelp of pain and pleasure, which morphs into a long moan the deeper I get until my cock reaches the hilt, with my balls pressed firmly against her ass.

Through a thin membrane I can feel Professor Taylor pumping in and out alongside me, and although the sensation is totally strange and unlike anything I've ever felt, it's certainly not bad. I can only imagine what this must feel like for Rosie.

Soon the three of us are all moving together in unison, our cocks thrusting in and out of my wife's tight holes in tandem while she hangs onto the wooden desk as firmly as she possibly can. Slowly but surely, our rhythmic slams begin to speed up until we are pounding her toned body with all of our might, railing into my wife's small frame while she edges closer and closer to orgasm.

"Oh my god!" Rosie finally gasps, her body beginning to tremble spastically as quakes of pleasure shoot through her. "I'm gonna cum so fucking hard."

She pushes back against me, letting out a powerful howl of delight while her eyes roll back into her head, like there's a lustful demon being exorcised from somewhere deep within her soul. Rosie's stomach clenches tight and then suddenly she flings herself forward onto Professor Taylor as we continue to pound her silly.

Seconds later, I find myself pushing past the edge of orgasm with her, the tension building and then finally breaking as I push deep and hold within Rosie, expelling my warm seed into her maxed out rectum. Pump after pump of milky jizz unloads into my wife, filling her up completely so that when I finally pull out the semen bubbles up and spilled from her reamed hole, running down the crack of her ass and across her pussy where the professor is about to blow his load, as well.

"Cum inside this college girl pussy!" My wife commands. "Shoot that fucking load up inside of me!"

Professor Taylor lets out a long, aching groan and then suddenly unleashes his pent up spunk within my wife, quickly filling her to the brim and then squirting out from the sides of her tightly plugged pussy. When he pulls out, his pearly semen pours into the desk below, mixing with mine in a delicious cocktail of man seed.

The three of us pause for a moment, panting in silence as we struggle to catch our breath, then finally Rosie grabs her trench coat and wraps it around herself once more. She looks back at Professor Taylor. "I trust you'll do the right thing." Rosie says.

A month has passed and the summer is in full swing, but I still can't get the visions of that night out of my head. It was an incredible experience, one that somehow managed to bring my wife and I even closer together. More importantly, it was depraved enough to fuel my fantasies for years to come.

I'm laying on the beach in a low, wooden chair with a drink in my hand and a good book by my side, looking out over the Pacific Ocean without a care in the world. Hawaii is even better than I expected.

Rosie is nearby, chatting on the phone with someone while her sweet voice carries across the sand on a warm tropical breeze. She hangs up and walks over to me.

"I guess I'll be heading back to school next year after all." She says.

"What?" I'm suddenly yanked from my tropical vibes by the news. "You didn't graduate?"

Rosie laughs. "No, no, no; I passed just fine. That was Professor Taylor, actually. He wants me to come back and be his teaching assistant."

A devilish smile slowly creeps across my wife's face.

BANG THE DJ

Thundering drums, throbbing bass and a delicious synthetic vocal hook slicing through the night air above a roaring crowd; this is what my wife, Mason, lives for. A DJ by trade, she loves everything about electronic music and the scene that comes with it.

Getting started, I wasn't sure if the whole DJ thing was going to work out for her because, after all, she'd never expressed any interest in making music before this, having given up on her guitar lessons a little after we started dating in college. But this was something that she could really sink her teeth into, spending hours upon hours behind the blue glow of her computer screen, arranging tracks and creating incredible remixes.

Despite my doubts about the project, I supported her. Never in my wildest dreams could I have imagined what was going to happen when she released her first record.

Home recorded and sonically perfected with the help of a few online video tutorials, the collection of songs sounded pleasant to my unrefined ear, but I'm just an average guy with average tastes. Neither of us got our hopes up, but instead we took pride in the accomplishment of finishing a project and releasing it out into the world, even if it was just a free download.

My wife finally got her songs online and then came to bed, falling immediately to sleep next to me after a frustrating day of trying to upload her record correctly to the online distributor. She sent out a few emails to friends, asking them to check out the record, and that was that.

The next morning, however, everything had changed. When Mason opened her laptop the incoming notifications were through the roof. Someone overseas had gotten a hold of her tracks and loved them, quickly forwarding them onward to a few select tastemaker blogs while we slept the night away in Los Angeles, oblivious to the commotion. The blogs were raving about Mason's record, released under the moniker DJ Blowbang, which I personally found to be pretty hilarious. At first I wasn't sure if she even knew what it meant, but when I brought up the name with Mason she explained that is was "controversial, so people will notice." I guess she was right.

Suddenly, managers and booking agents were coming out of the woodwork. Everyone wanted a piece of Mason and claimed they knew exactly how to take her to the next level.

Fortunately, the team she went with did exactly that, and before I knew it my adorable, unassuming wife was headlining festivals and getting flown out to raves all over the world. Talk about being in the right place at the right time. The world of electronic dance music was the hottest ticket around, and Mason was at the dead center of all of it.

Was I jealous at first? Maybe a little, but that came and went fast, quickly replaced with a sense of loving pride as I watched my wife move massive crowds from behind that same laptop that she once typed away on while watching trashy reality television.

Today, we are flying to London for a festival. Normally, I'd have to be working but I managed to the weekend off to join her out here on the road; or in the air, in this particular case.

We board at a snail's pace, filtering into the cabin behind a long column of slow moving passengers, before eventually arriving at our seats. As I'm loading our bags into the overhead compartment and attractive, dark haired young man approaches my wife.

"Are you her?" He questions.

Mason smiles, celebrity recognition still a relatively new thing. "DJ Blowbang?" She asks.

"Yeah! It is you, isn't it?" The guy laughs. "Can I get a photo?"

"Sure!" Mason replies, clearly excited about this entire situation.

The guy takes out his phone and holds it up, grinning into the camera as he pulls my wife close. As the light flashes, he turns and gives her a kiss on the cheek which makes Mason bust up laughing.

"Hey!" She shouts in mock anger.

"I'm sorry, I just had to." The guy says.

A sting of jealousy shoots directly into my heart, but I pull it back as much as I can muster. It's not so much the kiss on the cheek that gets me, it's the fact the my wife actually kind of likes it. She's basking in the attention now, letting the attraction flow back and forth freely between her and this handsome guy.

The fan turns around his phone and shows Mason the photo.

"Aww!" Mason coos. "That's cute."

"Thanks Blowbang." The guy says with a wink. "Maybe next time we'll have time for more than just a kiss."

"Hopefully." Mason responds with a giggle.

My jaw nearly hits the floor as I watch this exchange, but when my wife turns back around and sits next to me in our designated seats, she seems totally oblivious to anything even remotely unusual. Mason pulls out the in-flight magazine and starts to read.

"So… What was that?" I ask, slightly flustered.

Mason turns to me with a quizzical look on her face, then almost immediately realizes something and bursts into a wide smile. "Oh yeah! It's crazy, right? I can't believe I'm getting recognized now."

"No, I mean you flirting with him." I respond.

Mason shakes her head and rolls her eyes. "He was a fan!"

"So?" I respond.

"That's what you do." She tells me. "You've gotta treat your fans well, Victor."

I take a deep breath. "Yeah, I know. I'm sorry."

She turns back to her magazine and I try to move on, but for some reason I just can't get over the exchange that I had just witnessed. My wife has a point, she's in no position to be turning away the innocent requests from fans, but that one didn't exactly come across as all that innocent. I find myself engulfed in a green sea of jealousy that pushes and pulls me in every direction, no matter how hard I try to suppress it. Yet, lurking below the surface there is something else brewing, something even more powerful.

I try to put my finger on exactly what I'm feeling, but I can't quite pinpoint it until I look down and realize that my cock is rock hard within my pants. I may be jealous, but I'm also more turned on right now that I have been in a very long time, the envy morphing and changing into a strange, almost humiliating lust. The more I think about my wife flirting with this guy, the more I realize how much I actually kind of liked it.

"Whoa, what's going on here?" My wife asks, suddenly interrupting my thoughts.

Her gaze has wandered down onto my hard, bulging cock which tries desperately to break free from its cloth prison.

I can't help but laugh. "I don't know."

Mason glances back along the aisle to where the fan is now sitting. "Guess it turns you on to see me flirt with other guys?" She asks. "I've heard that was a thing."

"Not a chance." I lie, starting to tremble with arousal.

"You sure?" Mason asks, her hand wander over onto my leg and inching closer and closer to my swollen cock.

I swallow hard, so turned on that I can barely stand it. "I don't know." I repeat. "I mean, yeah I guess so."

Mason suddenly looks shocked, as if realizing that she's bitten off more than she can chew. "Really?" She asks, flustered. "I was just fucking with you."

At this point I could easily cover myself and pretend I'd been messing around, too. This is my first instinct, to run away from these confusing feelings that bloom larger and larger within, but before I answer I stop myself. I consider the trembling, overwhelming arousal that courses through my veins. Is it worth it to throw that all away just because I'm embarrassed by something I don't yet understand?

"Yeah." I finally say. "I don't get it, but it really turns me on."

Mason leans back into her chair, looking straight forward as the news settles in her mind. I try to refocus but I can't, questions still lingering above me and haunting my thoughts.

"Would you ever do it?" I ask. "Fuck somebody else?"

Mason laughs. "No, baby."

"What if I wanted you to?" I prod.

She falters for a moment, the idea clearly sparking her interest more than she wants to admit. "I don't know." My wife finally responds.

"What if I was there, too?" I ask, my cock so swollen that I'm worried it's going to burst.

"A threesome?" She asks.

"Yeah."

Mason lets out a long sigh, glancing one final time down the aisle at her handsome fan. "That sounds really hot." She finally confesses.

The arena is dark and the tension in the air is heavy, floating above the audience along with a thick mist from the nearby smoke machines.

Suddenly, a thundering low drone slices through the darkness, rumbling the entire stage and shaking my body with its incredible volume. The note starts to shift and change, causing the audience to burst into an uproarious cheer. This is Mason's cue to go on, and seconds later she runs up to her DJ booth and throws her hands out wide.

She's wearing a gold jacket and matching pants, specially made for the live show, and they glint playfully under the now flashing stage lights.

"What's up London!?" Mason shouts into a microphone, fully assuming the identity of DJ Blowbang. She presses a few buttons and suddenly the entire building is shaking from the sound of a powerful beat. The audience is swirling together, dancing like wild monsters as a throbbing mass of ecstasy-influenced ravers.

Mason glances over to me on the side of the stage and I give her a thumbs up. She flashes a smile and then turns her attention back to her computer; that's my girl.

The entire show I stay enraptured by her performance, so proud to be the loving husband of such a talented woman. Her command of the audience is astounding, and it's not long before I find myself nodding along to the beat, as well, despite her tracks being light-years away from the rock and roll I'm accustomed to.

The entire set flies by incredibly fast and, before I know it, Mason thanks the audience, gives a wave and then walks off stage to a torrent of deafening cheer. She heads straight for me and gives me a big, passionate kiss.

"I'm so fucking horny for you right now." I whisper in her ear, still reeling from the tension on the plane this morning.

"I know." She says with a smile. "Me too."

"So let's get back to the hotel!" I laugh.

Mason shakes her head. "I've got to do a meet and greet right now, but then we're going straight back and I'm going to fuck your brains out."

"Yes please." I say.

Mason grabs me by the hand and starts leading me down a long backstage hallway, while her manager talks quickly at her and has her sign a few documents. Moments later, we arrive at an inconspicuous door and push through it, greeted by a handful of fans who erupt into excited applause.

My wife laughs. "You're too kind."

The next twenty minutes are spent watching Mason chat with fans, take photos and sign autographs. I hang back, observing from the catering as I snack on some chips and dip.

"Hey!" A voice shouts out in recognition. It's strange sounding in its familiarity, and I quickly realize that I'm hearing a fellow American accent.

I turn towards the voice and stop in complete shock. It's the handsome fan from the plane.

"I remember you!" I laugh. "Holy shit!"

"This is crazy right?" The guy asks, and then extends his hand. "I'm Tyler, nice to meet you."

"Victor." I tell him.

"What are the odds?" He asks.

I nod.

"I can't believe you got to sit next to her on the plane." Tyler says. "I mean, I know we're all just people and I try not to buy into the celebrity thing, but good god, Blowbang is so fucking hot."

Suddenly, the strange feeling is back and it's stronger than ever. I sense my heart skip a beat, and my first instinct it to say something to assert my dominance over this guy, but somehow I hold off. "Yeah she is." I agree, as calmly as I can.

My wife, totally oblivious, turns to take a photo on the other side of the room, giving Tyler and me a great view of her ass.

"God damn, the things I would do to that thing." Tyler says.

"Oh yeah?" I ask, trembling. "Like what?"

"Like bend her over a chair and pound her up the ass until she can't walk straight." Tyler says, practically frothing at the mouth. "You know she's gotta be a freak in the bedroom."

"She is." I tell him.

"Well, maybe we should double team her then!" Tyler jokes with a hearty laugh.

"That can be arranged." I say.

Tyler's laugher quickly dies down. "What do you mean?"

"I mean I can ask her if she wants to double team us." I say, my cock throbbing for release.

"Ha! Sure." Tyler says sarcastically. "You'd get thrown out of here so fast that your head would spin. Besides, I heard she's married."

"She is." I tell him. "To me."

Tyler goes white as a sheet when I tell him this, suddenly stammering to find any words that he can. "I'm so sorry." He mumbles. "I was just fucking around."

"I wasn't." I say. "Do you want to fuck my wife with me?"

His expression freezes and then suddenly changes into a kind of confused shock. "Seriously?"

"Seriously." I tell him. "Just stay right here."

By now, the last of the fans are being escorted out by security.

"Can we have a moment?" I ask the main guard, who nods. I point over at Tyler. "He's cool." The guard leaves and closes the door behind him.

Now its just Tyler, my wife, and me in the room together. I walk over to Mason and hug her.

"Remember what we talked about on plane, baby?" I ask.

"You mean about a threesome with another guy?" She responds. "How could I forget?"

Suddenly, Mason sees Tyler and freezes, a series of realizations working their way through her mind. "Holy shit." She finally says.

"Holy shit." Repeats Tyler.

Somehow, we all come to terms with our situation at exactly the same time. No words are exchanged, no questioning of motives, no hesitation. The next thing I know, Tyler is approaching and Mason has squatted down between us, looking up with a frantic hunger in her eyes.

Tyler and me pull out or rock hard cocks in a feverish, lustful trance, and Mason takes them both in her slender hands. She begins to pump slowly up and down our shafts but then stops and looks up at me.

"Are you sure?" She asks.

I feel like I'm at the edge of a cliff, about to jump off without any means of coming back once it's done. If we do this our lives will be forever changed, for better or worse.

With my heart pounding in my ears, and the sight of my wife's fingers wrapped tight around another man's dick, I've never been so turned on in my entire life. The decision seems clear.

"Of course I'm sure." I tell her.

A devilish smile crosses Mason's face. "Good."

The next thing I know she is taking my cock into her mouth and swallowing deep, pushing me hard against her gag reflex and then pulling back for air. She immediately turns to Tyler and does the same thing, then quickly gets to work pumping up and down on his massive shaft while stroking me off.

I watch in complete awe of my wife's sexual skill. I know that she's incredible in bed, but there's nothing like seeing your beautiful bride with another man to remind you of her hotness. Mason continues to glide her lips across Tyler's length until finally collecting herself and plunging down as deep as she possibly can go. This time, she relaxes as the guy's cock hits the edge of her gag reflex, expertly letting it slide past and fill her throat entirely. She takes him until her face is pressed up hard against Tyler's abs, who quickly removes his shirt to show of just how incredible they really are.

I can her Mason moaning into the flesh of his cock as she teases him with the vibration, then works her way around his shaft with her wet tongue.

"God damn." Tyler groans. "I can't believe this is happening. I can't believe I'm having a blowbang with DJ Blowbang."

Mason pulls him back and takes in a huge gasp of air. "Is that all you want? A blowbang?" She asks seductively. "Or would you like to fuck this tight little pussy?"

Tyler doesn't even know what to say as my wife stands up and walks over to one of the greenroom couches. She unbuttons her pants and then slides them slowly off over the curves of her perfect ass while we watch. Her panties come next, and soon Mason is bent over the couch in nothing but her shiny gold stage jacket. She looks back at us playfully, and then gives a little wink. "Well?" She asks.

Immediately, Tyler springs into action, stepping forward with his gigantic cock and positioning himself behind my wife. Mason looks back at me nervously, biting her lip before silently mouthing, "I love you."

Then next thing I know, Tyler is thrusting into her, stretching out the tightness of my wife's wet pussy with his absolutely enormous rod. Mason groans loudly as he enters her, gripping tightly onto the couch in front of her as she braces against his slow, but powerful thrusts.

"Oh fuck." My wife whimpers. "That feels so fucking good. Keep fucking me just like that."

Tyler continues pumping into her from behind, keeping his angle perfectly aligned but steadily speeding up with every pound until, eventually, he's hammering into her at a thunderous pace, rocking the couch with every rapid slam.

My wife is screaming now and suddenly the green room door opens, stops, and then immediately shuts again. In true rockstar fashion, the guards know when to turn a blind eye. I can't help but laugh as I walk around to the front of Tyler and my wife, then position my cock directly in front of Mason's waiting mouth.

Mason swallows me gladly, wrapping her lips tightly around my shaft and then immediately getting to work, finding the rhythm of Tyler's plows from behind and then falling into it with her blowjob. Soon the three of us are completely synchronized, moving together like a beautiful sex beast as we moan and sweat our ways towards three powerful orgasms.

I can tell by the way that Mason is trembling she is already well on her way there, our new friend doing a fantastic job of railing her from behind. Her entire body is wracked with pleasure, which reveals itself spastically though a series of violent shakes that seem to pulse through Mason like waves. She looks up me with huge, satisfied eyes, my cock stuffed into her throat as she watches my expressions shift through every different kind of pleasure.

It could all end then and there, the three of us succumbing to the sensations within and exploding together in a powerful orgasm, but there's still one part of my fantasy we haven't tried yet.

I pull out of my wife's mouth and then walk around to the other side of the couch. Tyler immediately sees what's happening and removes himself as well, allowing me the space to sit down next to Mason and pull her over to me.

"Get on." I command.

Mason throws her leg over the top of me and then reaches down and grabs a hold oh my aching cock. She quickly aligns it with the entrance of her taut slit, then slides down gracefully onto my rod, sighing loudly as she's impaled. When she finally comes to rest against my hips, my dick fully inserted within, Mason begins to grind hard against me. She moves her body in elegant swoops, slow at first and then speeding up until she is slamming firmly onto my rod.

"God dammit, I love that dick." My wife confesses. "Thank you for letting me fuck another man."

I lean my head back and close my eyes, enjoying the incredible sensation of her riding me for a moment before reaching down with both hands and grabbing onto Mason's perfect ass. I grip each cheek firmly and then spread her open for Tyler to get a good look at her puckered asshole. He knows exactly what to do next.

Soon, Tyler is climbing up onto the couch behind Mason, placing the head of his cock right up to her back door and teasing against the tension. She's tight, especially thanks to my cock, which is already graphically stretching the limits of her pussy.

Tyler pushes forward, the rim of Mason's asshole not quite ready to give until the third try, when Tyler braces himself against the ledge of the couch and plows into my wife, breaking the seal and sliding all the way down to the hilt of his massive shaft.

Mason lets out a yelp of pain and pleasure, then hisses through a set of clenched teeth as we begin to push back and forth within her.

"That's so much dick." She moans. "Oh my god, I don't know if I can take this."

"You can take it." I tell her reassuringly.

"Fuck." Is Mason's only response.

Tyler and me continue to fuck her like this, slamming into my wife's holes back and forth as her small frame becomes accustom to our violations. Soon enough, the pain seems to subside and an incredibly potent lust takes its place. Mason is loving it; reveling in the way that the two of us men are overwhelming her body with our dicks. She is helpless between us, a powerless fuck toy who trembles wildly from the force of our dual penetration.

"You like those cocks?" I ask. "You like taking a fan up your ass while I pound you from below?"

"I love it!" My wife screams. "I love taking two dicks!"

Her frantic cries kick us into overdrive and suddenly Tyler and me are railing my beautiful wife with everything that we've got. We're pounding her gorgeous body so hard now that the couch scoots loudly across the floor, not built for such a brutal pummeling to take place on it's cushions.

Mason's spastic shaking has evolved into a full on tremor, rattling her body as she reaches down between her legs with one hand and begins to play with her clit.

"I'm so close!" My wife cries out. "Keep slamming me just like that!"

We do as we're told, keeping up the break neck pace until finally Mason just can't take it anymore and erupts in a powerful orgasm. She throws her head back and lets loose with a blood-curdling scream, her nails digging deep into my shoulders as she convulses on top of me. I can feel her stomach clenching tight and then releasing in a rapid series of movements.

It feels like her orgasm lasts forever, but eventually the waves of pleasure seem to pass and Mason quickly pulls the two of us out of her holes.

"I'm ready for you now." My wife says. "Cover me in your hot white cum!"

She immediately tears off her jacket and bra then squats down between us, looking up with her tongue hanging out like a hungry dog. Tyler and I stand on either side of her with our cocks in our hands, frantically beating off as we edge closer and closer to a glorious finish.

It's not long before we're blowing our loads. Tyler goes first, a thick rope of jizz blasting out of his shaft and splattering in a diagonal line across Mason's face. She manages to catch some of it in her mouth and swallows graciously, then turns her attention to me.

Seeing my beautiful wife covered in another man's jizz immediately pushes me over the edge and I'm instantly cumming hard, groaning loudly as my milky seed splatters across her chin and down onto her massive tits.

Now finished, Tyler and I collapse back onto the couch, while Mason stands and makes her way over to the green room shower. I listen to the quiet hiss of warm water as she steps inside.

"That was incredible. Thanks man." Tyler tells me. "You're a good husband to her, I'll tell you that much. She's lucky to have you."

I smile. "I'm the one who's lucky."

We sit in silence for a moment before Tyler stands and begins collecting his clothes.

"Hey, have you ever been to Brighton?" I ask.

The guy shrugs. "No, why?"

"That's where tomorrow's show is. I think there's room for one more name on the guest list." I tell him. "And room for one more cock inside my wife."

PLAYING DOUBLES

Eventually, all married couples will fall into a routine. On the surface this may sound a little boring and monotonous, but it's not always a bad thing. In fact, when it's finally time to settle down with the one that you love, the routine is something that you'll start to look forward to. It's different for everyone; some couples make dinner and watch a movie every night, some adventurous ones go camping together once a month. It can be anything, really, as long as it brings the two of you together and reminds you why you chose the comfort of each other's warm embrace over the cold, harsh wilds of single life.

The relationship routine of my wife, Liz, and me, is tennis. It started on whim, after seeing a deal online for half off lessons at the local courts in the park. Always health conscious, we figured it was something we could do together that was active and would get us out of the house, which is great for Liz as she works from home.

It has to be said, though, tennis is not as easy as it looks. Liz and me are natural athletes, having done sports ever since college when we met through our mutual love of track and field, but nothing comes close to the delicate finesse required for rallying a tennis ball. Hitting that little yellow sphere back and forth over the net seems simple enough, but when the slight angle of your racket comes into play, things can get out of control fast.

I have to admit, I'm not nearly as good as Liz, which is why I'm really not all that disappointed when I end of twisting my ankle five lessons in. I was just starting to get the hang of things, but my desire to trek all the way down to the courts for lessons was fading fast, while Liz was constantly begging to play more! Having spent the whole day inside, she would frequently try to get in a few matches after dinner, not realizing how exhausted I was from a long day at the office.

My ankle isn't bad enough for a cast or anything, and only really aches when I start running around frantically, which doesn't happen to often these days. All it does is keeps me off the tennis court.

One warm evening, I pull up to the house and notice that my wife isn't home. Confused, I call her name while pushing open the front door and receive silence in return. I know her all too well to be worried, though. Liz must be putting in some extra time at the courts.

Our house is not far at all from the park where we play, so I change out of my work clothes and make my way down the front steps, towards my wife's presumed whereabouts. The walk could probably do some good for my ankle, kicking it back into gear after a few weeks of trying to stay off of it.

The park is almost entirely empty, which is usual for an evening like this. Technically, our park is public, but it's nestled up here in the hills of the palisades and far from the view any average passers by. There are plenty of neighborhood activities during the weekend afternoons, like our tennis lessons, for instance, but when the evenings begin, the wealthy elite better things to do, apparently.

As I step closer and closer, I can hear the familiar hollow slapping of a tennis ball rallying back and forth across the hard ground; the squeak of shoes and the occasional grunt of someone slamming the ball as hard as they can. The noises themselves are almost sexual, in a way.

I cut through a few trees and then follow a path down towards the court, where its green, rectangular surface eventually comes into view through the woods. I immediately spot Liz, her long blonde hair bouncing behind her in a ponytail as she darts back and forth across the court, rallying fiercely. Her opponent, however, is unfamiliar to me.

I take a few more steps forward through the trees to get a look, but then stop short of revealing myself to the two of them.

The man that Liz is playing against is young and strikingly handsome, with dark features and a chiseled jaw. His face is boyish, just waiting to break into a smile after every rally as he encourages my wife's performance.

It's a smile that is apparently contagious, because Liz can't help but grin as well, clearly enjoying herself out here.

Immediately, a deep pang of jealousy strikes into the pit of my stomach. I feel a strange tingle across my entire body, a simmering anger that doesn't quite have enough fuel to ignite, but certainly would if it could. Despite their activities being totally innocent, I feel as though I have caught my wife with this man deep inside of her, giving her pleasure in a way that I never could. I suppose, thanks to my twisted ankle, he actually is giving her a pleasure that I'm not equipped for. I can feel my logical brain and a frantic, animalistic rage battling within me, each one vying desperately for the upper hand.

Finally letting my suspicions take hold, I hang back and watch them from a distance, analyzing every movement as my jealousy boils.

The man slams home a particularly well-placed return and my wife misses it, barely catching herself before falling over. She laughs.

"Damn! You got me!" Liz tells the mysterious man.

"That was close, though." The man says, encouragingly. "You're getting so good, it's incredible."

"Thanks." Liz tells him, picking up the yellow tennis ball and tossing it back over. "You've helped me so much, I really can't thank you enough."

"Are you kidding me?" The man responds. "I love playing with you, it's not often I get to practice my serve and get a little eye candy at the same time."

My heart skips a beat as he says this, and then kicks into double time when I see my wife laughing coyly in reply. She's clearly enjoying the attention.

Finally, I just can't take it anymore, my seething jealousy getting the best of me as I step out from the trees and approach the courts. Liz spots me and her expression immediately changes to one of familiar warmth.

"Jordan!" She calls out of me, running over and exiting the courts, then throwing her arms around me in a big hug. "How was work, baby?"

"Fucking boring." I tell her with a laugh. "I see you're working on your game! Are we still going out for dinner tonight?"

She freezes as I say this. "Oh fuck, what time is it?"

"Our reservation is in a half hour, but it's just down the road." I explain.

"I need to get ready!" Liz shouts, a wild look in her eye.

My wife immediately turns around and grabs her bag. "Thanks for playing!" She calls over to her handsome friend. "Same time tomorrow?"

The man nods. "Sure thing!"

"This is my husband, Jordon." She tells the guy frantically.

"I'm Keith." He waves. "Nice to meet you."

I return the wave but before I can say anything else my wife is dragging me back towards the house, desperately trying to shower and get ready before we miss our dinner reservation.

"That was close!" I say as we take our seats near the window of this swanky, newly opened restaurant. They call it New American, but I've never seen anything like it, my eyes darting across the delicious plates of our fellow patrons as we're lead to our table.

"I'm so sorry about that." Liz says with heaping sincerity. "I completely lost track of time."

We sit.

"That's okay, baby." I tell her, reaching my hand across the table and putting it over the top of hers. "Looks like you were having fun though."

The moment is suddenly interrupted by the waiter, who asks us if there's anything we'd like to drink. I order a nice bottle of wine and the waiter smiles.

"Is this a special occasion?" He asks.

Liz and me exchange glances. "It's our two year wedding anniversary." I tell him.

"That's adorable." The waiter responds, suddenly looking as though he's watching two puppies prancing playfully together in a field. "Well, thank you for choosing such a special night to celebrate with us."

"Of course." Liz says.

The waiter leaves and then suddenly we are dropped into silence, my wife and I taking in the beautiful view that lies out of the window before us. No matter how gorgeous this incredible sunset is over the water, however, I still can't push the nagging questions about my wife and this other man out of my head.

"So what's the deal with this Keith guy?" I finally ask.

"Oh." Liz starts. "Well, he was taking lessons too, and when you left I needed a new partner to rally with. He lives up the street and works from home, so we just started hitting the court in the early evenings for some more practice."

"Okay." I nod, not exactly sure how to express the strange swirl of feelings that brew inside of me. There's a question that I want to ask, but I'm not exactly sure what it is.

"You seem concerned." Liz finally says.

I laugh. "Maybe a little. I don't know, I mean he's a very good looking dude."

Liz declines to comment on this, but the flicker of girlish embarrassment in her eye tells me everything that I need to know.

I can feel my jealousy returning, blooming somewhere deep within as I struggle to contain it. Only this time the emotion is joined by something else, something strange and, I hate to admit, arousing. My body is trembling slightly, trying desperately to sort though all of the strange feelings that are battling for superiority within my mind. The creeping lust is slowly taking control.

"Do you want me to stop playing with him?" Liz asks.

"No way!" I tell her. "We're not going to have a marriage like that. Our relationship is wild, and free, and…" I trail off, trying to think of the word.

"Open?" Liz offers.

I laugh. "Well, maybe not open."

Suddenly the two of us are plunged back into our silence again, our thoughts racing a mile a minute. My cock is hardening in my pants, something that I can't even begin to understand, only knowing the emotions that overwhelm me feel amazing and that I want more of them.

"Would you be opposed to that?" Liz finally asks.

This time I don't laugh, just let her words hit me and then gradually seep into my soul. I know exactly where this is headed.

"Do you want to fuck him?" I ask, sounding angrier than I intend to. "Is that what you're saying?"

Liz chooses her words carefully. "I mean, me and you are a pretty adventurous couple."

I nod, my blood boiling with a lustful, aching jealousy. My wife has no idea, but I'm loving every second of this. "We are." I confirm.

"And you still owe me from that threesome with my roommate in college." Liz continues. She's right, one of the best nights of my young life was banging her and her gorgeous redhead roommate, Heather.

159

I let out a long sigh, barely able to believe the words that are coming out of my mouth. "Consider it an anniversary gift." I tell her.

Immediately, Liz's expression changes from concern to utter shock, blown away by the fact that I just agreed to this. I'm blown away myself, but I can't deny the incredible arousal that's been coursing through my veins ever since I saw her flirting with this other man at the park.

"Are you serious?" My wife asks.

"Baby, I know that you love me." I tell her. "It's just a little harmless fun and, honestly…" I lower my voice and lean in across the table. "The idea of you fucking another guy kind of turns me on."

"Really?" She gasps.

I nod. "I've only got one stipulation, I have to be there."

Liz smiles. "I wouldn't have it any other way!"

The next day when I arrive home from work, Liz is missing once again. Like before, I know exactly where to find her, but for different reasons entirely.

I take my time to change out of my work clothes and take a shower, letting the water run over my body and sooth me as my cock aches from excitement. I'm already stiff as a board, my imagination running wild.

As soon as I'm ready, I head out the door and make my way down towards the park, my body shaking from the overwhelming jealous desire that fills me to the point of bubbling over. If everything has gone according to plan, then my wife may already have another man deep inside of her, hammering away at her tight pussy or, better yet, slamming her perfectly toned asshole.

I reach the trees and head in, following a path through the empty park towards the tennis courts. As I step closer and closer, I can hear the familiar sound of my wife grunting and groaning, only now It's no longer accompanied by the noise of shoes squeaking across the court or rubber balls bouncing. Now mere yards away, I can faintly hear what appears to be a different kind of balls bouncing.

I emerge from the woods and stop dead in my tracks, not entirely prepared for the erotic vision that lies before me. My breath catches in my throat as I see my wife and her muscular lover, Keith, colliding together rapidly in the middle of the tennis court. Liz is wearing her white tennis outfit, the racket still in her hand, but she has been bent over the net while

Keith pounds into her from behind. She looks back at him with an expression of complete lust in her eyes, transfixed on his incredible toned body as he rails her with brutal power.

"Oh my god." My wife is moaning, her voice drifting over to me as I edge closer and closer. "Fuck me just like that! Just like that!"

I glance in either direction, making sure that the park is still empty, then immediately pull my throbbing cock out of my pants. I slowly begin to stroke myself off, my eyes transfixed on the sight of my gorgeous wife being pleasured so thoroughly by another man.

I can't believe that, just days before, this entire idea was nothing more than a strange flicker of arousal in the back of my head. Now the flame has grown, consuming everything in its path until it has become completely uncontrollable. It's out of my hands now and there is no turning back.

Eventually, Liz looks up and spots me off in the woods watching them. She flashes a devious smile when she sees me, then lets out a long, satisfied moan, closing her eyes and biting her lip as she slams back against Keith's rapid thrusts.

My cock is aching to cum, and although I could easily blow my load any second that I wanted to, I hold off, reveling in the overwhelming feelings that invade my thoughts. I'm shaking hard now, unable to control my body while it grapples with the sight of my wife fucking another dick. It's so innately wrong, but feels so good to experience the infidelity of my wife in such a visceral way.

Finally, I just can't take it anymore. I step out of the forest and head onto the tennis courts, where my wife and her lover look up but don't stop pounding each other.

"It's about time." Liz tells me with a giggle. "Get over here and let me suck that cock of yours."

I step around to the opposite side of the tennis net, so that Keith and I are divided onto either half of the court with my wife Liz bending over the middle. Liz looks up at me happily and then wraps her lips tight around my cock.

"Oh fuck." I groan, bracing myself for the movements of her head as she pumps and down across my shaft, propelled by the man fucking her from behind. Liz winks at me, then pushes down as far as she can, letting my cock slide all the way down to her gag reflex before she retches and pulls back.

My wife comes up with a gasp, collecting herself briefly before diving back down and trying again. This time Liz is ready, relaxing her throat as she plunges downward and somehow managing to slip past her gag reflex unnoticed. Soon, her face is pushed hard against my abs, my entire cock consumed within her. My balls rest against my wife's chin, bouncing lightly as she's railed from behind.

Liz holds there for as long as she can and then eventually starts to move across the length of my shaft in a steady rhythm, pacing herself with the pulsing slaps against her backside from Keith. We eventually start to move together gracefully, synchronizing our bodies into one incredibly pleasant sexual movement. Keith and I pump hard into my wife from either end, pushing her tight body back and forth across the net in a strange, lustful sex rally.

Liz starts to tremble and quake between us, her body not accustomed to the extreme sensation of two men at once. I can tell that Keith is hitting her just right, every thrust sending a powerful bolt of pleasure down my wife's body.

Lost in the moment, my wife suddenly pulls me out of her mouth and snarls, "Lie down. I need to ride that fucking cock."

I climb over to there side of the net and, after quickly stripping off the rest of my clothes; I lie on the hard, green court next to them. Liz maneuvers herself down next to me, throwing her legs around my toned abs and then reaching between to grab my cock, which juts out fiercely from my body. My wife lines me up with her wet slit and then slowly pushes herself down onto my shaft, slipping lower and lower as a soft whimper escapes her lips. She's so tight that I almost explode right then and there, ejecting all of my pent up sexual tension in a single pump, but I hold steady, clenching my teeth and trying not to focus too hard on the incredible sensation of my slutty wife's movements.

Liz slowly begins to grind against me, pumping her hips hard across my shaft in a confident series of deep swoops.

"Do you like sharing your wife with another man?" She asks me.

"I fucking love it." I confess. "I love seeing you take another dick."

"In my cute little tennis outfit?" She coos.

I nod, every nerve in my body seeming to fire off with extreme pleasure.

"Then hold my fucking ass open for that second cock!" Liz suddenly commands, a fierceness in her voice.

I immediately do as I'm told, reaching back and grabbing tight onto my wife's ass cheeks as I continue to pound up into her from below. I can see Keith climbing down into position behind Liz, aligning his massive cock so that the tip is pressed tightly against my rim of my wife's puckered asshole.

Liz looks back over her shoulder, wild with lust, and then hisses through her clenched teeth, "Shove it in there! I need you in my asshole right now!"

Keith thrusts forward, but my wife's tightness is unforgiving and refuses to give way to Keith's enormous cock. He grunts loudly and repositions himself, then tries again. Keith goes slower now, but his movement is much more firm and direct.

My wife yelps loudly as her asshole finally gives in to the pressure, expanding as far as it can go and enveloping Keith's giant dick. Liz grips onto me tightly, bracing herself against my body as expressions of pain and pleasure begin to cycle through her face. She seems confused by her own feelings, trying to grapple with this entirely new sensation until eventually she starts to warm up to the movements and a greedy smile crosses her lips.

Keith and I are pumping back and forth within my wife's tightness now, pounding her ass and pussy in tandem with our dual cock invasion as she trembles between us. Liz is filled to the brim with cock, pulled tight inside and out as we pulse together, moving slowly at first and then gaining speed. Before long, Keith and I are ramming into Liz with everything that we've got.

My wife reaches down between us and starts to frantically play with her clit, the trembling that courses through her body growing stronger and stronger until finally she throws her head back and let's out a howl that echoes throughout the park. I can feel her stomach clench tight as an orgasm hits her. All the while, Keith and I never let up with our brutal double fuck.

"Oh my god." Liz cries. "I'm cumming so hard! Don't stop!"

My wife's body is convulsing now between us, simply unable to withstand the onslaught of pleasure that flows though her in a rhythmic series of powerful waves.

Finally, Liz collapses between us. I fully expect her to be finished, her body completely spent after being so thoroughly fucked by massive cocks, but Liz has other plans.

Immediately, she pushes Keith away, groaning loudly as his cock slips out of her now reamed asshole.

"Give me that racket." My wife commands.

Keith does as he's told, handing Liz a nearby tennis racket and then the next thing I know, Liz is positioning the handle at the entrance of her tight back door.

"You want to see how slutty I can get out here on the tennis court?" She asks me playfully.

"Show me." I beg.

Liz pushes the tennis racket up into her asshole, the handle stretching her tightness as it plunges deep inside. Meanwhile, Keith has maneuvered himself around to the front of us. As my wife screams out in pleasure, Keith takes her by the head and then shove's his huge cock into Liz's mouth, cutting her off and turning her screams into a strangled gargle.

My wife pumps the racket handle in and out of her to the rhythm of my dick, continuing the double penetration that we had already been so greedily enjoying. I can feel the movement of the handle as it slides in and out next to me, separated only by a thin layer of membrane.

Now plugged in every hole, Liz is crying out like a wild animal, unable to contain her desires within her small frame. I'm losing control as well, just about ready to cum when suddenly Keith beats me to it, pulling out of Liz's mouth and ejecting a hot blast of spunk right across her face. He moans loudly, leaning back with his eyes shut tight as pump after pump of jizz covers my wife above me.

The sight of her with another man's seed all over her is more than enough to push me over the edge as well, and almost immediately I'm blowing my load up inside of her, filling her pussy with my milky white cum. I push deep within her and hold tight, reveling in the sensation as I lose my entire load. There's so much semen that my wife quickly runs out of room, the jizz spurting out from the sides of her tightness and running down her legs onto me.

"Fuck!" I cry out, bracing myself against the torrent of overwhelming pleasure until it finally passes.

I collapse back onto the court and Liz stands up, pulling the racket from her ass with a smile. The three of us are completely dazed and confused, struggling now to collect our wits after such and intense encounter.

From the edge of the court, we suddenly hear clapping.

I look up to see two very fit men standing nearby, smiles plastered across their faces as they applaud our performance. I'm too blissed out to be worried, but I'm still unsure of how this situation will unfold. After all, we are in a public park committing very vulgar acts.

"That looked fun." One of the guys calls over. "You play here often?"

Liz manages a smile. "Depends on what you mean by play."

The two guys exchange glances, and then look back at us. "I guess what we're asking is, do you have room for two more?"

Liz looks over at my cock, which is already hardening at the thought. "I think we can work something out." She calls back. "Who says tennis can't be a team sport?"

PIANO LESSONS

"I think I want to start playing an instrument." My wife, Jane, tells me. We're sitting in the breakfast nook of our apartment and she's focused hard on something online, staring intently at her laptop.

"Oh yeah?" I ask, slightly amused. I love my wife, but she's always going on about some new activity or another. It never lasts, and soon her attention will be elsewhere, but for the time being it looks like Jane wants to be in a band.

"Yeah, don't you think that would be fun?" She asks.

Jane is so excited that I can't help but smile. A beautiful blonde bombshell, my wife has been a constant source of joy in my life; she's fun, flirty, and most of all loyal. I really don't know what I would do without her.

Jane turns her computer so that I can see the screen, revealing a streaming video of some all girl rock band playing in a sold out venue. The place is packed with people who are all singing along at the top of their lungs.

"Oh yeah." I tell her with a nod, then take a long sip of my coffee as I watch her bright eyes bouncing back and forth across her screen. There's something truly admirable about Jane's enthusiasm for life, and I often wish that I could share it. However, I'm the realist in our relationship, and no matter how hard I try, I just can't overlook certain things.

"Isn't this amazing? I'm gonna be a musician!" Jane says happily.

"Well, don't get ahead of yourself now." I caution. "I mean, you need to take lessons first, right?"

166

Jane rolls her eyes. "Well, yeah."

I look back down at the video of the girls thrashing around violently on stage, a growing concern suddenly blossoming deep in the pit of my stomach. "So, what instrument are you going to play?"

Jane thinks for a moment. "Drums."

My reaction is immediate and visceral, but I try my best to hide it. "Those are pretty… loud." I tell her. "You really want to play the drums?"

"Yeah!" Jane confirms. "Wouldn't that be cool?"

She watches my face for a reaction and soon her expression slowly fades, morphing into one of concern and disappointment. "You don't think I could do it?" My wife asks.

"Oh baby, that's not it at all." I tell her. "I'm sure you'd be great at the drums. What about, like, the piano though?"

Jane's face is totally blank. She looks down at the video playing on her computer screen once again, then back up at me. "The piano?"

"Yeah, it's really soft and nice." I tell her.

"What the fuck are you talking about?" Jane responds, busting up laughing. "I want to rock."

Finally, I let it all come out, frustrated with the way this conversation is headed and trying to shut it down quick. "I'm gonna be honest with you, if you try to get a drum kit into this apartment I'm going to lose my mind. And besides, the neighbors would kill us."

My wife frowns, but doesn't say a word. Instead, she just gets up from her chair and heads out of the kitchen.

"Aw, come on!" I call after her, feeling like I just kicked the world's more adorable puppy. "Where are you going?"

"I just need to get ready for work." Jane tells me. "It's fine."

She leaves and I sit in silence for a moment, sipping my coffee and feeling like a massive jerk. In most cases, our personalities really balance each other out, in fact it's what makes our marriage work so damn well. Other times, though, I just feel like a giant grey cloud of realism here to rain on her happy little parade.

I take Jane's laptop and spin it towards me on the table, scanning my eyes down the long list of music lesson classifieds that are open in her second tab.

The drums are too loud, and guitar seems a little too expensive.

Finally, near the bottom I find an ad titled, "Piano lessons: price negotiable and beautiful grand piano provided."

I open the link and start writing an email.

As we drive up into the hills of San Francisco my wife doesn't know what to think, her eyes darting back and forth across the beautiful homes that only get nicer as we climb. I look over at her in the passenger seat and smile, the awkwardness of this morning a far and distant memory. Jane is back to her usual, excited self, and she's going to be even more excited when she sees what I've arranged for her.

"Can you give me a hint?" Jane asks, literally squirming in her seat with excitement.

I think for a moment, and then finally give up. "If I give you a hint then it's just going to give the whole thing away."

"Please?" My wife begs. "Just one?"

I let out a long sigh. "Okay, fine. It has something to do with our talk this morning."

Jane's eyes go wide and she immediately sits back, trying to contain herself.

My GPS instructs me to turn left into the nearest driveway, so I do it and immediately end up in front of a gorgeous, looming mansion unlike anything I've ever seen. We park in the roundabout and I turn back to Jane.

"Ready for your music lessons?" I ask.

"Drums!?" Jane shouts.

I immediately cringe as she says this, knowing that there is sure to be disappointment coming close behind. I was hoping to meet her halfway, but as I watch the excitement on Jane's face with the knowledge that I'm about to completely crush her joy, I wish I would've just gotten the fucking drum lessons instead.

"Actually." I say, trying to think of some way to spin this so it doesn't seem like such an utter failure on my part. I stammer for a moment and the eventually give up and just come out with it. "I got you piano lessons."

Jane seems totally confused at first, and then with her understanding comes a tragically forced smile. "Okay." She says awkwardly. "Thanks, Kyle."

We sit in silence for a moment as I reel from the realization of just how hard I've been blowing it lately. "Well, I'll be back in an hour to pick you up." I tell her. "Have fun."

Jane gives me one last strange glance and then steps out of the car. She looks up at the massive mansion, taking in its incredible size, and then starts making her way up the front walk.

Now alone in the car, I take a deep breath and try desperately to think of some way to turn this situation around. Jane and I have never really had any problems in our relationship, but recently our differences have become less and less charming. She's the greatest thing that's ever happened to me, and I'll be damned if I'm going to lose that to my own bizarre awkwardness.

I pull out of the driveway with a lot on my mind, ready to work it out on the road for a while. I promise myself that when I get back to pick her up, I'm going to have something for Jane that will make up for all of this, I just don't know what it is yet.

When I arrive back at the mansion Jane is still inside, but it only takes a few minutes for her to come bursting outside through the massive front door. She's as giggly as ever, a complete shift from her attitude from when I dropped her off.

"Thanks again!" My wife calls over her shoulder to the man who waves from the doorway.

When I see him, my heart almost stops. The guy is perfect, somehow boyishly handsome and utterly masculine at the same time. We make eye contact for a brief moment and he waves, then starts following Jane out to the car.

My wife hops in next to me and her piano teacher approaches my window, which I roll down.

"Hey there." The man says with a perfect smile. He extends his hand towards me. "I'm Brad."

"Kyle." I tell him, giving him a firm handshake. The guy is even more stunning in person, his welcoming face perfectly framed atop an impeccable physique.

"Your wife here is a natural talent." Brad tells me. "She's already way ahead of some students I've had here for years."

"Really?" I ask.

"Oh, absolutely." Brad continues gushing. "Anyway, I just wanted to introduce myself." He turns his attention to Jane. "Nice work today, I'll see you next week."

Jane smiles. "Can't wait!"

Brad heads back to the house and I sit for a moment, completely stunned by my wife's shift in attitude. It could very well be that she's honestly discovered a new love of tickling the ivories, but I'm fairly certain her enthusiasm is due to something else entirely.

"So you had fun?" I ask.

Jane is already staring out the window, completely lost in thought. She doesn't hear me until I repeat myself a second time.

"Oh sorry!" Jane says, turning to face me. "Yeah! I really liked it."

"Because I was thinking; we can switch you to the drums. I'll pay for it and everything." I inform her.

"No way!" Jane interjects. "I like this."

I can't help raising one eyebrow at her, unable to hide my curiosity as I start the car and pull back out onto the road.

"I think you just like Brad." I finally blurt.

Jane doesn't say a word. At first, I think she just didn't here me, but when I glance over, I see that I have her full attention and she's just desperately thinking of how to respond. "Why would you think that?" She asks, avoiding the question.

"Because he's a handsome guy." I tell her. "I mean, I'm handsome too, but that guy is pretty ridiculous."

Suddenly, Jane bursts out laughing. "Okay, yeah. Fine."

"You can't keep anything from me!" I say jokingly.

"I know, nor would I want to." She tells me. "Remember what we said when we first got married? We will always give each other total honesty."

"Total honesty." I repeat back.

Rows and rows of palm trees pass on either side as we make the descent back to our apartment on the other side of town. The sun has finally set, casting the entire scene with a beautiful purplish glow. I'm not sure if it's the scenery or the situation, but an unusual emotion is creeping over me as we drive. I'm a confident guy, so it's rare that a guy like this would get to me, but for some reason I actually find myself a little jealous of my wife's attraction to him. Even more surprisingly, I find myself kind of liking it in a weird way. Somewhere deep down inside of me, there is a compulsion to hear more about it.

"So did he hit on you or anything?" I ask, as nonchalantly as I can.

My wife bites her lip, a dead giveaway that I've struck some sort of chord.

"What did we just say about being honest?" I laugh, trying not to show how fast my heart is pounding. I nervously adjust my grip on the steering wheel.

Jane sighs. "I know. I just don't want you to get upset and quit paying for my lessons." She admits begrudgingly.

"I'm not going to get upset." I assure her, keeping my eyes on the road. My cock is swelling in my jeans now, something completely unexpected that I'm still trying to fully understand.

"Well," Jane starts. "We were having our lesson and at one point he put his hand over mine, and then I looked over at him and we…" She hesitates. "We kissed."

Her admission hits me like a punch to the gut and I'm immediately forced to pull over on the side of the road. I feel a swirling cocktail of emotions within me, from rage to jealousy to a deep strange lust.

"I'm so sorry." Jane tells me. "But that's all that happened, I swear. I told him that I had a boyfriend and he stopped."

Desperately trying to sort my thoughts, I find myself sifting deeper and deeper though the emotions that have been stacked onto my heart. The anger is fleeting, a shock to the system upon realizing that the woman I love could actually do this to me, but once the anger is gone only jealousy remains. The jealousy is easier to deal with, and as it consumes me I find myself slowly becoming accustomed to its aching weight. I let it wash over me and adapt to it, my cock continuing to swell larger until it feels like it's about to burst.

It's only then that I'm faced with a startling conclusion. I'm turned on by my wife's sordid indiscretions.

"Tell me again about how he kissed you." I suddenly ask.

"Baby, no." Jane tells me. "Why would you want that?"

"I just want to hear about it." I tell her.

Jane quickly realizes that something strange is going on, hesitating before she reaches across the center console and runs her hand along my leg. We lock eyes, as if checking in to make sure this bizarre situation was unfolding the right way, and after a moment I give her a slight nod.

Jane unzips my jeans and pulls out my throbbing member, causing me to throw my head back in ecstasy at the second her hand wraps tightly around my dick. Jane begins to pump her fingers slowly up and down on my shaft as she watches with lustful excitement, thrilled to be giving me such intense enjoyment, however unusual.

"Tell me about how you kissed him." I beg, not even understanding the situation myself, just going along with how I feel.

"Well, he leaned in," She starts, dropping her voice down to a seductive coo. "And pressed his lips against mine, and then he slipped his tongue into my mouth." Jane reveals, still jerking me off.

"More." I beg.

"I…" Jane stammers. "That's all that happened."

"I need more." I tell her again, my entire body trembling.

Jane keeps stroking but a confused look crosses her face. She loves the connection that we're having just as much as I do, but she doesn't have any idea where to take it. This is uncharted territory for the both of us.

Suddenly, Jane reaches for my phone and takes it in her hand. She hesitates for a moment, eyeing me with suspicion.

"Are you sure you want more?" Jane asks.

I nod. "Yes."

"How much more?" She prods.

By now I have a vague idea of what she's planning, and I'm fully aware that it could change our relationship, our marriage, forever. The lustful cravings that pump though my body, however, are much more powerful than any sort of solid logic at the moment.

Even more importantly, though, I owe her. For as much as I've been fucking things up between us, my wife deserves something truly special. "Just do it." I finally tell her.

Jane immediately flicks through the recent calls on my phone and dials a number. The phone begins to ring throughout the car speakers, connected wirelessly across the tense air that surrounds us.

"Hello, this is Brad." A voice suddenly booms through the stereo system.

"Hey there Brad." Jane coos, still keeping a good pace with her hand across my cock. "This is Jane. What are you up to?"

"Just about to make some dinner." He says. "Is everything alright?"

My wife hesitates for a moment, looking over at me for one last check in before changing our lives forever. She sees the aching look of desire on my face and then smiles.

"Everything's fine," My wife says. "I was just wondering if I could come back over there and fuck you silly while my husband watches, maybe even joins in."

There is silence on the other end of the line, and for a brief moment I suddenly think that we may have made a horribly embarrassing mistake. My heart is nearly pounding out of my chest as we wait for his response.

"Yeah." Brad finally says. "Come on back, I think I can help you out."

As we walk through the doors of his huge mansion, Brad is already ready and waiting for us. He's sitting at the piano bench in a vast living room where the lights have been dimmed.

"Are you ready for your lesson?" He asks with a devilish smile.

"I'm ready." My wife tells him.

Brad laughs. "No, him." He says, pointing at me. "I'm going to teach you how to fuck your wife just right."

The rage that boils within me could not longer even be considered anger at this point, churning and mutating into something weirdly pleasant and aching that fills my body. Every word of dominance that Brad speaks sends a sensual chill down my spine. Never in my wildest dreams would I ever have thought I'd end up in this position, but right now I want nothing more than to watch this man fuck my wife, and fuck her good.

I sit down on a nearby couch and then nod to Jane, who approaches Brad. Brad leans back against the piano and unzips his pants, unsheathing an absolutely enormous cock that juts out towards my wife's face as she crouches before him. My chest is tight as I watch them, bracing myself for the inevitable feelings that will wash over me when my wife finally takes him into her mouth.

Jane looks back at me over her shoulder. "Do you want to watch me suck off this huge cock?" She asks.

I don't even hesitate. "I do."

Jane smiles, then opens wide and swallows Brad's length. She pushes down as far as she can across his shaft, relaxing her gag reflex and taking him in a skillful deep throat. Soon enough my, wife's face is pressed hard against Brad's stomach, and Brad immediately removes his shirt to show of his incredible muscular body.

Jane holds here for a moment, with Brad's balls resting firmly against her chin, then finally pulls back and takes in a huge gasp of air. She looks absolutely maniacal now, a lust in her eyes that I haven't seen in years.

With Brad's hands planted firmly on the back of her head, Jane immediately gets to work pumping her wet lips up and down his rod at a rapid pace, trembling with excitement. Soon I see her reach down and unbutton her skirt, then slip her fingers within. She starts to play with herself, moaning into the flesh of Brad's cock while she sucks him off.

I look down and suddenly realize that I've been stroking myself this whole time, as well, a movement that seemed so natural in the situation that I didn't even notice it was happening. My cock is hard to the point of hurting, but the pleasure that I feel as I pump my hand slowly up and down it is unlike anything I've ever experienced.

Suddenly, my wife pulls Brad out of her mouth and looks up at him with her pleading eyes. "Your cock is perfect." She tells him. "But I want more."

"Are you a hungry little slut?" Brad asks, dominating her right in front of me.

"I'm so hungry for cock." My wife tells him.

Brad looks over at me. "Get over here and let's show her what we can do." He commands.

I immediately stand up and walk over to them, stripping off my clothes as I go. Soon we are all stripped down completely, with the exception of my wife who happened to be wearing a lacy black lingerie set beneath her clothes. She removes her panties but leaves the rest on, showing off the fantastic way that it frames her body.

I kiss my wife deeply on the mouth and then moments later Brad springs into action, pulling out the piano bench and guiding her away from me. Without a word, Brad pushes Jane down so that she's laying across the bench, then begins to align his cock with the tight, wet slit of her pussy.

"Oh my god, shove it in!" Jane demands, looking back over her shoulder at Brad with that crazy look in her eyes. "And you!" She turns, looking at me. "Get over here and slam that dick of yours into my throat."

I don't need to be told twice, climbing around to the other side of the bench and then kneeling down before her. I place my rock hard shaft against her soft lips just as Brad pushes forward from the other end, impaling Jane onto his massive dick.

"Fuck!" My wife moans, reeling from Brad's substantial girth as he pushes into her and holds deep.

"You like that?" Brad demands to know, slapping Jane hard on the ass.

My wife doesn't get a chance to answer however, as she greedily opens up and swallows my rod.

I lean back and let out a long, satisfied moan as Jane goes to work on me, tracing her lips up and down along my hard shaft. Her movements are strong and slow, propelled forward onto me by every slam that Brad makes against her backside.

Eventually, though, the three of us begin to speed up, finding a rhythm together as me and this other man rail Jane from either end. My wife groans and whimpers onto my cock, her sounds coming out as a muffled gargle while Brad pounds her perfectly. I can feel Jane trembling between us, her body trying desperately to handle the sensations that consume her. She is gripping tight against the piano bench beneath her, frantically trying not to lose control of herself during this overwhelming cockfight that she's hosting within her body.

Seeing another man give Jane this much pleasure is something that I'm still getting used to, but by now the anger and jealousy has all slipped away into something more primal. I find myself helpless against the incredible lustful insanity that drives me to push this farther and farther; to watch my wife in even more depraved, slutty situations.

Suddenly, inspiration strikes, and there's no turning back now.

I pull my cock out of Jane's beautiful mouth and then lie down onto the floor next to the piano, my dick jutting out stiffly from my body.

"Come fuck me." I command.

Jane does as she's told, rising up from the bench and climbing down onto the living room floor. She opens her legs and throws them over my toned abs, reaching down and grabbing my cock as she positions me for entry. Once she's all lined up, Jane begins to lower herself slowly down onto my rod, letting my cock slide up into her tightly toned body while she bites her lip playfully.

"God damn, that feels so fucking good." Jane whimpers, rocking her hips slowly across me in a long powerful swoop, followed by another and another until eventually she's fucking me at a confident pace. I reach back and grab my wife's perfect ass with each hand, taking her cheeks and spreading them open so that Brad can see everything.

Brad knows exactly where I'm headed with this, and moments later he's crouching into position behind Jane, his massive cock poised and ready.

My wife feels Brad grab onto her hips and turns around abruptly, confused by the arrangement of our bodies until she senses Brad place the head of his shaft up against her tightly puckered asshole.

"Two at the same time?" Jane groans, an air of frantic concern in her voice. "I don't know if I can take it."

"You can take it." I tell her.

Jane looks back down at me and our eyes meet for a brief moment of marital encouragement. My wife smiles, "Yeah, I can take it." She repeats.

Brad pushes forward and Jane's expression immediately changes, contorting before me as her rectum is stretched wide. She struggles to accommodate Brad's giant member.

"Holy fuck!" Jane shouts, a long shudder coursing down the entire length of her body. "Holy…" She starts to repeat herself and then stops, her eyes rolling back into her head with ecstasy.

I can feel Brad pumping in and out of my wife right next to me, our members dueling back and forth within her body. Everything is super tight, filled to the max by our rods as we slowly gain speed.

Soon enough, Brad and I are absolutely pummeling Jane, hammering into her with everything we have in a brutal double penetration. My wife is screaming now, her feelings vocalized into a twisted howl of pain and pleasure that eventually melts away into something wholly indescribable. She reaches down between her legs and starts to frantically play with her clit as her eyes roll back into her head.

"I'm gonna cum." My wife starts to moan. "Oh my god, your two big dicks are gonna make me cum so hard."

Jane's trembling has become a full on quake, her body spasming between us as Brad and me continue to pound her. We don't let up for a second, taking her to the edge of orgasm and then flying off into oblivion. Jane screams and suddenly throws herself forward onto me, clenching tight as wave after wave of sexual bliss pulses through her body. Tears stream down her face as she shakes, the sensations simply unable to contain themselves within her small frame.

I hold Jane tight until the trembling stops and Jane rolls off of me onto the floor. She looks utterly beside herself, fucked silly and swimming in a cock drunk haze.

"Cum on me." Jane commands. "Cover me with those hot white loads."

Me and Brad immediately get into position on either side of my wife, kneeling so that our cocks are aimed and ready at her beautiful young face. Jane looks up at us and giggles playfully while we beat off above her.

It doesn't take long for Brad to explode, ejecting a hot rope of milky white semen across my wife's open mouth. She catches as much as she can while the rest of it splatters across either side of her face, running down her cheeks in long, beautiful trails of spunk.

The sight of Jane wearing another man's seed so proudly is more than enough to push me over the edge, and almost immediately I'm cumming as well. It hit's me hard and I buckle forward slightly, gritting my teeth as the onslaught of sensation overwhelms me.

"Fuck!" I cry out as my jizz blasts across Jane's lips, mixing with the load that came before it.

She gives me a wink and then proceeds to suck the rest of my spunk out of me, finishing off with a gleeful swallow. I fall back onto the bench, exhausted.

It's hard to look back and remember what things were like before our first encounter with Brad; to live out our ordinary lives of monogamous sexual fun. Don't get me wrong, Jane and I had some fantastic times, but once you know the pleasure of sharing your wife with another man, there's no turning back.

It's safe to say that we both started to learn a little something from Brad's lessons.

We're back in the breakfast nook one morning when Jane turns to me with a devilish twinkle in her eye.

"What is it?" I ask, before she can even say a word.

"Well…" Jane starts. "Me and Brad we talking about how well I'm doing with music."

I nod. It's the truth, my wife as become quite the piano player, not to mention her anal skills are through the roof. I couldn't be happier.

"What did he say?" I ask.

"He thinks that I could easily switch over to guitar if I wanted, or even drums, finally."

I roll my eyes. "Not drums."

Jane smiles. "Well, how about he just invites the whole band over for my next lesson and you can… watch." She coos. "See if you like it."

A smile slowly crosses my face. "Maybe I can get into the drum lessons after all."

LIFEGUARD ON DUTY

My wife is every guy's fantasy, and I'm lucky to have her. I know that it's my job as her husband to say that type of thing every once in a while, to talk her up and let the world know what it's like to have such an incredible woman in my life. That's all well and good, and it's the truth, but I'm also not just saying that for the sake of saying it.

There are quite a few archetypical fantasies to go around in the brain of your average American man. The naughty schoolgirl, the slutty secretary, the bimbo cheerleader; but nothing seems to quite hit the spot for erotic arousal like a busty blonde lifeguard.

My wife, Rachel, plays this role perfectly. In her tight red bikini swimsuit, she spends her days running up and down the beach helping the fine people of Santa Monica not die in the undertow. Of course, I'm oversimplifying. Every once in a while there is a rescue, but for the most part she seems to find herself relaxing at the lookout station, leaning back into her wooden chair with shades on as she scans the water for a waving hand of distress.

Rachel's body may be relaxed during this time, but I know for a fact that her mind is focused, sharp-as-a-tack and ready the spring into action should the need ever arise. During these moments the absolute worst thing I could do would be to stop by and say hello to her, interrupting her intense train of thought when she's hard at work guarding lives.

It's hard not to go check in on such an incredible beauty, but I do my best. Our apartment is near the water, just a few block down from her lifeguard post, but when I find myself walking by I rarely do more than throw over a friendly wave. She's busy; I get it.

We both work a lot though, so there is plenty of mutual understanding in our relationship when it comes to being professional. While I'm slaving away in my office on 3rd street, she's down by the water taking in the rays, but we're both working our asses off and when we finally come home after a long day, there is nothing but chemistry between us. I couldn't be happier.

It's a perfect marriage, and after two years of this partnership I have no doubt that we are in for plenty more; until today.

"What do you mean you're feeling constricted?" I ask, trying to hide the desperation in my voice. "I barely get to see you these days."

Rachel looks across the table at me without a hint of dismissal or anger, just solemn confusion. She doesn't seem to know what she's saying either, just somehow feels like it needs to be said. "I just have this emotion." My wife tries to explain. "It's like…" She trails off, looking out towards the water from our table on the restaurant's patio.

"It's like what?" I question.

We sit in silence for a moment, looking out from our spot in the shade at the bustling beach crowds, happy people completely oblivious of our blindsiding marital woes. I have a deep sinking feeling at the pit of my stomach, an anxious gnawing that I never expected to feel in regards to my loving wife.

"There's nothing really… wrong." Rachel explains to me. "I mean, I'm so happy."

"I'm happy, too." I tell her, looking deep into those beautiful blue eyes. I believe what she's saying, she's honestly just as in-the-dark about this as I am.

"But, something is missing." Rachel says.

I shake my head in complete confusion, simply unable to comprehend this situation as it unrolls before me. I was expecting a pleasant lunch on the boardwalk with my wife, and now the whole thing has devolved into this; and I don't even know what *this* is.

"Are we breaking up?" I finally ask, bluntly.

Rachel looks at me for a moment, as if scanning my face to see if I'm joking. When she realizes that I'm not her entire expression changes. "Oh my god, Ken! What?" She shouts, almost laughing. "No!"

A wave of relief washes over me almost immediately, taking all of the anxiety with it. Whatever this is about, Rachel and me can work through it.

My wife shakes her head and puts her hand over mine. "I love you, baby."

"I love you, too." I tell her.

Rachel lets out a long sigh. "I really don't know what it is, but I need to get back to work. Can we talk about this later?"

I laugh. "Do I have a choice?"

My wife flashes a half smile. "I'm sorry, I'll make it up to you."

She stands up and gives me a quick kiss goodbye, then hurries off. Back down the beach my wife goes, disappearing into the crowd as I look on with a forlorn expression of anxious fear.

I pick at my food for a moment longer and then finally stand up. Thankfully, I don't have to work today, but I need to get my feet moving because there's a lot on my mind and the longer I sit, the heavier it gets.

Instead of heading back to the apartment I decide to take a long stroll down the boardwalk and blow off some steam. I have so many questions and thoughts swimming around in my head that I don't even know where to begin with pulling them apart. Does Rachel plan on leaving me? Have I let myself go? What's happening with us?

I look down and place my hand on my stomach, making sure that my toned abs are still there and then sighing with relief. By all appearances, I'm just has handsome as I always was, and there's no reason for Rachel to be losing interest physically.

I make my way down from the restaurant in a slow saunter, taking my time and checking in with all of the booths that line the long strip of cement before me. There are all sorts of venders; people selling home made incense, carved works of art and various items of bold jewelry. I'm a little clean cut to be shopping amongst the stalls here and they know it, basically ignoring me until I finally reach the end of the line.

"Hey there!" A fresh-faced young woman, just barely out of college says to me. She smiles sweetly as she approaches, holding out a candle for me to smell.

I lean in and take a long inhale of its pleasant scent. "Oh whoa, that's really nice." I offer. "Did you make these?"

She nods. "All of these candles are hand dipped by me."

There is something about this girl that I find incredibly alluring. She couldn't be any farther from my type; a sweet little pixie with curly brown hair who clearly has more than a few magic crystals and dream catchers in her apartment, but I rarely get a chance to flirt with someone like her and the variety is intoxicating. I would never actually cheat on my wife, and certainly don't see myself ever loving another woman like I love Rachel, but the excitement is still there.

"How much are they?" I ask.

The hippy girl laughs. "For you? Ten bucks a piece."

I reel at hearing the price. "That's the cool guy cost?" I ask. "What do they run when you *don't* like me?"

The girl eyes me up and down, biting her lip slightly. "The same. I just know this isn't for you. You're handsome enough to take it for free, but I know that you're buying it for a girlfriend."

"Wife." I correct her.

The girl's eyes go wide. "Well, that's just a shame isn't it."

My heart is racing a mile a minute now, blood pumping desperately out across my body in response to the blossoming arousal. It suddenly hits me that, regardless of how much I love my wife, I've missed this kind of back and forth banter. Love is incredible, and certainly can't be replaced by something as fleeting as the rush from a flirtatious hippy girl, but that doesn't mean there's not a time and a place for this.

I suddenly realize what I've got to do.

"It really is a shame." I tell her, putting the candle back down with a smile. "Thank you."

Immediately, I turn and start heading back down the boardwalk towards my wife's lifeguard outpost.

When I arrive, Rachel is not as excited to see me as I would have hoped.

"What are you doing here?" She asks, pulling off her shades as I climb up the wooden tower in the sand.

"I have the best idea!" I blurt. "I've been thinking about what we talked about."

Suddenly, an incredibly muscular, tan guy emerges from inside the outpost. He's got short cropped hair and an amazingly handsome face.

"Hey, what are you doing up here?" The male lifeguard asks, then immediately turns to Rachel before I can answer. "Is this guy bothering you?"

I almost bust up laughing right then and there, but Rachel handles the situation quite nicely with a look of utter shock.

"Bret, this is my husband." My wife explains. "Ken, this is Bret."

I reach out and we shake hands firmly.

"Sorry about that." Bret says, only slightly embarrassed and somehow just as skeptical as ever. The two of us eye each other like wild animals invading one another's pride.

After an awkward moment of silence my wife suddenly interjects again. "Like I was saying, you can't be up here, Ken, we're working."

I start to say something and then stop myself, realizing that she's absolutely right, and the longer I'm here with my crazy relationship ideas the more Rachel's just going to get annoyed with me.

Besides, I can see that the proposition of allowing her to flirt freely isn't even close to the kind of strong sexual intervention that we need in our life. She's already taking care of that on her own.

As I climb back down the latter of the lifeguard tower and can hear Rachel and Ken talking in hushed voices, giggling and laughing at some inside joke that I wouldn't understand. She is already flirting as much as she'd like, which is just fine with me, but bringing it up isn't going to do anything for our relationship.

Walking back across the sand, however, I find my mind racing with all sorts of crazy ideas, starting innocently enough but slowly becoming more and more depraved as I go. Strangely, the more depraved my thoughts become, the more aroused they make me.

What if I let my wife make out with another man while I watch? Or what if she gives him a blowjob?

The thought makes me queasy at first, but the longer I sit with it, the more it starts to change and morph within my mind, becoming something else entirely; something arousing. My cock already rock hard in my shorts, I take it a step farther and imagine what it would be like to allow Rachel one night with another man. I picture her small, beautiful frame bouncing up and down on Bret's massive shaft, his cock impaling her perfectly as she sucks me off at the same time.

Never in a million years could I have predicted that the thought of sharing my loving wife would get me so worked up, but right now it's all that I can think about. It could also be the solution to all of our problems.

Bret's shift ends a little before Rachel, who has to stick around at her outpost until sunset. I watch from afar as the two of them part, sharing a hug that lasts only slightly too long to be entirely friendly.

I'm waiting on the sidewalk when Bret finally reaches me, and he looks up with an expression of slightly confused recognition.

"Hey!" He says. "Ken, right?"

I nod. "That's right."

"What's up, man?" He asks, a slight glimmer of fear lurking somewhere deep within his eyes. It suddenly hits me that he probably expects me to punch him out at this point, driven mad by his casual flirtation with my wife. Bret couldn't be any more incorrect, however.

"I wanted to talk to you about something." I explain, finding a spot on a nearby bench. "You got a minute?"

Bret nods and sits down next to me.

"Baby! I'm home!" My wife calls out as she pushes through the door of our apartment. "Listen, I'm so sorry about today, I know things got weird and that's my fault, not yours."

Rachel, still in nothing but her red swimsuit, strolls casually around the corner of the living room and then stops abruptly, a look of utter shock and amazement plastered across her face.

Bret and I are waiting for her, totally nude and gladly showing off our tan, muscular bodies. We're standing at attention in the center of the living room, waiting with our cocks semi-hard and quickly swelling at the appearance of my beautiful blonde wife.

"I forgive you." I tell her with a smile.

"What's happening?" Rachel asks, both confused and excited by our appearance. She seems completely flustered, almost driven to glance away from the sight of our massive and quickly growing cocks.

"I think I know what's been going on with us." I explain. "I know that we love each other, but we need variety in our lives. Sometimes it's okay to have a little fun."

Rachel is frozen now, her mind racing with all of the possible meanings that I could be getting at. "What kind of fun?" She asks, still not capable of believing the obvious.

"In the bedroom." I tell her. "Or even out here in the living room."

I'm trembling now, unable to control the powerful lust that flows through me. Even though I've had plenty of time to prepare for this moment, I still can't quite believe that I'm standing here about to treat my wife to another man. If we follow through with this, then moments from now Rachel will have Bret's cock inside of her, pleasuring her in a brand new way. I take a deep breath and try to calm myself, preparing for what comes next.

"Do you want me and Bret to fuck you?" I ask her plainly.

Rachel is beside herself, trying to find the words but failing.

"Are you sure that's okay with you?" She finally asks, stumbling over her words.

"Do I look like I'm okay with it?" I counter, my cock throbbing with anticipation as I stand before her, completely exposed.

Rachel closes her eyes and then opens them again, as if checking to see if she's dreaming.

Finally, Bret speaks. "Get over here." He commands. "I know you want this."

Slowly, my wife begins to step towards us, her gorgeous body looking toned and sleek under the red swimsuit. Eventually, Rachel is standing right between Bret and me, her chest heaving with excitement.

"You're sure?" She asks me again, looking deep into my eyes for any signs of doubt.

"Yes." I say, my voice trembling slightly. "I'm sure."

My wife kisses me hard, with more passion than I've felt in a very long time. The two of us embrace for a moment and then she pulls away, turning her attention towards Bret. She reaches up and, with a hand on his cheek, kisses him deeply as well.

I look on in awe as their bodies begin to press into each other, my wife's hands wandering slowly down Bret's ripped stomach until they finally reach his mammoth dick. Moments later, Rachel is stroking him off with a series of long, firm movements, her fingers wrapped tightly around this other man's aching shaft.

I suddenly feel as though I'm going to pass out, not nearly prepared for what the sight of another man with my wife was going to do to me. I'm about to lose my balance when suddenly I feel Rachel's other hand close around my cock and start to stroke, which instantly brings me back into the moment.

My wife gradually lowers herself down into a squat between us, looking up with her big blue eyes as her strokes become faster and faster. As her pace quickens she seems to become more and more aroused, eventually entering a state of completely cock-drunk abandon.

"God dammit, I want you both so bad." Rachel growls.

I close my eyes and lean my head back, reeling from the sensation of her firm grip as, suddenly, the sensation changes. I look down to see my wife frantically sucking me off. Her head bobs up and down across my shaft, lips running in tight pulses over the head of my cock.

"Oh fuck." I moan, placing my hands behind my wife's head and helping to guide her up and down.

Meanwhile, Rachel is still beating off Bret to the side, but after a moment she turns her attention to him completely, releasing me from her depths and then engulfing Bret's cock with her mouth.

Instead of pumping up and down, however, Rachel continues to push herself deeper and deeper over Bret's enormous rod. I watch as she struggles to take this other man past her gag reflex, her body rejecting his substantial length as she gives up, pulling back and gasping for air.

"Come on, baby!" I coax in lustful support. "You've got this."

My wife glances at me and gives a playful wink, then tries again. This time she relaxes even more, taking Bret's shaft down her throat slowly and carefully. There are no problems as his dick reaches, and then passes, her gag reflex. Rachel pushes further until eventually her face is pressed firmly against Bret's toned stomach.

Bret let's out a long satisfied moan, holding my wife there for a moment while he enjoys the feeling of being fully inside of her neck. His balls resting against her chin, Brit begins to pump ever so slightly in and out of her depths, before eventually pulling her back up.

Rachel let's out an even bigger gasp than before, trying desperately to get some air into her lungs. She's not at all displeased however, and clearly enjoys the rough treatment that Bret is giving her.

After a good while of moving back and forth between our cocks, Rachel finally grabs the coffee table and pulls it out into the middle of the living room. She immediately lies down flat across it with her ass in the air, then reaches back and pulls the bottom of her red swimsuit to the side.

"Fuck me!" My wife demands. "Slam this tight little pussy right now and don't stop until I tell you to!"

Bret doesn't have to be told twice, and immediately squats down into position behind her. My wife glances up at me with a devilish look in her eye, enjoying herself even more than she ever imagined was possible.

I watch in a trance as Bret aligns his tight rod with the entrance of my darling wife's slick pussy, the muscles of his arms rippling while he positions himself at just the right angle, and then pushes forward.

Rachel grips the coffee table tightly and braces herself against Bret, moaning loudly as he enters her. His cock is absolutely massive, and I can tell that Rachel is just barely able to handle his girth as the large man begins to pump slowly.

"Fuck, that's a tight little pussy!" Bret offers, then looks up at me. "You're a lucky guy."

"You're both lucky!" My wife interrupts. "Now fuck me from each end like the dirty slut that I am!"

I immediately kneel down at the other end of the coffee table and soon enough my wife has been granted her wish. I push my cock between her lips and immediately get to work pulsing back against the movements of Bret. Together, we quickly gain speed within Rachel, ramming her hard enough to shake the table loudly. My wife is trembling with pleasure between us, her body unable to contain the sensation of having two men slamming her at the same time. Soon she begins to groan with ecstasy, her cries vibrating against the swollen flesh of my hard cock as it stays firmly planted within her mouth.

It's hard for me not to think about how innocent I once saw her, the way that Rachel looked on our wedding day or when we wake up in each other's arms. Clearly, she's not as innocent as I once thought, but the juxtaposition of these memories with the hedonistic display before me is so sexy that it's hard to keep myself from just blowing my load right then and there.

We slam my wife like this for a while as her shudders of pleasure grow larger and larger, until suddenly Rachel pushes us away and desperately stands up from the coffee table. She quickly strips off her swimsuit and then, in a stammer of desperation, she demands, "I need you both inside of me. My ass and pussy need your fucking dicks."

"Double penetration?" I ask, exchanging excited glances with Bret. Even now, my wife still continues to surprise me.

"You fucking heard me." Rachel confirms.

Almost immediately, she jumps up onto me, almost knocking me over.

I stumble back and then catch myself, hoisting my wife up as she wraps her long slender legs around my waist. I lift Rachel up and then position her directly above my cock, which juts off from my body towards her tightness.

"Fuck me!" Rachel commands.

I immediately drop my wife down and impale her tiny frame onto my cock, causing her to howl with lustful excitement. I begin to pump Rachel across my rod, using the power of gravity to raise and lower her over my entire length. Every thrust is as deep as it can get, taking her completely to the hilt of my sturdy flesh post.

"More!" Rachel commands like a spoiled little brat. "Give me more cock now!"

Bret steps up behind my wife and I raise her up for a moment, letting this other man place his huge dick against the tight entrance of her puckered back door.

"Do you want this dick up your fucking ass?" Bret demands to know.

"Yes!" My wife cries out, her encouragement of another lover sending a sharp chill of arousal down my spine. "Double fuck me!"

I lower her slowly over Bret's cock, appreciating the way that I can feel his enormous member pulling my wife taut against me from the inside. Her ass is struggling to take him, but eventually she manages to relax and let Bret's dick slip right up inside next to me, our cocks separated only by a thin membrane within.

"Holy shit!" Rachel groans, repeating the words over and over again as me and Bret lift her up and down over out double barreled cock insertion.

As before, we start slow, letting Rachel become accustomed to the overwhelming sensation of being stretched by two dicks at once, but eventually our animalistic lust becomes too much to contain and we speed up drastically, hammering my wife down onto our cocks at an increasingly rapid speed.

Soon, Bret and I are railing Rachel with everything that we've got, pounding up into her sweet tightness like two jackhammers as she screams with bliss. Rachel is quaking wildly, her legs kicked out straight to either side of me, which I immediately recognize as a sign of impending orgasm.

"I'm gonna cum!" My wife starts to chant, confirming my suspicions. Rachel reaches down between her legs and frantically plays with her clit, her eyes closed tight and her teeth clenched as the pressure builds and builds and then finally releases. My wife throws her head back and let's out a guttural howl, her entire body clenching and spasming in wild fits of pleasure.

All the while, Bret and I don't even let up for a moment, continuing to give my wife everything that we've got. It's not long before the two of us are ready to blow as well, and, as soon as my wife comes down from her heavenly sexual trance, we lower her onto the ground where she kneels happily between us.

"Give me those fucking loads." My wife begs as we beat our cocks frantically above her smiling face. She reaches over and rubs our balls with each hand, trying to coax us along until eventually Bret and I are exploding across her beautiful face.

We cum all over my wife's face almost simultaneously, the jizz mixing together as it splatters in beautiful patterns on her tan skin and then runs down her cheeks in milky white streaks. Rachel licks the spunk from her lips playfully and gives us a little wink.

"I think you're right about this helping out our relationship!" My wife offers to me cheerfully, another mans cum still dangling from her chin. "Looks like you're the real life saver here after all."

TEAMMATES

It's hard not to worry about the ones that you love. You trust them, and you give them space, but every once in a while they'll get in a little over there head and there's not a lot you can say about the matter.

When my wife wanted to join the community football league, this is exactly how I felt.

"I'm sorry, what?" I ask her, stunned as we sit next to one another on the living room couch, the big game on mute in the background.

"Yeah, I was thinking about joining." My wife, Nora, says. "It looks fun."

I glance back at the screen and see the quarterback suddenly obliterated by a tackle, the ball flying from his grasp as he smashes to the ground under two equally massive men.

"Don't you think that's a little dangerous?" I ask her.

Nora scoffs, definitely trying to prove a point. "What? Because I'm a woman?"

"No, I'm not saying that." I protest. "I mean… kinda. You never even liked football before this."

"What are you talking about? I watch the game with you all the time!" She tells me. "Don't you think it would be fun to see me play in one?"

I eye my wife suspiciously. The funny thing is, for as strange as all of this seems it's completely within the normal realm of her personality. Nora is a wild child, always finding something new to get excited about, but unlike most people, she actually follows through with it.

Last year we watched a documentary about Spain, and the next thing I knew my wife was planning a trip for us. We went, and it ended up being an amazing time that I'll never forget.

However, playing football sounds like there is a massive medical bill lurking somewhere in our not-so-distant future.

"Do they even have a women's league?" I ask. I know the community group that she's talking about because I've seen them in the park down the street, but for the life of me I don't think I've ever seen a woman playing.

"They don't actually have a women's league." Nora explains. "It's co-ed."

I look back at the screen, noting the difference in size between these massive, muscular men and my tiny little wife.

"Oh my god, Luke!" Nora finally cries out. "Stop worrying! I'll be fine."

I try my best to accept her assertion, to trust her now like I've trusted her before and just let this thing play out how it's going to. It's not like she's joining the professional league, after all; these are just some dude's in the park. Besides, maybe this is the one time that she actually doesn't follow through with her grand idea.

"Practice is in a half hour!" Nora shouts as she bursts through the front door, a yellow sheet of paper in her hand. "Gotta run!"

"What's that?" I ask, walking in from the kitchen to meet her.

"Medical waver!" Nora responds, giving me a quick kiss and then rushing past me towards our bedroom to get changed. "It's so I can't sue them if I get hurt!" She shouts from the other room.

"You mean *when* you get hurt." I mutter under my breath, shaking my head.

Seconds later, Nora comes back out wearing her usual workout gear.

After all these years I'm still blown away by the sight of her toned body, an absolutely perfect example of the female form. I still don't know what I did to deserve Nora, but I'm thankful every day to wake up with her next to me in my bed.

"Quit staring." My wife tells me, laughing as she breaks my concentration.

"I'm sorry. You're beautiful." I explain. "Don't you need pads and stuff?"

"They're got them down at the park." Nora explains, already headed for the door. "You coming or what?"

I had just started to make dinner but it can wait. Now that I've accepted the fact that my darling wife is going to put her ass on the line like this, my fear and apprehension has blossomed into a strange curiosity. Maybe she'll actually be pretty good. After all, Nora was a track star back in college. If we're lucky she'll run fast enough to never actually get tackled.

"Yeah, sure." I say, grabbing my coat and heading out the door behind her. "Let's go."

It's a quick drive down to the park and as we cruise Nora and me catch up on our time apart from one another today. She's stressed from work, feeling like she could use come kind of release from the daily grind. It's been a while since we've been able to take a vacation together, and it sounds like that's really getting to her. The more that I hear from my wife, the more I start to think that this whole football thing might actually be on okay idea. It's great stress relief, as long as she doesn't break an arm.

We pull into the gravel parking lot and Nora hops out immediately, grabbing her things and running across the grass to meet her team. They greet her warmly, one of the men passing over some pads, a helmet and a uniform.

There is a small restroom at the park with showers and a changing room, so Nora excuses herself and heads inside to get ready. In no time at all she emerges in full uniform, running out to huddle up with the team before the game starts.

I find myself a place on a set of relatively empty metal bleachers.

"Alright!" I shout excitedly, "Let's do this!"

Suddenly, Nora's team is taking the field and my anxiety blossoms into an uncontrollable tension across my entire body. I really don't want my wife to get hurt.

A few minutes later the ball is snapped. Nora is sprinting down the field as fast as she can, whipping past other players as the quarterback looks for an opening. He fakes to the left and then immediately switches directions, hurling the ball an incredible distance across the open field towards my wife.

My breath catches in my throat as the ball rotates perfectly through the air. The moment seems like it lasts forever until suddenly Nora is reaching out her arms as far as she can, leaping upwards while she runs and snagging the football from the air.

I literally burst up out of my seat, screaming for her to run as my wife continues down the grassy expanse and then, a few tense seconds later, scores a touchdown. Her very first play, and this is what happens. Maybe Nora's a natural after all.

The rest of the game plays out much like this, with my wife running several successful plays and their team dominating for a win of twenty-eight to nothing. By the end, she's earned her team's respect and admiration, and I'm proud of her.

Nora pulls off her helmet as she runs over to me on the sidelines, her long dark hair sticking to her head.

"That what amazing!" I shout, "Good job, baby!"

"Thanks." She says with a smile, panting.

"Are you ready to roll?" I ask, already starting to lead the way back to the car.

"Oh no." My wife stops me, "We're gonna shower off first."

I'm not sure if I heard her correctly, but my confusion is enough to stop me in my tracks and involuntarily flash my wife a quizzical look. We stand there looking into each other's eyes, neither one of us speaking until I finally break the silence with a simple, "What?"

"We're gonna shower off!" Nora says, laughing and completely oblivious as to why I would have a problem with this. "I'm so sweaty right now, look at me."

I laugh. "It sounds like you're saying there's only one co-ed shower over there."

"There is." My wife answers bluntly.

I feel like I've been punched in the gut, my heart rate immediately kicking into double-time.

"Are you serious?" I finally ask.

Nora looks genuinely confused. "Why wouldn't I be serious?"

"Why don't you just shower at home?" I question.

Nora lets out a frustrated sigh. "Luke, this is how you do it when you're on a team." She insists. "You shower together."

Suddenly realizing that my wife is dead serious, I get a deep sinking feeling that washes over my entire body. "No way." I tell her.

"What?" She asks, incredibly offended. "You're just going to tell me what I can and can't do now?"

"Nora." I say, reaching out for her, but my wife pushes me away, clearly upset.

"You can just drive home then, I'll get a ride." She tells me.

I think about this for a moment, trying my best not to show how livid I am about this whole thing. I'm literally trembling now, my body unable to contain the fear and anxiety I'm being thrust into at the thought of my gorgeous wife showering with these large, muscular men.

"Hey Nora!" One of the guys shouts from across the field. "Come on!"

My wife looks back at me and then shakes her head in disappointment. "I always worried about this with our relationship. You're so jealous."

"I'm not." I say, begging for her understanding.

"If this is going to be and issue for us then I don't know what I'm going to do." Nora tells me. "I'm heading to the showers, if you're not here when I get out then I'll get a ride with someone else."

I try to say something to stop her but, by the time I manage to assemble the words, my wife is gone, sprinting towards the showers and leaving me to stew in my own aching emotions.

Being with someone who's such a free spirit is hard, and this type of freedom had long been a point of contention between us. I'm naturally a little on the jealous side, but I've worked to maintain a healthy amount of trust with Nora so that I can allow her to be this wild woman who I love. Of course, it can be stressful sometimes, but nothing that my wife has done has ever tested me like this.

I watch as she disappears into the public shower building and then I walk back to the car, beside myself with aching fear. Climbing in, I start the engine and then sit for a moment, trying to decide what to do.

The thing is, I love Nora, and I have no doubt that she loves me. No matter what happens between us, I can always count on her love.

I almost settle in with this thought, slowly calming myself down until suddenly another image enters my head. I'm picturing my beautiful wife surrounded by the other players, warm water running down her incredibly toned body. I imagine the way that their eyes trace across her tan skin, taking in her curves as they run their gaze up and down her slight frame.

I'm picturing the way that their cocks would grow hard around Nora when suddenly mine starts to do the exact same thing, swelling within my pants as these horrifying images swirl across my brain.

At first, I'm confused by my own bodies reaction to the painful idea of my wife messing around with other men, but the longer that this jealousy pumps through my veins, the more I start to actually enjoy myself. It's only then that I realize my feelings of anxious discomfort are not the only thing lurking deep within my psyche. There's something else there, something powerful that is slowly but surly making it's way to the surface.

"Fuck." I moan aloud to myself as my dick finally becomes completely engorged. "Why do I like this?"

My cock is begging to be touched, pressing relentlessly against the fabric of my pants as I wait for my wife to emerge from the showers and desperately wonder what's happening inside it's cement walls.

I grab my phone and try calling Nora, which is a desperate move since I know that by now her phone is probably nowhere near her. There's no response, which was wholly predictable but still manages to make my blood boil.

Finally, I just can't take it anymore, unzipping my pants and pulling out my cock as I sit and wait in the driver's seat of our car. At this point, some of the freshly showered men have started to leave the small gray building at the end of the field, wishing each other well before heading off in either direction.

With no sign of my wife, it's easy to fantasize. In my imagination, she's being pushed up against the wall of the shower room, mist filling the air as some hunky other man rails her from behind. I'm quaking with ecstasy as my mind is flooded with all kinds of hardcore positions between my wife and her new lover.

Eventually, though, my fantasy begins to push up against reality, and hard. The players all appear to be long gone, yet for some reason my wife is still inside.

I want so badly to just cum right then and there, to get this whole entire thing out of my system, but my curiosity finally gets the best of me and I zip up my pants.

I climb out of the car and immediately begin making my way across the green grass field, the shower room growing closer and closer with every step. My heart is pounding a mile a minute, slamming within my chest at a break-neck speed while a approach until, eventually, I'm standing right outside of the building.

I can hear water rushing within, but that's it. No laughing, no chatting, just water.

My first instinct is to call out, but I stop myself abruptly and opt instead to sneak inside as quietly as I can.

I slowly round the grey cement corner and stop. There before me is my wife and another man; large, muscular and black skinned. They are kissing passionately under the stream of warm water, their bodies pressed together hard as their hands roam across one another.

The second that I see them I feel as though I'm going to fall over and pass out, immediately reaching over and grabbing onto the nearby wall to catch myself. For as much as I had been fantasizing, I never truly imagined that this could be happening. Yet here I am, faced with unequivocal proof of my wife's infidelity right before my very eyes.

My brain is enraged, but my cock has other ideas.

I find myself suddenly at a crossroads, two aspects of my emotional state furiously battling it out within me. The most obvious direction to take things is to sink deeper into the anger, let the fury that builds within me explode in a fit of yelling, cursing and crying.

However, there is something way too arousing about this situation for me to deny any longer. I want nothing more than to prove to Nora that I can be the exciting, free, and adventurous man that she's always wanted me to be. I want to show her that I can be just as wild as she can.

I open my mouth to speak, then hesitate, not entirely sure I can go through with this. But, as I watch my wife and this other man carcass each other, completely oblivious to my presence, I know exactly what I have to do.

"Mind if I join you?" I finally ask.

Nora jumps in surprise and then spins around to face me, a look of complete shock on her face.

"Oh my god, Luke." She shouts. "I thought you drove home."

My wife begins to step towards me but I stop her.

"No." I say, holding up a hand.

"Luke, please let me explain." Nora begs.

A smile crosses my face. "No, let *me* explain. You deserve someone who can love you for exactly who you are, a fun, exciting, crazy woman. You might think that I can't keep up with you any longer, but I can." As I speak these words to Nora, I begin slowly stripping my clothes away from my body; my shirt first, followed by my jeans.

"What are you doing?" Nora questions.

The expression on her male partner's face makes it apparent that he's probably wondering the exact same thing.

"Showing you that I'm not just another jealous guy." I tell my wife.

By now I'm completely naked, standing before them with my cock at full attention. I step forward, entering the steam of the room as my wife suddenly realizes what's about to happen. She had admitted before that being with two men at the same time was one of her ultimate fantasies, but I had shut it down immediately. Now, things have changed.

The next thing I know, Nora is dropping down into a squat between her muscular black teammate and me. She takes both of our cocks into her slender hands and immediately begins to pump up and down across our shafts.

"Oh fuck." The other man moans, reeling from the sensation of my wife's expert strokes.

Nora looks up at me with a fire in her eyes, her expression one of completely reckless lust. "I want both of you." She gasps excitedly, as if possessed by the demon of cock-drunk arousal. "I need your dicks!"

The next thing I know, my wife is taking her teammates rod deep within her throat, pushing him down as far as she can until his balls rest firmly against her chin. Nora holds the man there for a while, letting him enjoy the sensation of being completely consumed, and then finally pulls back and takes in a giant gulp of air.

Immediately, she turns her attention to me and does the exact same maneuver, swallowing my rod all the way down into her neck. She's clearly been practicing, because her gag reflex seems like some long forgotten memory, not even a consideration as she services me. I can feel Nora's tongue swirling around the shaft of my cock within her mouth, then she pushes it forward and lets the pink tip of it just barely pass her lips enough to tickle my balls.

All the while that my wife is pleasuring me with her mouth, she continues keeping a steady pace with her hand over her teammate's big black cock, and visa versa.

Nora switches back and forth between whose cock is crammed into her mouth. Eventually, in her frantic tornado of blowjobs, Nora shoves us both between her lips at the same time, our dual invasion filling her face completely.

My wife let's us battle for position within her throat for a while and then abruptly pulls us out to command. "Fuck this tight little pussy right now."

Nora stands up under the torrent of water and bends over, her perfect round ass directed towards this other man while her head lowers closer and closer towards my crotch.

"What are you waiting for?" My wife demands to know of her dark skinned teammate. "Shove that cock into this pussy and show my husband what kind of slut I really am."

The man obliges, quickly aligning his huge shaft with Nora's pussy and then immediately thrusting forward to impale her on his rod.

"Shit!" Nora cries out, not entirely prepared for his massive size. "That dick is so fucking big."

The football player grunts in acknowledgement and then begins to pump in and out of my wife, slowly at first but then gaining speed within the tightness of her pussy lips. Nora immediately opens her mouth wide and swallows me once again.

Now penetrated from each end, my wife quickly starts to moan and groan with pleasure, her body trembling between us as her teammate and I slam Nora back and forth across our rods. She's trapped between us, unable to do anything other than accept the cocks that we are now railing her with at either end. I can see her reach a hand down between her legs and frantically begin to help herself along, the slight trembling throughout her body quickly turning into a full on seizure of pleasure. Nora's eyes roll back into her head, blissfully hanging over the edge of orgasm when suddenly her black lover pulls out and slaps her ass hard.

"We're not done with you yet." My wife's black teammate informs her.

The man immediately pulls her upright and then spins her around so that they are standing and facing one another. Now that I'm up close, the size discrepancy between them is even more apparent; my small, slender white wife pressed up against a hulking, muscular black man.

Nora's teammate lifts her up in his barrel arms, easily hoisting my wife into the air as she wraps her slender legs around this other man. The football player's giant dick is perfectly aligned with Nora's pussy, and slowly the handsome black man lowers her down onto his hard, throbbing shaft.

"Oh my fucking god!" My wife cries out, her grip tightening around her teammates broad shoulders as he enters her fully. "You're so deep!"

And deep he is. From where I'm standing I can see the player slide

Nora down completely to the hilt of his shaft, stopped only by the fact that there is simply nowhere left to go. Using his powerful arms and the force of gravity, the huge black football player immediately gets to work raising my beautiful wife up and down over his rod in the warm, falling water of the shower.

Nora's legs are kicked out wide now and she's clearly enjoying herself, swearing like a sailor under her breath as the ferocious pounding continues from below.

"You gonna get in on this ass or what?" My wife's teammate says, nodding towards me. He reaches down and grabs Nora's cheeks with two giant black hands, then spreads them apart to give me a perfect view of her puckered hole. It's just waiting for a cock to fill it.

Nora looks back at me over her shoulder. "You heard the man, double fuck me right now in my pussy and ass!"

I step forward and join the two of them, positioning my cock at the tight entrance of Nora's asshole. Her teammate lifts her up and holds her there for a moment so that I can get myself situated, and then seconds later he drops my beautiful bride and impales her directly onto both of our massive flesh rods.

Nora howls in a mixture of pain and pleasure, her head thrown back in an expression of shock and her fingers clenched tightly into her teammates back.

Me and my wife's lover give her only a brief moment to settle though, and soon enough we are pumping into her just as hard as before.

"Is this enough adventure for you?" I ask Nora with a laugh.

My wife is utterly beside herself, her body seizing with overwhelming pleasure as we hammer up into her pussy and ass. "I love taking two fucking dicks!" She screams.

The sensation within her is unreal. Nora had always been incredibly taut in both her pussy and asshole, but filling them together creates a tension that has to be felt to be believed. With the football player pumping in and out next to me, as well, there is a whole other layer of pulsing tightness that I've never even dreamed of.

After a good while of fucking my wife like this, I begin to notice her screams of pleasure changing shape, morphing into a familiar tone that only happens when she's just about ready to cum. Nora reaches down and starts to play with herself again, and it looks like this time her teammate is ready to oblige her.

"Oh fuck, I'm gonna cum!" My wife cries. "Keep fucking me just like that!"

We continue to double pound her ruthlessly until suddenly Nora is exploding in a fit of wild spasms, her legs quaking in the air and her teeth clenched tightly together.

"I'm cumming!" My wife hisses.

Nora's teammate and I don't let up for a second, railing her toned little body until finally she collapses between us in a state of fucked silly exhaustion.

The next thing I know, my wife is climbing down onto the shower room floor and kneeling between us, looking up with lust filled eyes as the water splashes around her.

"Give me those fucking loads!" Nora commands, reaching up with her hands and cradling our balls as we beat off above her. "I need your cum all over my face!"

Nora's teammate begins to moan almost immediately, his stomach muscles clenching tight as he suddenly lurches forward and ejects a massive rope of hot white cum across my wife's beautiful face, which she catches hungrily on her tongue.

The football player lets loose with two or three more impressive pumps of jizz, and then falls back as I step up to the plate.

Seeing my wife covered in another man's load is an incredibly potent image, and the next thing I know I'm blowing a pearly splatter of my own across Nora's face.

The two loads swirl together on the pallet of my wife's tan skin, running down her cheeks in warm white lines as she smiles up at me and the big black football player.

"Thanks guys." My wife says with a smile.

Nora's muscular teammate grabs her by the hand and helps her to her feet. "Welcome to the team."

THE GROUPIE

When I'm driving, the sound system is all mine.

I'm not too picky about many things, but when it comes to what we listen to in the car, I just don't understand my wife's taste. She's not exactly a huge music fan, but when something she likes comes on the radio all bets are off. Suddenly, she's the queen of the world, belting her heart out to some top forty hit like it's the last thing she'll ever do.

If we're at a stoplight and the windows are rolled down, heads are certain to turn and check us out, passers-by straining to see the woman who's all too wrapped up in her vapid pop song. It's mortifying, but in some ways I actually admire the lack of self-awareness in Heather, my incredible wife.

Heather truly doesn't care what anyone else thinks of her, completely confident to be herself whether it's singing to the radio or trying out a new outfit that pushes to the edge of fashion. Of course, it's easy for someone as stunning as her to not give a damn. If I was a woman that drop dead gorgeous, long blonde hair and a cute, girl next door smile, I wouldn't see the need for mirrors either.

However, that also just leaves the rest of us to worry about how we look while she's in the passenger seat acting a fool.

Tonight is Heather and my two-year wedding anniversary, so despite the fact that I'm driving, I've decided to let Heather do whatever she'd like with the stereo as we head off towards the fancy restaurant that I've picked out for us.

I'm nervous about the tiny box that sits tucked away in my jacket pocket, snug and warm within the fabric. I've given Heather a lot of gifts over the course of our relationship, but rarely are they worth this much money; other than our wedding ring, of course.

If I could make it through proposing, I can make it through this, I think. The diamond necklace I've picked out for Heather is absolutely stunning and I know that it will take her breath away, so that's not really the problem. The problem is that I'm a fucking idiot.

Let me back up for a moment, because I'm sure your first reaction is to tell me I'm being too hard on myself.

Fine. I'm not dumb, not by a long shot, I just have a very, very specific problem when it comes to hanging onto valuable things. I lose them.

I've installed a location device on my car keys, thank god, which keeps me going from day to day but, as far as the other small items of value in my life, there really is no hope at all. Wallet, left at the bar; important presentation for work, back at the house; it never ends. Even when I proposed, I reached into my pocket to find that the ring had been left back in our room. Luckily, I played things off coolly and managed to keep Heather from noticing my strange kneel until back in the hotel where the real thing went off without a hitch. Still, the terror of that night will stick with me for the rest of my life.

Because of this, I keep pressing my hand against the necklace's box within my jacket pocket, compulsively making sure that it's still there.

"What are you doing?" Heather suddenly asks, suspicious of my strange movements.

I glance over at her from the driver's seat, "Oh! Nothing."

Heather narrows her eyes and gives me a suspicious smile. "You're acting so weird right now."

I shrug. "Guess I'm just happy to be your husband. Two years is a long time."

"Aww!" Heather purrs, leaning over the center console between us and giving me a quick kiss on the cheek. "That's very sweet, Jordan."

Suddenly, Heather's face contorts into a vibrant look of surprised elation. She's screaming, not out of fear or alarm but pure joy, and it's so loud that I have to cover my ears.

"This is my song!" Heather yells, reaching over and turning up the radio to as loud as it can go.

I've heard this song before but I couldn't tell you the name. The chorus just repeats the words, 'You rock me with your style, baby.' So I'm guessing that's probably it. Heather seems to know every inflection of the crooning vocalist, singing along with all of the passion that she can muster.

Suddenly, I'm wondering if letting her be in charge of the radio was such a good idea, but I hold my tongue, forcing a smile as I glance over at my beautiful, but horribly out of tune wife.

To be honest, the song itself really isn't that bad. It's pop disguised as hard rock, but the guitars are loud and fun and then singer himself actually has some great chops.

"Who is this?" I shout to Heather over the deafening sound of the music.

"What?" She asks.

"Who is this?" I repeat.

Heather holds her finger up and cuts me off just as the final chorus kicks in, shouting out as we pull up to a stop light. A guy in the car next to us exchanges glances with me and I simply shrug, which seems good enough for him as he turns his attention back to the road before us.

"And that's why I'll always love you!" Heather sings as the final crashing note rings out through the vehicle. She seems satisfied with herself, as if something very important had just been accomplished.

"Alright!" Comes a wildly excited and overly enunciated voice on the radio. "That was Billy Tucker and the Noise with their hit single, 'You Rock Me With Your Style'!"

"I love Billy Tucker." My wife says gushing. "Oh my god, he's so hot."

I can't help but shoot her a glance as she says this and Heather notices, immediately covering it up with a quick, "But not as hot as you, baby."

I'm not at all the jealous type, in fact, quite the opposite, but something about anybody worshipping celebrities like that is always going to be slightly annoying to me. They're just people, nothing more or less. Sure most folks in the limelight have some amount of talent that deserves to be admired, but they're not gods.

"If you're still listening right now then you are in luck!" The radio announcer cuts in with his assertive tone. "Because we about to do our Billy Tucker and the Noise VIP giveaway!"

Heather screams again and I recoil in shock. "Oh my god." I mutter.

"Listen up fans, because this is how it works." The radio announcer continues. "We've got two tickets here for the Billy Tucker show tomorrow *and* for the show down in San Diego the day after. If you can answer the trivia question correctly, you'll see both shows and you are your guest will get to ride the tour bus from one show to the other with Billy and the band!"

Heather looks like she is about to pass out at this point, breathing heavy as she scrambles for her phone in her purse.

"Alright, here is the question." The radio announcer begins. "What is the name of the secret track at the end of Billy Tucker's debut album?"

"That's so easy!" Heather erupts, dialing the number for the radio station immediately.

Meanwhile, I've somehow managed to drive us to the restaurant amid all of this chaos, and now we sit idling in the parking lot.

Heather's phone rings once, twice, three times before someone picks up and there is a loud screech of feedback over our car radio. I immediately turn the volume all the way down.

"Hello?" Heather is shouting. "Hello?"

"Hi! This is Nick the Wildman, you're on the air! Are you ready to win two tickets for the Billy Tucker VIP experience?"

"I was born ready." Heather says with confidence.

"Alright." Nick the Wildman starts, "What is the name…"

"Girl, You Want It." Heather interrupts. "That's the name of the song."

There is a long pause, my wife frozen in her seat as she waits for confirmation from the radio host. After all of this wild cacophony, the silence is deafening, so tense that I don't dare say a word that would interrupt it prematurely.

"Hello?" Heather says quietly, finally breaking the tension. "Are you still there?"

Suddenly, Nick the Wildman is back on the line. "Yes, we're still here and you just won two tickets to the Billy Tucker VIP experience!"

Heather is immediately losing her mind, screaming and thrashing about in the seat next to me like a belligerent fan girl. I can't even remember the last time I saw her this excited and I try not to let it get to me, but it does as I reach into my jacket pocket and check for the box once again. It's still there, but my anxiety remains. There's no way she's going to like my necklace better than the prize she already won tonight, regardless of how much money I spent.

It takes a few minutes for Heather to calm down, and when she finally does we head inside. The server greets us and leads Heather and me to our table, which is a killer little spot right out on the patio that overlooks Los Angeles.

"Whoa, this is beautiful." I say as I stare out across the twinkling city lights, taking it all in and thankful to have a moment of calm with my darling wife.

Heather doesn't say anything in response, and I look over at her curiously. She's staring off into space, clearly not listening to a word that I'm saying. When she sees me looking her direction she glances and offers a concerned, "What?"

"Never mind." I say with a laugh. "What's on your mind?"

"Nothing." Heather lies. "Just this."

"You're excited about meeting Billy Tucker tomorrow, aren't you?" I ask.

A sly grin creeps across my wife's face, despite her best efforts to stop it. "Maybe." She admits.

"I would be, too." I joke. "You know who you're going to invite along yet?"

"You!" Heather laughs. "You goofball! Who else would I take?"

"I don't know, one of your friends." I offer.

Heather reaches across the table and puts her hand over mine. "You're my best friend, though." She says.

As she says this I feel a wave of love and understanding wash over me, relieving me from any sort of doubt or concern I could have possibly had about the state of our relationship.

It might sounds like I'm jumping to conclusions, but I can honestly say that, even before winning the tickets, Heather has been distant. We haven't been having sex as much lately either, which is pretty normal when you've been married two years, but I'd rather it wasn't the case.

I've tired getting my wife to talk about her fantasies so I can bring some excitement into the bedroom, but Heather is fairly closed off when it comes to that kind of stuff.

None of that matters now though because in this moment, with her hand over mine, I know that Heather loves me no matter what. It doesn't matter what obstacles are thrown our way, we are going to overcome them together; regardless of how cold our sex life gets or how many times I forget something important at home.

Which reminds me, I haven't checked for a while.

Suddenly, panic strikes as I reach for my pocket to make sure that the necklace box is still there. It is, and I breathe a sigh of relief.

"Okay, seriously now." Heather starts, rolling her eyes. "Why do you keep doing that?"

I let out a long sigh. I might as well give Heather her present now, otherwise I'll probably lose it here just sitting at the dinner table.

"Alright." I finally succeed, pulling out the box and setting it down in front of her. "It's an anniversary present."

Heather smiles and looks at me as though I've suddenly transformed into the most adorable puppy that she's ever seen. "Jordan, this is so sweet, baby!"

I shake my head. "No, you're worth it. You're the best thing that's ever happened to me. This is the least I could do."

Heather carefully opens the small oblong box and lifts the lid, staring down in wonder until suddenly she stops and her face morphs into one of extreme confusion. "I don't get it." She says, turning the box towards me so that I can see inside. "There's nothing in here."

"Oh fuck." Is all that I can manage, reeling as I realize that the box is, in fact, empty.

"You didn't seriously lose the…" She trails off.

"Diamond necklace." I answer.

"Diamond necklace!" Heather repeats back, yelling. "Are you fucking kidding me?"

A few of the other patrons take notice of our conflict, shooting worried glances my way.

"I'm sorry." I tell Heather, "I know I should have checked the box."

Heather just shakes her head solemnly. "This is just getting kind of ridiculous." She tells me, exasperated. "How many times are we going to get locked out of our car, you know? How many times are you going to spend a fortune on diamonds and then lose them?"

"I know." I say, lowering my head. "You're right, but I'm gonna make it up to you."

Heather looks at me skeptically, "Well alright, let's start with a replacement gift."

I shake my head. "I don't have anything, I mean, those diamonds were worth a lot of money."

Heather rolls her eyes. "Let's just drop it then."

The waiter eventually comes to take our orders but, other than that, the rest of the meal remains almost entirely silent. Heather and I are both lost in thought, a myriad of different questions swimming around in our heads.

I know that I've messed things up, and I want to make it better but I just don't know how. If I knew what it was I would just do it, a miracle cure that could fix it all in one fell swoop.

I bet Heather wouldn't have these problems if she was dating Billy Tucker.

Suddenly, an idea hits me that is so outrageous, so dangerous and wild and exciting, that I actually have to keep myself from gasping out loud. I let myself process the thought, weighing the benefits of what I'm considering against the simmering jealousy that boils up inside of me, just below the surface.

I open my mouth to speak, then stop, questioning if I really want to go through with what I'm about to say. I'm not sure I completely understand it yet, but something about my devious plan is actually kind of arousing to me. I'm also well aware that it will be very exciting to Heather, too, regardless of how much she tries to play it off as nothing.

Once I put it out there, I know that there's no turning back.

"I have an idea." I finally say. "A present for you that will make up for all the fucking up I've been doing lately."

Heather immediately switches into a caring nurturer the second that she hears the defeated tone of my voice. "Oh baby, it's okay. You don't need to get me anything else."

"It's not okay." I insist. "And I'm not getting anything, I'm allowing you to do something."

My wife is suddenly intrigued, listening intently. "Oh yeah?" She asks.

I swallow hard, and then continue. "So… things have been rough with us in the bedroom. I keep trying to spice it up but I don't know what your fantasies are and you won't tell me, so it's kinda difficult."

Heather nods with understanding.

"But there's one fantasy that I know for a fact you're into… fucking Billy Tucker."

My wife giggles and blushes at this. "Oh my god, Jordan do you have to be so blunt like that?"

I shake my head. "Come on, be serious."

"I'm trying." Heather tells me. "Just spit it out, what is your present?"

I take a deep breath. "I want to fuck you with Billy." I tell her.

"What?" Heather shouts, "Are you serious?"

I nod.

Heather doesn't even know how to process what I'm telling her, completely flabbergasted that I could even consider the idea of sharing her beautiful body with another man, even if he is a rock star. "What's the catch?" She finally asks.

"No catch." I tell my wife. "I owe you, for the necklace, for everything. Besides, I think this could be the push that we need to breathe a little bit of excitement into our sex life."

Heather is silent for a moment and it suddenly dawns on me that she's actually considering it. I try not to let this simple fact bother me but I'm only human, and once again I can feel that aching jealously start to course hot through my veins. This time, however, there's something else, something even more powerful; desire.

I realize then that my cock is rock hard in my pants, throbbing with a dull lust at the thought of my wife fucking another man in front of me. It's not a fantasy that I've ever had before, but at this very moment, as I look across the table at Heather's gorgeous face and huge, incredible tits, I'd love nothing more in the world than to double team her.

"Well?" I finally ask, my voice trembling. "What do you say?"

"You're sure that you're okay with this?" Heather asks me one final time.

"I'm sure." I promise.

Heather hesitates, then opens her mouth, "Let's do it."

I have to admit, the show was incredible. Billy and his band we're absolutely stunning on stage, real performers with a true sense of connection to the audience. It was a night to remember, and for a moment as we watch from the sidelines I completely forget about what is coming next until, of course, I notice Billy himself making eyes at my wife right in front of me.

Heather loves it, swooning passionately and flirting back with a wink and a wave of her own. It's on.

The band finishes up and the whole group of us is lead back to a pack of busses that are parked behind the arena complex. The band has a bus to share between them while Billy Tucker has a bus of his own, with plenty of room. This is where my wife and I will be riding.

After saying goodbye to the rest of the band, we climb up the steps and onto Billy's bus. A rotund driver greets us, shaking our hands and directing us towards a set of two bunks in a hallway of many.

"Which one is Billy's?" My wife asks.

The driver just nods straight back. "He doesn't sleep in a bunk. Billy stays in the back lounge most of the time, he's already in there if you want to say hello."

"Oh, I wouldn't want to interrupt." Heather explains.

The driver shrugs. "Whatever. We're about to leave now. He'll probably come out and say hello at some point."

Eventually, the bus exits the arena parking lot and starts rumbling down the road. Billy is nowhere to be found, remaining locked away in the back lounge for the first several hours of the ride.

"Maybe he's just fallen asleep." I suggest to Heather, whose eyes drop in disappointment.

"Our plan is never going to work now." She says.

Her frustration breaks my heart in some strange way, and I try to be encouraging. "Why do you go check on him?" I finally say.

"Really?" Heather asks.

"Why not?" I tell her. "It can't hurt. I mean, who doesn't want to get woken up by a beautiful woman."

"But what if he invites me in?" Heather asks me, concerned. "I mean, he is a rock star after all, that's what happens on these busses."

My heart is pounding a mile a minute now, nearly beating right out of my chest, but I nod in acceptance. "Then I'll be very happy."

Heather eyes me for a minute, trying to understand my actions until finally giving up. "You're amazing." She says, giving me a quick kiss before standing up and making her way to the door of the back lounge. She knocks twice and waits.

From where I'm sitting, all I can see is the door slide open and my wife exchanging a few words with Billy, she looks back over her shoulder at me for a moment, considering something, and then finally steps inside. She closes the door behind her.

Now I'm alone, sitting on a couch at the front of the bus and watching the scenery float by. I feel sick with jealousy, but also overwhelmingly horny, a confusing cocktail that nearly overloads my senses.

Ten minutes pass, then twenty, then thirty; my mind racing with all of the dirty depraved things that could be happening to my wife just behind that door. I feel as though my soul is about to break when suddenly the door to the back lounge opens up and my gorgeous wife sticks her head out.

"Jordan!" She calls to me, giggling. "Come here."

I stand up and make my way down the long hallway of the bus towards Heather, my cock painfully erect.

As I reach the door, I realize that Heather is completely naked, but before I have time to react my wife grabs me and pulls me inside.

"Hey baby." Heather says, kissing me deeply. "I talked to Billy about your gift and he thinks it's a pretty good idea."

I glance over at the rock star, who sits shirtless with his pants unbuttoned on the edge of a large bed that takes up most of the back room.

"Cheers!" Billy says, lifting a glass of something stiff into the air and pounding it in a single gulp. "Let's rock her world."

My whole body is trembling now but Heather takes charge of the situation, dropping down into a squat as Billy stands and walks over to us. My wife reaches up and immediately gets to work undoing my belt, then moments later she reaches in and unleashes my swollen dick.

Billy's cock is also ready to go, and Heather wastes no time getting to work between us as she pumps her hands up and down over our thick rods. I let out a long, satisfied moan at the pleasant sense of her touch, my body craving release for so long.

When I look over and see my wife's hand wrapped around another man's cock, however, I don't know what to think. Part of me is immediately furious; an instinctual reaction to the sight of his girthy shaft between Heather's slender fingers, but the underlying arousal is still there and growing larger than ever. I can't help but think about the intense attraction between them, my wife and this other man, and it sizzles through my brain with a powerful, lustful electricity.

"Do you like that fucking dick?" Billy asks. "Why don't you shove it in that pretty little mouth of yours?"

I watch in awe as Heather opens wide and takes this other man down her throat, pushing him as deep as she can and then retching loudly as Billy hits her gag reflex.

My wife pulls back and takes in a huge gasp of air, then tries again. This time she's ready, relaxing enough so that when Billy's enormous shaft presses against her limits it can eventually slide pass and enter the depths of her throat. Soon, my wife's face is pressed hard against Billy's toned abs, his mammoth dick completely buried within her.

All the while, Heather doesn't stop beating off my cock with her free hand, servicing both Billy and me with equal skill. When she finally finishes with the rock star's dick she trades our position within her lips, taking me down to the base and holding my rod deep within her. I can feel her tongue dancing playfully around the edge of my shaft, lapping expertly against my hanging balls that rest on her chin.

I can't remember the last time I saw this kind of erotic fire behind my wife's eyes, and as she look up and me I'm more than impressed with her ability to turn it on. Soon Heather is moving her head back and forth between me and Billy, servicing us one after another and sometimes both at once, somehow managing to fit each of our hefty cocks between her lips at the same time.

Eventually, though, the passion becomes too much for Heather to contain and she stands up, kissing us in turn and then climbing up onto the bed with her ass in the air. My wife gives a playful wiggle as she crawls into position, then looks back over her shoulder and winks. "How about you guys take turns in this tight little pussy?" Heather offers.

Billy and Me don't need to be told twice, immediately taking a position on either side of her. I move around to the front and let Heather wrap her lips tightly around my rod once again. Meanwhile, Billy positions himself at the entrance of my wife's tight wet slit.

The rock star aligns his cock carefully and then slowly but firmly thrusts forward into Heather's aching tightness. My wife let's out a long moan of satisfaction, the sound muffled by my cock as it sits firmly planted in her throat, then starts to move with Billy.

Eventually, the three of us find a pleasant pulse together, our bodies rocking back and forth in perfect harmony.

We begin to speed up amid a chorus of moans, our bodies craving more from one another. Heather pulls me out of her mouth just long enough to look up and command, "Harder! Faster!"

I do as I'm told, continuing to hammer away at her until me and Billy are absolutely pummeling my wife's body with dick, slamming Heather with everything that we've got. Every thrust into her mouth from me propels Heather back onto Billy's rod, and every slam from him pushes her back towards me.

"Oh my god." My wife starts repeating, the words vibrating over and over again through my fleshy rod in her mouth. "Oh my god, oh my fucking god."

Heather is trembling hard now, unable to contain all of the erotic feelings within her small frame. I know her movement's well, and it's more than apparent that my wife is about to cum. Heather, however, isn't interested in taking herself there yet. Instead, she has other plans.

"Lie down." My wife instructs me suddenly, pushing me back and positioning me down on the bed in front of her. She removes Billy from her pussy and then climbs on top of me, wrapping her toned legs around my torso and running her hands down my ripped chest.

Eventually, Heather's hand reaches my cock and she grabs a hold of me firmly, then aligns my rod with her slick entrance. My wife lets out a soft moan as I slide up into her, biting her lip and closing her eyes as her body fills with pleasure. She immediately starts to ride me, bucking her hips in deliberate, powerful movements across my body.

"Fuck, that feels so good!" I tell her, grabbing onto Heather's hips and helping her along. "God damn, my wife is such a good little slut."

"You think that's good?" She says with a smile. "How about this?" Heather immediately turns and looks back over her shoulder at Billy, who has been watching with his cock in his hand. "Get over here." Heather commands.

Billy comes forward and maneuvers himself around behind my wife. He gives her ass a hard slap.

"I want you to double fuck this hot little body of mine." Heather says. "Shove that big fat dick up my asshole right now."

Billy positions his cock at my wife's puckered entrance and then slowly but surely pushes past the tightness of her rim. I can feel him enter Heather from inside, a sensation so fantastic and unusual that it makes my toes curl.

Heather is screaming now, unable to control herself in the face of such brutal penetrations. Billy and me quickly get to work pumping in and out of her, our thick dicks working in tandem as we slam into her body. I'm in absolute ecstasy, the idea alone of sharing my wife with another man almost too much to handle, let alone the shockingly tight sensation against my rod. Heather is completely maxed out down below, stretched to her limits as we pound harder and harder.

Again, my wife starts to shake, convulsing wildly between us. She reaches down between her legs and starts to rapidly play with her clit, giving herself just the slightest push over the edge and then suddenly she's cumming hard, her entire body clenching tight and releasing over and over again as she howls with pleasure. Heather's eyes roll back into her head, completely lost in the moment.

Almost immediately, Billy and me start to cum, as well. The rock star goes first, pushing deep and holding within the depths of Heather's tight asshole. I can feel his cock twitching hard through the thin layer of membrane that separates us, filling my wife's ass with every ejection until there's just not enough room and the milky white spunk squirts from the edges.

I'm following just behind, holding on tightly as I unload a massive blast of jizz up into Heather's pussy. I cry out and then clench my teeth tightly as the sensation washes over me in powerful waves.

Eventually, the three of us all collapse in a pile, then remove ourselves from one another and try to stand in a fucked silly daze.

"That was amazing." Heather says, collecting her clothes.

I nod in agreement. "And that was a great show tonight, too."

"What? You're leaving just like that?" Billy asks.

"You can go again?" I question in astonishment. "That's impressive!"

Billy shakes his head and laughs. "No man, I'm not a superhero, but what about we try this again tomorrow?"

"We've gotta leave." Heather explains him, "The contest was for us to only stay with you for one night."

"Fuck the contest!" Billy shouts jovially. "How'd you two like to come out on the road for a while!"

A DANCER'S BODY

There's plenty to appreciate about the body of an attractive woman; be it her long legs, heavenly tits or perfectly toned ass. The thing is, a truly exquisite body is so rare that we almost never see it in real daily life. Sure there are commercials, television actresses and billboard models to wet our appetite for bare skin, but when it comes to the real world, that type of genetic prowess is almost impossible to find.

That is, of course, unless you're lucky enough to be married to a professional dancer.

In general, dancers are an interesting bunch, as I've learned over the last three years of marriage to my darling wife, Alana. They run in a tight nit social group and always seem to be busy, although when you ask them exactly what it is they're doing the answer is always pretty vague.

"Working on something." My wife usually says before she heads out the door to her dance studio, which she co-owns with a friend.

They teach lessons and put on all sorts of shows, ranging in dance styles that span the globe, but focused mostly on variations of basic hip-hop. It's a great artistic outlet for Alana, and she enjoys it a lot, which, of course, makes me a very thankful husband. Of course, there is also the nice bonus of having a wife with a body that's damn near supernaturally toned.

We have a great life, and I couldn't be happier.

"What are you doing Sunday night?" Alana asks me.

"Nothing, yet." I tell her, sitting down next to my wife on our deck that overlooks downtown Los Angeles. The sun hangs low in the sky, casting a beautiful blooming purple across the clouds and causing the buildings to take on the form of powerful, looming silhouettes. We sit out here a lot and watch the sunset, each in our own special deck chair. Usually, we're both sipping ice cold beers as we do this, but Alana has a night class that starts in a half hour.

"I had an idea." Alana tells me, her eyes still transfixed on the beautiful urban view that stretches out before us.

"Oh yeah?" I question, popping the cap off of my drink with a loud hiss. "Tell me."

"My advanced class is doing really good." Alana explains. "Like, really good, probably the best I've ever had. We're all getting so…" she trails off, struggling to find the words. "Close."

"That's great!" I say, unable to keep myself from smiling at the twinkle in my wife's eye. I love it when Alana gets excited like this, so much passion is such a tight little dancer's body.

"I guess dance can do that to you." Alana continues, speaking her thoughts as they come to her, riffing now the same way that she would freestyle to a song. "It's like, you get to know these people so intimately, their bodies, the way that they move."

"Damn." I laugh. "It sounds like you're fucking them."

Alana glances over at me for a moment, a strange look in her eye that I can't quite put my finger on. For a brief moment, it's actually kind of awkward, but then seconds later my wife cracks a smile and joins in with the laughter. "Yeah, I suppose that it kind of is. Anyway, I was just thinking that it feels so weird when my classes end and my students just go away, especially the really good ones."

I shrug. "I guess that's just kinda what happens, right? That's what it's like when you're a teacher, eventually your students leave the nest."

"Yeah, I know." Alana agrees. "But I want to see them off, not just shove them out and hope that they can fly."

I finally can't help it and longer and roll my eyes in exasperation. "Okay, enough with the metaphors. What's up? What's your idea?"

"I was thinking that, at the end of each season, we could invite my best student over for dinner or something." Alana suggests. "I'm just sick of getting so close to these people and then one day they're gone without a trace."

I nod in agreement. "That sounds like a great idea!"

"So… Sunday then?" Alana asks again.

"Sure thing, I'll be here." I tell her. "Whose the lucky girl?"

My wife pauses for a moment. "Lucky guy, actually."

I'm a little shocked to hear this. Almost all of Alana's students are women, for whatever reason. I can't even remember the last time she had a male student in any of her classes. "Whoa, okay." I answer. "That's awesome. Is he pretty good?"

Alana seems lost in thought for a moment, as if recalling some beautiful memory and transporting herself there. "He's incredible."

There's something that, if I'm going to be perfectly honest, makes me a little uncomfortable about the way that Alana says this. I can't exactly put my finger on it, but my wife is definitely not being entirely upfront about the entire situation, and I know it. Still, I'm not worried. Alana's sexual apatite may be voracious, but she'd never ever cheat on me. I'm sure her feelings of admiration for this particular student are strictly professional, nothing more.

"Well, I'm excited to meet him." I tell Alana, taking another long sip of my beer.

We sit in silence for a while longer until my wife glances down and notices the time. "Shit!" She cries, hopping up to her feet. "Class is about to start. I'm gonna be late!"

Alana grabs her purse and gives me a quick kiss, then heads straight towards the door of our apartment. "Love you, Ian!" She shouts over her shoulder.

"Love you, too!" I tell her.

The second that I hear the door close behind her my imagination begins to run wild.

I try to contain the thoughts at first, not at all wanting to transform into the overbearing, jealous husband that we all have lurking somewhere deep inside of us, but it's hard not to when you have a prize like mine on your arm. What could it possibly mean when Alana got awkward about her student? Was she hiding something?

There is a wicked knot twisting and turning at the pit of my stomach, rolling up into a ball and then stretching out again as I try desperately to keep my mind under control. I trust Alana, I tell myself, repeating it over and over again within my head like a mantra. I have no reason not to.

The jealousy puts up a valiant fight however, and soon the big green monster starts to envelope me. I begin to actually consider opening up my wife's email and seeing if I can find anything suspicious, but I force myself to push those thoughts away and lock them up tight.

Stranger than the jealousy, however, is the intense feeling of lust that comes along with it. I have no idea why, but the thought of Alana messing around with this student of hers is actually kind of a turn on, in some strange way. The more my thoughts focus on my beautiful wife's infidelity, the harder my cock seems to get in my pants until, finally, I just can't take it any longer.

I unzip, right then and there on the deck, and pull out my aching rod, beating it slowly. Closing my eyes, I imagine my wife resting on her knees, servicing some faceless other man down at the dance studio. I picture them sprawled out on the mats, his dick buried deep inside of her tight little asshole as she squeals, her wedding ring off and resting on the counter nearby.

It doesn't take me long to cum, blowing my load hard as I cry out loud and then falling back into the chair. I feel as though a Pandora's box has been opened within my soul, and there's no going back. I've finally discovered how much I enjoy the thought of my wife with another man and, as much as I don't understand it, the fantasy is too overwhelming to ignore.

"Ian, this is Carter." Alana says, introducing me to her young and incredibly handsome student as he comes walking through the door of our apartment.

"It's nice to meet you." Carter says with a big, broad smile.

Even being objective as I can be, Carter is breathtakingly handsome, a muscular frame that leads up to his boyish face and a perfectly chiseled jaw.

"It's nice to meet you, too." I tell Carter, shaking his hand firmly. "I've heard you really know what you're doing with my wife."

Carter and Alana stop abruptly, suddenly uncomfortable with the way that I phrased that.

"On the dance floor." I add. "That's what you call it right? The dance floor?"

Alana rolls her eyes and starts to push me over to the table. "Don't mind him." She calls back to Carter. "My husband is a little strange."

I laugh. As awkward as I can be, it's good to know that my wife is still amused by it.

Alana pulls out two chairs at our round table and motions for Carter and me to sit, then heads back into the kitchen and starts finishing a few things up.

"I'm sorry, it's almost ready I promise." She calls out to us.

Carter looks around our place, clearly impressed. Despite the killer money that my wife makes with her dance studio, I'm still the breadwinner of the family, and our apartment definitely reflects a lifestyle that can only be attained by a fortunate few.

"This is a really nice place." Carter gushes, trying his best to make small talk.

"Thanks." I say. "Wine?"

Carter nods and I pour him a glass.

From the other room we can hear Alana banging around with some pots and pans, clearly working hard to provide us with something very impressive. Moments later, my wife emerges with a hot plate of delicious smelling eggplant parmesan, serving us up and then sitting down to join us.

"Before we dive in." I announce loudly, lifting my glass. "I just wanted to say how great it is to share our home with someone new tonight. Sharing is something that I hope me and Alana can do more often."

My wife flashes me a strange look, but then recovers nicely and joins in with the toast. "Cheers!" Alana adds.

The wine continues to flow over the course of the meal, loosening everyone up enough so that, eventually, the conversation takes a natural turn towards sex.

"You know, the great thing about you dancers is that they know how to use their body in the bedroom." I say, winking at my wife.

"Yeah, I think that's defiantly true." Carter agrees.

"I can only imagine what it's like when two dancers get it on with each other." I continue, and then look deep into Alana's eyes. "Have you ever thought about that? What it would be like to fuck another dancer?"

Alana looks mortified as I say this, clearly not finding my bluntness the least bit entertaining. "Ian, can I see you in the kitchen for a moment?" She asks sternly.

"Sure." Tell her, standing up and following my wife into the other room while Carter remains awkwardly posted at the dining table.

The second that we get out of earshot Alana spins around with a fire in her eyes. "What the fuck are you doing?" She hisses.

"What?" I counter. "I'm just having fun."

Alana shakes her head. "You're acting so… jealous."

I'm absolutely shocked when she says this. "Why?"

"You won't stop talking about sex!" Alana says. "So he's a cute guy, so what? That doesn't mean that I want to fuck him!"

I laugh as Alana says this and go in for a hug, which my wife accepts graciously. "Oh no baby, that's not it at all." I tell her. "I'm not jealous, I'm actually kinda…" I trail off, not exactly sure how to tell her.

"Kinda what?" Alana asks.

"Into it." I finally say. "I've been thinking about it a lot and, honestly, the idea of sharing you with another man has been really turning me on."

Alana looks absolutely dumbfounded, her jaw literally hanging open as she stands in shocked silence. "Wait, are you serious?" She asks.

I nod.

"You want to share me?" My wife clarifies, still having trouble processing this new information. "With Carter?"

I nod, again.

Alana leans back against the fridge, looking as though she's about to pass out. I'm not sure if her exasperation is out of confusion or arousal as she struggles to collect herself, but eventually she pulls it together enough to finally tell me, "That's so fucking hot."

"Really?" I ask, my eyes lighting up.

"Yeah." Alana nods, "I can't even fucking tell you how hot that is."

"Then let's do it!" I beg her, unable to contain my excitement.

Alana narrows her eyes. "What's the catch?"

"No catch." I promise.

My wife considers it all for a moment and then finally nods in the affirmative. "Okay." She says.

We make our way back into the dining room and find that Carter is already at the door of our apartment, pulling on his jacket and turning to leave.

"Hey!" I shout. "You don't have to go! Come on now."

"No, it's okay, really. I feel like I'm interrupting something." Carter explains. "Besides, I really need to go work on the new choreography."

"It's fine!" Alana chimes in. "Stay."

Carter shakes his head, clearly a little flustered. "Nah, I really should work on this tonight."

He starts to leave but, before he can, Alana offers one final suggestion. "Wait! Why don't you come down to the studio and work?"

Carter pauses. "It's all closed up for the night, though. Isn't it?" He asks.

"You're having dinner with the owner." Alana laughs, "I've got the keys right here and the studio's only a block away. We'll walk you over and open it up for you."

Carter looks from Alana to me and then back again. "Are you sure that's okay?"

"Positive." She tells Carter.

We all grab our jackets and then head out into the night, walking briskly towards my wife's nearby dance studio. Although we haven't yet continued the sexual discussion, I can tell that there's an electricity in the air between the three of us. In some ways, it's slightly uncomfortable, but I'm beginning to think that the discomfort comes mostly from the fact that, deep down, we all secretly want the same thing so badly.

Finally, my wife steps up and makes her move. "So Carter, about that question earlier." Alana starts in.

"Yeah?"

"You ever been with another dancer?" My wife asks.

Carter nods. "Yeah, of course."

"How was it?" She continues, looking back over her shoulder with a playful smile as Carter follows us along the downtown sidewalk.

Carter nods. "It was good. Same as dancing, you just need to find the flow with your partner and then you just go for it."

"Yeah, that sounds about right." Alana muses. "But what if it wasn't just you and a partner, you think you could flow like that with three people?"

Suddenly, the tension between us all seems to dissipate. Carter, Alana and me are all on the same level and we know it. He doesn't even have to answer because we all get what the others are actually saying. We want to get weird tonight; to have some fun and experiment. We want to double-team my wife.

"Here we are." Alana says, walking up to the front door of the studio and pulling out her keys. She goes through the ring until she finds the one that she's looking for and unlocks the door, pulling it open and flicking on the light inside.

The fluorescent overheads sputter to life, illuminating the wide-open dance studio, complete with padded floors and an entire wall covered in mirrors.

We've only taken two steps inside before, suddenly, Alana is all over us, pulling both Carter and me towards her and making out with each of us in turn. Not one to reject a beautiful woman in the troughs of passion, Carter and I begin to run our hands up and down across my wife's body, enjoying the feeling of her toned, perfect curves.

"Oh my god." Alana moans, closing her eyes tight. "I can't believe this is happening."

The three of us push and pull each other towards the center of the empty studio where we eventually stop. Alana quickly drops to her knees and frantically unzips our jeans, an insatiable hunger brewing behind her eyes.

"I need those fucking cocks." My wife commands. "Give me your dicks right fucking now."

Seconds later, the shafts of Carter and me spring forth from their denim cages, bouncing in the air as they jut out above my wife's beautiful face. She smiles happily and takes one rod in each hand, then immediately begins to stroke in slow, deliberate movements.

The sensation is absolutely incredible, causing my entire body to break out in a powerful tremble of pleasure. I close my eyes tight and lean my head back, letting out a loud, satisfied groan.

"You like that?" Alana coos. "Do you like watching me stroke off another guy right in front of you?"

I look down at my wife, entranced by her slutty encouragement. "I love it." I admit.

"How about if I suck him off?" Alana asks me, "Would you like that?"

I don't even have time to answer before my wife opens her mouth wide and engulfs Carter's massive rod. She can barely fit him between her lips, struggling to take the hung dancer's massive shaft but, once she does, all bets are off. The next thing I know, my wife is pumping her head up and down his cock, deep throating every inch of Carter's incredible shaft.

Carter places his hands behind my wife's head and takes control, maneuvering her forcefully over his length. Meanwhile, Alana is completely at Carter's mercy and loving every second of it, the student now becoming the teacher.

My wife hasn't let up for a second on her rapid stroking of my cock, pleasuring me in tandem with the sloppy blowjob that she's providing our new friend.

The sight of my beautiful wife's lips around another man's massive rod is incredible, still strangely anger inducing, in a way, but also profoundly arousing to the point that the other emotions stop mattering. I don't even begin to try and understand it, just continue to go with the flow as Alana continues to push the envelope farther and farther.

Soon enough, my wife turns her attention to me, licking my cock from the balls to the tip and then giving me a few playful sucks. Eventually, she pulls me out of her mouth and then takes me by the hand, pulling me down so that my dick is still level with her as she climbs onto her hands and knees.

Alana looks back over her shoulder at Carter. "Now let's see what you can really do with that cock of yours!" She laughs.

Carter kneels down behind my wife and aligns his massive rod with her slit, positioning himself for entry as he grips her tightly by the hips.

"Fuck me!" Alana demands, growing inpatient. "I need that fucking dick right now!"

Carter pushes forward, impaling my beautiful wife on his extra thick cock and causing her to squeal out with pleasure, holding firmly onto the mat beneath her. He immediately gets to work pumping in and out of her pussy, slamming over and over again into Alana's incredibly toned body.

Not wasting any time, my wife opens her mouth and swallows my rod, sucking me off while she's pounded from behind. She moans loudly against the flesh of my cock, her sexual cries distorted into a strangled gargle as she picks up the pace.

Soon the three of us are all pumping together with a solid rhythm, Carter and me ramming back and forth while my wife skillfully takes it in the middle. I watch as Alana reaches down and plays with her aching clit, pushing herself closer and closer to the inevitable orgasm that lies somewhere in her near future. I can see the muscles of Alana's lower back tense up as she approaches her breaking point but, instead of tipping over the edge, Alana pulls back and saves herself.

My wife pops my cock out of her mouth. "Get on the mat." She demands. "I want to ride that fucking dick of yours."

I fall backwards, flat on the ground as my cock juts out from me like a pink tower of sex. Moments later, Alana is climbing atop me. She spreads her legs and straddles my toned abs, then reaches down to wrap her fingers around my rock hard dick. I shudder and groan, arching my back against the soft mat below.

"You like that?" Alana asks.

"I do." I tell her, my entire body trembling with the anticipation of entering her tight little pussy.

"Then you'll love this." My wife says, lowering herself down so that my cock slides right up into her wet slit.

"Oh fuck." I moan as Alana begins to ride me, moving slowly at first with powerful swoops and then building speed as she pumps up and down against my body. Soon Alana's riding me with everything that she's got, slamming her hips against mine over and over again in a frantic, wild fuck.

"I'm ready." My wife starts to pant. "I think I'm ready." Alana looks back and beckons Carter over, then reaches behind her and spreads her asshole open for him to get a good look. "I've been fantasizing about doing this since the day you first walked into class." She admits.

The fact that she's been yearning for this other man for so long should bother me, but right now I'm too overwhelmed with passion to give a single fuck. The nastier and sluttier the better; there's not much my wife could admit at this point that wouldn't turn me on.

"You've fantasized about doing what?" Carter asks.

"Getting pounded up the ass by that huge fucking cock of yours." Alana tells him. "Now shove it in."

Carter is happy to oblige, placing his rod at the rim of my wife's backdoor and then slowly thrusting forward. The muscles of Alana's sphincter resist at first, but then moments later her body gives in and accepts Carter's incredible girth, stretching her out as we fill her with a brutal double penetration.

My wife clings onto me below her, clenching her teeth as she tries to allow her body a moment to adjust. I hold her tight, glancing over at the three of us in the studio mirror, a heaving mass of bodies in utter ecstasy. I'm so happy to share this moment with Alana, a expression of a fantasy so deep and suppressed it could have easily never seen the light of day. Now, however, we've brought it to the surface, and I can honestly say that we are closer in every way because of it.

"You've got this." I whisper into Alana's ear.

My wife kisses me deeply, slowly beginning to pump against me once again, only this time with a second rod stuffed firmly up her asshole.

"Oh my god." My wife moans. "My fucking holes are so maxed out."

Our thrusting quickly becomes faster and even more deliberate, the trepidation giving way to a powerful, passionate dance that all takes place within this pile of bodies in the middle of the studio floor.

The sensation is incredible, my wife's pussy feeling absolutely incredible as Carter's cock slides in and out of the asshole next to it.

It's not long before I find myself aching to blow, unable to contain all of this blissful sensation within my quaking body.

"I'm gonna cum." I start to moan. "Oh fuck!"

Almost immediately Alana pulls me out of her and rolls over onto the mat, sticking out her tongue teasingly as Carter and I kneel over her beautiful face. Moments later, the two of us are exploding across my wife with a spectacular torrent of jizz, ejecting rope after pearly rope onto her waiting tongue.

Meanwhile, Alana reaches down between her legs and starts to rapidly rub her clit, almost immediately joining us with a powerful, simultaneous orgasm.

"Oh my god!" My wife screams, jizz still dangling from her chin as her entire body clenches tight against the oncoming waves of pleasure. "I'm gonna, I'm gonna…" Alana doesn't have time to finish her sentence, suddenly writhing back against the mat in a fit of ecstasy. Carter and me watch her body contort and spasm before us, completely covered in a swirling cocktail of our pearly spunk.

When the sensation finally passes, my wife collapses back onto the floor as Carter and I quickly join her, lying out on either side of Alana's perfect, nude body.

"That was incredible." My wife says aloud, to no one in particular.

"The best dance I've ever seen." I add with a smile. "I think you two should work together more often."

SPOILED BRAT

Even in the early stages of dating Mary, the woman who would eventually become my wife, I knew she was going to be trouble. Mary wasn't necessarily rude, but she certainly knew that she was cut from a different cloth than most of the people around her. She couldn't help but look down on everyone else, even me.

It would be one thing if Mary was simply hot, which she certainly is, but add endless money to the equation and you get a real monster.

But she's my little monster, and I love her.

It's hard to talk about Mary honestly without making her sound like a horrible person, so it should be stated again loud and clear: my wife is incredible. She is loving and absolutely gorgeous, funny and fun to be around, but she is also spoiled rotten.

Who could really blame her, though? An heir to the Monte Clark fortune, Mary was born with more than just a silver spoon, she had the whole dining set. Her family consists of some of the richest people on the planet, never having to work a day in their life for at least three generations back. It's a type of wealth that I could never have imagined living with and, like most people, find it slightly appalling in some strange, subliminal way.

Its not like Mary *asked* to be born into this fortunate situation, it just happened, and the things that this kind of freedom does to the mind of a young woman are powerful. Mary doesn't understand what it is to work, to save, or to starve. She has never experienced a hard time in life where things were truly down to the wire, never yearned for a purchase that was just out of reach.

At least she *tired* to live like the common people every once in a while, which is precisely how we met.

Years earlier, Mary and I had been in the same English class in an esteemed east coast college, where she was attempting to shed her silver spoon image. There were murmurs around the school that Mary Monte Clark was attending, but to be honest I would have never recognized her in a million years had we not sat right next to each other. Even then, I only understood that there was a vague familiarity about her.

I soon discovered that the familiarity I felt was from years of seeing her smiling face on the cover of various tabloids, but I'd like to chalk it up to love at first sight. I guess I'm just a hopeless romantic.

Dating Mary was difficult when I realized that there was nothing I could really do to impress her. The girl had it all; even if I splurged on the fanciest dinner in town, my girlfriend could easily just buy the restaurant right then and there.

But as soon as I let go of all that nonsense, our relationship truly blossomed. Mary liked me for me, not because I needed to provide her with gifts or tokens of value.

Eventually we were married, having one of the most incredible ceremonies I could've ever imagined. The Monte Clark family spared no expense, from the world famous wedding band to the flowers shipped in overnight from Paris; the whole thing was extravagant beyond belief.

Now we live in married bliss up in the hills above Los Angeles, our massive, modern home stretching out across the ridge of a mountain that looks down on the twinkling lights of Hollywood. Mary enjoys her various hobbies by day while I work as an author, and we meet in the evenings for dinner and to catch each other up on our respective days.

To be honest, I find myself looking back and unable to remember the last time I actually did something I didn't want to do, but now I personally know the same curse that Mary has grappled with her entire life; supreme boredom. When you don't have to work for anything, it all starts to lose value. You find yourself buying more and more stuff to fill the void, to make yourself feel like you did when you were younger and you worked all summer to buy an old used bike or a ticket to a concert. I miss that feeling.

Mary, on the other hand, never knew what it was like to yearn, and that difference is finally starting to draw us apart.

"Is that a new car?" I ask my wife as she walks in the front door, a stern frown plastered across her otherwise beautiful face.

I've just finished up dinner and was waiting for Mary to come home, lounging in our living room that could probably fit the entire house of most middle class families within it's walls.

"Yeah." Mary says, throwing her keys onto the counter and walking over to sit next to me on our small white couch in the middle of this vacant, open space. "But the thing doesn't fucking work."

"Are you serious?" I ask out of courtesy, but fully aware she's completely exaggerating some minor problem. "What's wrong with it?"

"I just feels weird when you drive it, I don't know." Mary explains.

"Like, weird how?" I continue.

"I don't know, just not like my old car." Mary tells me.

I look at her blankly. "So what happened to the old one?"

"I don't know." Mary says. "I guess I just left it there at the lot."

I let out a long sigh. "Baby, that is so wasteful."

Mary can't help but start laughing at my distain for her economic carelessness. "It's fine, Travis." She tells me. "You know we don't have to worry about that kind of thing."

"It's the principal." I tell her, a little frustrated.

Mary considers this for a moment and then eventually sides with me. "You're right, I shouldn't be so wasteful."

I lay back onto the couch, satisfied with this but not completely. Trouble still brews somewhere deep within my mind.

Mary lies back with me and snuggles up, wrapping one of her arms around my body and sighing as she rests her head against me. I look down at her and smile; we may have our differences, but god damn I love my wife.

"Everything else okay?" Mary asks, immediately sensing that not all of the tension has been totally cleared between us.

"Not exactly." I sigh. "Your birthday is coming up in a few days."

"I know!" Mary says excitedly. "You don't want to come to London?"

"I do." I tell her. "It's not that."

My wife sits up and looks me in the eyes, trying to figure me out. "Well, what is it then?"

"I can't figure out what to get you." I tell her. "I mean… you have everything."

"Whatever. Get me a card." Mary says. "It's the thought that counts."

"I know for a fact you don't believe that!" I tell her.

"I do!" Mary insists.

I shake my head. "No way, not falling for it this time. Every year I get you a card and write you something nice, and every year you act like it's all you ever wanted. I know you're lying." I explain.

Mary doesn't protest, just listens and lets her silence speak for itself.

"This year is going to be different." I tell my wife. "This year I'm gonna get you something that money can't buy."

I spend the whole evening and next day trying to brainstorm ideas but I still come up empty handed. Even when I think that I've finally found something clever I quickly realize that it's just too cute and sentimental, which is the last thing that Mary is interested in.

Desperate for an idea before we leave town tomorrow, I head down to Hollywood and meet Carter, a mutual friend of Mary and I, for a drink.

I find Carter sitting alone in the corner of an upscale rooftop bar, which apparently doubles as a pool party on the weekends as young, hot men and women wander past us in bathing suits.

"Travis!" Carter says as he sees me, standing up to give me a powerful bear hug. "You excited for tomorrow? Passport ready?"

I shrug. "Yeah, sure man."

Carter cracks a sly grin. "Oh god, what is it?"

"I don't know what to get her." I admit.

My friend laughs and turns back to the bartender. "Can I get a beer for this guy? Thanks."

"I don't suppose you have any ideas." I ask, completely exhausted.

"I've got plenty of ideas!" Carter says. "Why don't you just write her something nice on a card?"

I roll my eyes. "I do that every year. Listen, there is a time and a place for being sentimental, but this year is not one of those times. Mary has always had more to give then I have, and for once I want to turn the tables."

Carter nods in understanding as the bartender hands me a beer. I take a long pull, actually getting worried for the first time in a long time. I kind of like it.

Carter is an actor, and a good one. After a string of successful television spots he finally landed a movie lead and it turned out to be a surprise blockbuster, catapulting Carter into fame and fortune. He's not nearly as wealthy as Mary, or me by way of marriage, but he's not doing too bad for himself these days.

"What do people get you for your birthday?" I ask Carter. "You're rich."

Carter laughs. "Dude, you're freaking out about something that doesn't matter. She's going to be fine with whatever you get her. People get me all sorts of stuff and I don't really care what it is because it's the thought that counts."

I shake my head. "There is a big difference here, a huge one. You're a guy who came from nothing so you appreciate the effort, Mary is a spoiled brat."

Carter can't help but crack up as I say this, and seconds later I join him. The entire situation seems so absurd but it is all absolutely true.

"Alright." My friend finally says, his eyes wandering across the ass of a cute young girl who struts by us in her bikini. "You really want to know the best thing I've ever gotten for my birthday that didn't cost a dime?"

My eyes light up. "Yes! Tell me!"

Carter leans in. "The best thing I ever got was when my girlfriend arranged a threesome."

His words hit me like a brick, almost knocking me backwards off of my chair. I hadn't even thought of something sexual like that, but it's perfect for Mary who loves adventure and especially loves pushing her boundaries in the bedroom.

"Okay." I nod. "But where are we going to find a girl that wants to have a three way in London?"

Carter just stares at me blankly, looking as though my head is full of rocks and pebbles that rattle around everywhere inside. "You can't be serious." He finally asks.

"What?" I respond, not quite getting it.

"Another girl?" Carter laughs. "Dude, this is *her* birthday not yours!"

When my ignorance finally dawns on me I start to laugh myself. "Oh shit, you're right. So another guy?" I think about this for a moment, imagine what it would be like to share my beautiful wife with another man. At first, the thoughts are incredibly off putting, but the more a picture her gorgeous, toned curves sandwiched between me and someone else, the more I start to think the idea sounds pretty hot.

Most importantly, though, I know that it's the perfect gift for Mary.

Immediately, I start to scan my brain for options of who I could possibly ask to join us in such a perverse and private encounter. It would have to be a guy that Mary knew and thought was attractive, so just finding some random cock was out of the question. It would also have to be someone that I trusted, not only to be cool about the whole thing but to keep all of this a secret, because if the tabloids got wind we would never ever hear the end of it.

I suddenly realize that the perfect answer is sitting right in front of my face, staring back at me.

"Are you game?" I ask Carter who, at first, does an amazing job of pretending he has no idea what I'm talking about. The guy is an actor, after all.

"Game?" Carter asks.

"Will you fuck my wife with me?" I question, cutting right to the chase.

Carter takes a drink of his beer, his expression cracking a little as he tries to hide his smile behind the glass. "Yeah man, let's do it."

By the time we all arrive in London I am a living, breathing ball of anxiety. I try my best to enjoy the experience of partying in the United Kingdom with all of our friends, but regardless of the adventure unfolding around me, I simple cannot shake my awareness of the *real* adventure scheduled for later tonight.

Thankfully, I somehow managed to catch a few hours of sleep on the plane, so I'm not completely out of it as the group of us make our way to the swanky hotel in a caravan of private cars. Along the way we get a nice view of the British countryside, which stretches out its rolling green brilliance on either side of us. I finally manage to center myself.

It's one thing to talk about sharing your wife with another man, but actually going through with it is another story entirely. I look across the car at Mary, who meets my gaze and smiles with genuine warmth before mouthing "I love you."

In my quest to satisfy the woman who has it all, was I risking it all in the process? I can't help but consider this a possibility, but the longer I think about it, the more another powerful emotion begins to seep into my thoughts. There is just something so hot about imagining another man's hands roaming across Mary's toned body, the thought of my wife trembling as a foreign finger massaged her clit, or slipped deep into her aching pussy.

This is a fantasy that I've never before had, but right now it is utterly overwhelming, causing my cock to grow harder and thicker within my pants. Of course, part of me is also consumed by sheer jealousy, but somehow that emotion only adds to the cocktail of lust that swims and swirls within.

I suddenly realize I'm trembling and avert my thoughts to anything else that could possibly calm me down.

"Jet lag?" Mary asks, reaching her hand across and putting it on my knee.

"Yeah." I tell her with a nod. "I'll be fine."

Soon enough we arrive at our hotel, an incredible luxury tower in the heart of London. Our group has eight in total, and for the first while we all split off into our individual rooms to rest up and get ready for dinner.

I find Carter and we head to his room to discuss the plan, my body filling with equal parts blood-boiling jealousy and powerful, throbbing arousal.

My heart is pounding hard in my chest as Mary climbs into bed next to me, both of us sufficiently buzzed after our drinks at tonight's first of many birthday dinners. She has no idea that Carter is waiting right outside our hotel room door for his cue to enter.

Mary kisses me deeply and an electricity flows through my body in a way that I haven't experienced for quite some time. Everything seems more important when you put it all on the line, and that's exactly what tonight is about.

I pull back and look up at my wife, a sly smile crossing my face. "I've got a present for you." I tell her.

Mary laughs. "And it can't wait until we're done fucking?"

I shake my head.

My wife eyes me with suspicion now, immediately sensing that something is up. She looks absolutely gorgeous tonight in a bright pink lingerie set, her outline framed in the dim light by the extravagant trappings of our luxury penthouse. "It's not just a card is it?" Mary asks.

I shake my head. "You're so spoiled! What if it *was* just a card?"

Mary rolls her eyes and kisses me once again, then sits up. "Then I would still love it, baby. You know I'm just messing with you."

I sit up with my wife and grab her by the shoulders, suddenly changing the mood as I push her down onto the bed; trading places so that I'm now the one in control. I hold her by the wrists against the plush, furry bedding below us. "You're a spoiled brat and you know it." I tell Mary. "Always wanting more."

Mary clearly enjoys the fact that I'm taking control now, writhing seductively below me. "What's wrong with wanting more?" She asks playfully.

"Nothing." I tell her. "And tonight, more is exactly what you're going to get."

"Really?" My wife asks, confused but intrigued.

"Close your eyes." I tell her.

Mary does as she told and then moments later Carter uses his spare keycard to slip into our room. He makes his way over to the bed and undresses.

"Now, you have to promise me that, no matter what, you're not going to open your eyes until I tell you." I instruct Mary.

My wife nods and I glance over at Carter, who climbs up onto the bed next to us. I can immediately sense Mary's breath catch in her throat as she realizes that we are no longer the only people in the room, but she stays true to her word and keeps her eyes shut tight.

I remove what's left of my clothing and suddenly find myself kneeling next to one side of Mary's face while Carter kneels at the other, our rock hard cocks pointing directly at her beautiful smile. I reach down and take my wife's hand in my own, then place it around my shaft. Mary grips tightly, waiting while I take her other hand and then place it onto Carter's cock. When my wife feels it she gasps, but her eyes remain closed.

"Oh my god." Mary says. "You weren't kidding about giving me more tonight."

"Nope." I laugh.

My wife immediately starts to stroke our dicks, running her hands up and down the length of our massive shafts. Her grip is tight and her movements perfectly executed.

"Fuck." I moan, my body tensing up as Mary's movements grow faster and faster. I look over at Carter who is enjoying himself just as much as I am, his eyes transfixed on my wife's incredible body below him.

Seconds later, Mary opens her mouth and takes Carter's cock deep, pushing him down as far as she can into her throat. My friend lets out a long moan as Mary cradles his balls, servicing him perfectly while she hold him deep. Carters hard abs are pressed up against her face, his balls resting against her chin until finally my wife just can't take it anymore and pulls back in a frantic gasp of air.

After collecting herself, Mary turns her attention over to me, taking my rod between her lips and giving me an equally pleasant treatment. She pushes down as far as she can, deep throating me elegantly but, instead of holding there, my wife starts pumping her head up and down my shaft and sucking me off with a series of wild, lustful pulses.

All the while Mary continues to beat off Carter right next to me. I watch as he trembles with pleasure, my jealousy damn near boiling over in the most incredible of ways.

Eventually, Mary is completely overwhelmed with desire and shoves both of our cocks into her mouth at the same time, filling herself completely with an unbelievable double barrel blowjob.

After a while of this, Mary pulls us out and climbs up onto her hands and knees. "I need you inside of me right now." She demands. "I need to get fucked."

My first instinct is to jump right in, but somehow I manage to hesitate and nod at Carter, signaling for him to go first. My friend smiles and then climbs into position behind my beautiful wife, aligning his cock at the entrance of her tight, wet slit.

Moments later, Carter is pushing forward, Mary bracing herself against the bedding below her as her pussy stretches to accommodate his massive size. My wife lets out a long, satisfied moan of ecstasy, a visible tremor making its way along the length of her body as Carter begins pumping in and out of her.

"Do you like that other cock?" I ask, stroking myself off while I watch the scene unfold.

"Yes!" Mary cries out. "I love the way it feels to fuck another man! Thank you, baby!"

"Do you want to see who's in your tight little pussy right now?" I continue.

"Yes!" My wife begs.

"Open your eyes." I tell her.

Immediately, Mary looks back over her shoulder at the man who so diligently takes her from behind, and she couldn't be more happy to see him. "Oh my god, Carter!" My wife cries, then looks back to me. "Baby, this is the best present I've ever gotten in my life."

I feel a rush of adrenalin as she says this, thankful all of the trouble that went into arranging such an encounter has finally paid off.

"Now, come let me suck you off some more." Mary commands.

I crawl across the bed and then lay back against the pillow, my huge cock jutting out directly towards Mary's beautiful lips which she immediately wraps around my shaft. Soon enough, Carter and I are plowing my wife from either end, finding a pleasant rhythm with one another as she convulses between us. Mary is screaming now, unable to keep herself from vocalizing the incredible pleasure the flows through her body despite the cock that plugs her throat. Her cries come out warped and weird, a strange sexual gargle that cuts in and out with every pound of my dick in her mouth.

Soon, Mary pulls Carter out of her and climbs up onto me, straddling my body with her long, slender legs. She runs her hands down my muscular torso, lower and lower until she finds my shaft and grips it tightly.

"I need you inside of me." She says, lowering herself down and pushing my rod directly up into her sweet pussy. It feels so good to impale her gorgeous body, like the first time all over again as my wife begins to ride me. Mary swoops down in a series of deliberate hip movements, slowly at first and then speeding up until breaking into a full throttle ride. My wife grips the headboard tightly with her hands, using it to maneuver herself as forcefully as she can across my cock.

As Mary fucks me Carter begins to climb into position behind us, his massive dick poised and ready. At first I'm a little confused at what exactly he's attempting, but the second I realize my eyes go wide with lustful excitement.

"You looking for more?" Carter asks my wife. "More is always better right?"

Mary whips her head around as our friend aligns his cock with the puckered rim of her asshole. My wife gasps aloud, then immediately reaches back with one hand and spreads her butt open for him.

"She's a spoiled little brat." I tell Carter. "Shove it in there and teach her a lesson!"

"Do it!" My wife demands, echoing my sentiment. "More cock for the birthday girl!"

Immediately, Carter pushes forward and groans loudly as my wife's asshole stretches to accommodate his enormous size. The tightness of her pussy is immediately amplified as Carter rocks in and out of Mary, our cocks separated by nothing but a thin layer of sensitive membrane that is already drawn to its limits.

Carter and I immediately get to work pounding my wife from the top and bottom, railing her holes in tandem as we find a powerful rhythm together. Mary is completely at our whim, a rich little fuck toy who can't help but love every second of our confident double pounding.

"Oh my god!" My wife is screaming now, unable to control herself as she convulses between us. "Oh my god! Oh my fucking god!"

"Do you like those dicks?" I demand to know.

"I love them! Don't stop fucking me!" Mary shrieks.

Carter and I heed her warning and don't let up for a second, absolutely reaming my wife's aching holes. Mary reaches down between us and finds her clit, helping herself along as the pressure builds and then moments later she is cumming hard. Mary throws her head back and lets out an earth-shaking howl of utter bliss, her eyes closed tight as her taut body is hit with wave after wave of powerful orgasm.

"I'm cumming!" Mary screams. "I'm cumming from two dicks and I fucking love it!"

Carter looks ready to blow, as well, and moments later he pushes hard into my beautiful bride's ass and holds tight, his teeth clenched as he expels a massive load up into her. I watch in awe as Carter fills my wife with his spunk, so much that it actually comes squirting out from the edges of her tightly packed asshole and then runs down her crack in pearly white streaks.

Seeing another man unload his jizz into my wife immediately pushes me over the edge, and soon enough I find myself cumming along with them. I let out a cry of passion as I eject hard into my wife's pussy, filling her up with rope after rope of hot semen.

Completely spent, the three of us collapse into the bed in utter exhaustion.

"Well, I think that's my cue to leave." Carter says, sitting up and pulling his pants back on. He leans down and kisses my wife on the cheek and then gives me a high five. "See you guys in the morning."

Mary and I watch Carter go and then roll over to face each other.

"Thank you." Says Mary. "That was the best gift I've ever received."

"I guess I finally figured out what to get for the girl who has everything." I tell her with a laugh.

Mary smiles and kisses me. "I can't wait to see what you come up with next year."

I think on this for a moment. "Well, our anniversary is right around the corner." I say. "And then there's Valentines Day, and St. Patrick's Day… 4th of July."

Mary starts to laugh. "I like this idea."

"I like it, too." I say with a smile. "I like it a lot."

ABOUT THE AUTHOR

Hannah Wilde is an erotica author and graphic design student currently living in Los Angeles, California, where she spends most of her time writing, playing with her cat or traipsing around Disneyland. She started writing after discovering that she could entertain friends by improvising wild stories about them and claiming they'd actually occurred while drinking. Sometimes friends would actually believe her, and Hannah's love for storytelling blossomed from there.

Printed in Great Britain
by Amazon